HATE YOU ALWAYS

JENNIFER SUCEVIC

Hate You Always

Copyright© 2023 by Jennifer Sucevic

Cover Design by Mary Ruth Baloy at MR Creations

Editing by Evelyn Summers at Pinpoint Editing

Proofreading by Autumn Sexton at Wordsmith Publicity

Home | Jennifer Sucevic or www.jennifersucevic.com

CHAPTER 1

JULIETTE

"*I* had a really good time tonight," Aaron says, gaze pinned to mine with an intensity that has me wanting to take a quick step in retreat.

Instead, I force a smile. "Yeah. Me, too."

It's not a total lie. I did have a good time. But that's all it was—*good.* Kind of like when we study together at the library or grab coffee at the Roasted Bean before class.

He glances away and shoves both hands into the pockets of his perfectly pressed khakis. "I hope we can do this again." There's a pause before he tacks on, "Soon."

I'm treated to a long, soulful stare that leaves me feeling borderline uncomfortable.

Yeah…I'm pretty sure that's not in the cards for us.

Aaron is nice.

Really nice.

Super-duper nice.

There's just no spark between us.

I'm searching for that elusive little tingle you get at the bottom of your tummy whenever you're near that person or even catch a glimpse of them from across a crowded room. It's the kind of irrepressible energy that sizzles in the air, charging it until drawing a full breath into your lungs feels impossible.

No matter how much I might wish otherwise, Aaron and I just don't generate that kind of chemistry.

There's only one person—

No.

I take a deep breath, slamming the door closed on those thoughts.

What I feel for that guy isn't attraction.

It's irritation.

Annoyance.

Aggravation.

Trust me, if you gave me enough time, I could come up with a laundry list of descriptive words that start with a vowel.

I blink back to awareness, only to realize that Aaron is patiently awaiting a response.

Oh, right. He wants to do this again.

As I open my mouth to let him down gently, the words stick in my throat. The last thing I want to do is lead him on, but at the same time, I don't want to hurt him either. What I need to do is strike the perfect balance. We have several pre-med classes together this semester. If I'm sick and can't attend class, Aaron is the one who catches me up to speed and makes sure I have all the notes.

They're usually color coded and placed in order of importance.

If there's been one lesson learned this evening, it's that I should avoid dating guys I see on a daily basis.

As Carina, my roommate, would say—don't shit where you eat.

She's right about that.

He inches closer. "If you're in agreement, I'd like to move this relationship forward. I like you, Juliette." He glances away briefly before his muddy-colored eyes refocus on me with a mixture of heat and intensity. "I'm probably getting a little ahead of myself here, but I think we could be a real power couple. We share similar aspirations— both of us have set our sights on furthering our studies in medicine and becoming physicians. I've never found someone who fits so perfectly into my five- and ten-year plan. It's almost like we were made for one another."

My eyes widen as a garbled sound escapes from me.

A little ahead of himself?

Five- and ten-year plan?

We've been out precisely three times, and the chances of there being a fourth have dwindled to the single digits.

I need to tell him that this—whatever he thinks *this* is—isn't going to happen. "Aaron..."

He perks up and sways closer. "Yeah?"

There's so much hope and expectation packed into that one word.

Argh.

Why does this have to be so difficult?

The problem is that he really *is* a nice guy. And what he said is absolutely true, we *do* have a lot in common. It's the reason I talked myself into giving him another chance.

And then a third.

There are a lot of douchey guys at this school who are only inter-ested in sleeping with a chick before moving onto the next warm body. Sometimes within the span of the same evening. They don't have five- or ten-year plans that involve one specific girl. They don't even have twenty-four-hour plans that involve the same female.

So, when you happen to find a guy who has the opposite mindset, you need to take the time to delve deep and really get to know him before tossing him back into the wild for someone else to snap up.

"I had a nice time, too," I say carefully.

"Good." The tension filling his narrow shoulders drains as he beams in relief.

Aaron has a wiry build. His limbs are long and lean, much like a runner. Unlike some of the football or hockey players that strut around campus with their muscles on display as if they're god's gift to the female species.

Ugh. They seem to be everywhere.

As I stare into his earnest eyes, I make a last ditch effort to convince myself that he's exactly the type of guy I'm attracted to.

Deep down, in a place I'm loath to acknowledge, I know it's a lie.

Carina, damn her, would also tell me that the worst lies are the ones we tell ourselves.

That girl really needs to stay out of my head.

His hands reemerge from the depths of his pockets before rising to my face. It would be difficult not to notice their slight tremble. I force myself to stand perfectly still and not evade his touch at the last moment. And if that doesn't tell you everything you need to know about this situation, I'm not sure what will.

His eyelids droop to half-mast. "I'm going to kiss you now, Juliette," he mutters thickly. "I hope that's all right."

And with that, the mood has officially been killed.

Not that there was much of one to begin with, but still...

Unlike him, my eyes stay wide open as he moves toward me in slow motion. I steel myself for impact instead of flinching away.

Maybe I'm wrong.

Maybe Aaron will surprise the hell out of me and will end up being a phenomenal kisser. I'll magically lose myself in the caress as time and space cease to exist.

It's tentatively that his lips settle over mine. They're dry and papery to the touch. It's kind of like being pecked by a distant aunt or uncle.

Everything inside me deflates with the knowledge that this isn't going to end any other way than me carefully letting him down, because there's no way in hell I can do this again.

In fact, I'd pay good money to never do *this* again.

I press my palms against Aaron's chest to push him away when someone clears their throat. Aaron jumps back as if he just stuck his finger in an electrical outlet.

My gaze slices to the tall, muscular blond guy who has ground to a halt beside us.

Ryder McAdams.

My belly does a strange little flip before I swiftly stomp out the sensation.

Dark blue eyes pin me in place for a drawn-out heartbeat, making it impossible to breathe before shifting to Aaron. It's only when I'm released from his penetrating stare that the air trapped in my lungs rushes from me and I realize there are five more oversized hockey players crowded in the hallway outside my apartment door.

Ford Hamilton, Wolf Westerville, Colby McNichols, Riggs Stranton, and Hayes Van Doren are seniors on the Western Wildcats hockey team. Wherever they go, fangirls are sure to follow. I glance around only to realize they're all by themselves. It's weird not to see their entourage trailing after them.

Is it possible that hell has officially frozen over?

Colby flashes an easy-going grin as he snags my gaze. "Hey, McKinnon. Looks like someone has a hot date tonight." Like Ryder, he's blond and entirely too handsome for his own good.

His dimples are lethal to any female with a beating pulse in the vicinity.

Present company excluded.

Heat scalds my cheeks until it feels like they've caught on fire. The last thing I need is for the pretty hockey player to open his big yap to my brother.

Like I need the fifth degree from him.

Hard pass, thank you very much.

I might be the older sibling by fifteen months, but that, apparently, doesn't matter. Maverick takes his protective brother duties seriously. Dad drilled that into his head when he arrived at Western the year after I did.

Before I can snap out a response, they jostle and joke their way down the hall to the apartment next door. Ford lives there with Wolf and Madden while Ryder and five other teammates have a place located a couple blocks off campus known around school as the hockey house. For the last three decades, the residence has been exclusively occupied by Western hockey players. The current group of guys who rent the property will select the teammates who live there the following year.

It's a whole thing.

Eyeroll.

Thankfully, my brother lives off campus at the house. He's the only junior who was invited to do so and that has everything to do with Ryder. They've been tight since elementary school. I seriously don't think I could handle having him in the same building. He's all up in my business enough the way it is.

My skin prickles with awareness when I realize that Ryder hasn't followed his friends down the hallway. His gaze is still locked on Aaron, who looks seconds away from pissing himself.

And I get it.

Ryder McAdams can be intimidating.

Especially when he glares.

Which is exactly what he's doing at the moment.

Poor Aaron. In comparison, he looks like a scrawny, underdeveloped high schooler.

Awkwardness descends.

My date clears his throat before mumbling, "I, ah, should probably go."

There's a pause before he hesitantly sways toward me again. He only gets a few inches before Ryder crosses his thickly corded arms over his brawny chest. Aaron's movements stall as his face turns ashen.

"Umm..." He releases a high-pitched laugh that's strained around the edges. "How about a hug instead?"

When Ryder's eyes narrow, Aaron gulps, his throat muscles convulsing with the movement. In the silence of the hallway, the sound is deafening.

He finally reaches out, wrapping his sweaty palm around my hand before giving it three hearty pumps and promptly releasing it. I don't even get a chance to say goodbye as he swings around and races to the elevator like the hounds of hell are nipping at his heels.

He stabs the button a bunch of times and glances over his shoulder at us warily. When the bell chimes, announcing the car's arrival, he shoves his way inside before the doors have a chance to fully open, disappearing from sight.

Once the metal contraption closes, I scowl at Ryder. "Why'd you do that?"

One thick brow slinks upward. It's enough to have me gritting my teeth.

"Do what? I never said a word."

True enough. But still...

I'm aggravated with him for messing with my date. There was absolutely no reason for it.

"You purposefully stood there and made him feel uncomfortable."

Why am I picking a fight?

It's not like I wanted to kiss Aaron. If anything, I should be thanking Ryder for his timely interruption.

I almost snort, because there's no way in hell *that's* going to happen.

"How'd I do that? By standing here and patiently waiting for an introduction?" His gaze stays locked on mine as he tilts his head and scratches his shadowed jaw. "Seems kind of odd."

I bare my teeth before swinging away to dig through my purse for the apartment key. As soon as my fingers wrap around cool metal, I yank it out and jamb it in the lock with more force than necessary. The door reverberates on its hinges as I step inside and swivel to face Ryder once more before promptly closing it with a loud bang.

CHAPTER 2

RYDER

"Well…can't say I've ever seen a girl slam a door in your face," Ford says with an easy laugh as he claps me on the shoulder. "Looks like there really is a first time for everything."

I glance at him, unaware that he'd witnessed the terse exchange. I'd assumed he took off with Wolf and the others.

Although, why am I surprised?

That's exactly what Juliette does to me. She blinds me to the people and things around me. For a Division I hockey player who's supposed to have his head on a constant swivel, it's not a good thing. I force my muscles to relax and hitch my lips into a loose interpretation of a smile. The last thing I need is for this motherfucker to sense that I have any real interest in Maverick McKinnon's sister.

That would be bad for business.

My business.

Even though Ford and I have been friends since freshman year of college, he has no problem pressing on a tender spot if he just so happens to find one. Can't say I wouldn't do the same.

What's the point of having friends if you can't fuck mercilessly with them?

"Then you haven't spent much time around Juliette."

He shrugs as we fall into line and walk down the hallway. As tempting as it is to glance over my shoulder at the apartment the pretty brunette shares with her friend, I keep my eyes focused straight ahead.

It takes a herculean effort on my part.

"Can't say that I have. She's never been one to party much, has she?"

"Nope." And that's for the best. It would probably kill me to see her out and about, flirting or going home at the end of the night with other guys. I crack my knuckles to relieve the pressure building inside me. Even the thought of her hooking up with another dude is enough to piss me off.

"I've run into her at the library a handful of times," he says conversationally.

"Yeah, she hangs out there a lot. She's pre-med." I clear my throat and tack on offhandedly, "I think."

And smart as fuck.

Way too damn smart for the likes of me.

"Huh. Smart and hot. Now there's a wicked combination."

My heads snaps around so fast that I nearly give myself whiplash. "What the hell did you just say?

He pops a brow before studying my expression. "I said that the girl is both smart and hot. It's not like I'd say it to Mav. He'd probably give me a beatdown."

There's no *probably* about it.

Definite beatdown.

He'd give any guy who looked sideways at his sister a beating. And if I'm being perfectly honest, I'd gladly jump into the fray to help dissuade any further interest as well.

Luckily, most of the guys on the team have gotten the memo without Mav having to crack too many skulls together. It was a real pleasure to watch.

"Well, I don't wanna hear it either," I grumble. "She's practically like a sister to me."

A smirk simmers around Ford's lips as we grind to a halt outside his door. "Is that so? It's all sisterly feelings on your part?"

Apparently, those comments are sus.

"Yeah, that's right." With a frown, I dig in a little deeper. "I've known her since we were kids. We're neighbors, and our families have been good friends for years."

A sly look settles on his face.

It's tempting to punch it right off.

"Then you wouldn't have a problem if I asked her out, right?"

I straighten like someone just rammed a two by four up my ass and scowl. "The fuck you say?"

A shit-eating grin overtakes his expression as he wraps his fingers around the silver handle and shoves the door open. "Yeah, that's what I thought."

The asshole doesn't even bother to wait for a response as he strolls into the apartment as if he doesn't have a care in the world, leaving me to stand alone in the hallway, narrowed gaze pinned to his back.

Boisterous voices spill out from inside.

"You gonna get your ass in here or what?" Riggs asks, raising a green bottle of beer to his lips and taking a long pull.

With a grunt, I stalk into the entryway before slamming the door shut. Almost all of the senior guys are squeezed into the three-bedroom apartment. A few are standing around and drinking while others have settled on the couch and chair. They're focused on an intense game of NHL being played out on the high-def big screen television that takes up most of the far wall.

"Help yourself to a cold one," Colby adds as he does the same. "After that practice, you deserve it, man."

Even though he only walked in minutes before I did, there's a girl tucked under each arm. I almost shake my head at how quickly he works. Over the years, his nickname as the baby-faced assassin has been well earned. I've never seen a guy get so much pussy. He's like the pied piper of it. Crazier still, girls leave his bed just as happy as they went to it. It's like he's able to cast a spell over them or something.

Must be the dimples.

I've seen plenty of guys get their asses chewed out by spurned chicks who were hoping for more than just a one-night stand.

Not Colby.

It's almost like he's able to convince them that a casual hookup was their idea, and he was just doing them a solid. I've watched the guy in action. The way he's able to talk his way out of any situation is seriously impressive. I've whipped out my phone a time or two to take notes.

There's only one thing that can take my mind off the mahogany-haired girl in the apartment next door, and that's hockey.

More specifically, our new coach.

The hardass who seems to have it out for me.

As good as a beer would taste, I'm not in the mood.

It's funny...

Well, not exactly funny.

In fact, it's not amusing at all.

When senior year began a couple of months ago, I'd assumed everything would fall neatly into place just like it had the previous three seasons I'd been playing for the Wildcats. Being named captain along with being a top defensive pairing was a no brainer. Especially since I was assistant captain of the team last season.

And Coach Kasminski?

The guy fucking loved me. If he could've adopted my ass, he would've. He's the one who recruited me during high school, promising a full athletic ride.

It wasn't long before he was waving me into his office and asking for my thoughts regarding other players or for my opinion when it came to power plays and our opponents. Sometimes, we'd kick back in his office with a pizza and watch game film for a couple of hours.

So why wouldn't senior year just be more of the same?

I'd skate through the season without a care in the world, kicking ass and taking names. Then, to top it off, we'd bring home another Frozen Four Championship title. Senior year would be the cherry on top of an epic college career before moving up to the pros.

Except...

Kasminski up and quit a week before we headed back to campus. He accepted a position as an assistant coach for a professional team. I didn't even realize he'd been applying for other jobs. The dude never said a word.

Do I necessarily blame the guy for wanting to move up in the world?

Hell no. We all have our dreams, right?

And if you don't go after them, they certainly aren't going to chase you back.

It's just that he unwittingly screwed me over in the process.

Western swiftly hired another head coach to fill the vacancy.

Reed Philips.

He played in the NHL for more than a decade before sliding into an assistant coaching position and then a head coaching job at a Division II university. Now, he's here.

It only took a couple of practices to surmise that the guy is a real dick. For some reason, he took an instant dislike to me. If I even look at him sideways, he reams me out in front of the entire team.

It's been a bitter pill to swallow.

The arena has always been my happy place.

And it could be any arena. They're all the same. From the snap in the crisp air to the smell of the ice and the feel of the smoothness under my blades when it's fresh after the Zamboni.

There's nothing better in this world than hockey.

And I didn't think anything could ruin it for me.

Unfortunately, I was wrong.

Reed Philips has snatched it away quicker than he could blow his whistle and tell us to get our asses on the blue line.

And no amount of beer will change that.

CHAPTER 3

JULIETTE

I slam the apartment door shut with more force than necessary and stalk through the tiny entryway into the carpeted living room. Carina glances up from the paperback she's reading on the couch. One look at my face sends her brows skyrocketing across her forehead.

"That good a date, huh?"

"The date was fine."

Sort of.

All right…maybe that's a bit of an overreach.

"Okay." She stretches out the second syllable so that it sounds more like *okaaaaay*.

With a huff, I toss my keys and purse onto the table before dropping down on the chair parked across from where she's curled up. It's her favorite reading spot. Whether it's a textbook or one of the romance novels she enjoys devouring, this is the place I usually find her.

"I won't be seeing Aaron again." I wave a hand and amend that statement. "I mean, obviously I'll have to see him in class, but we won't be going out on any more dates."

"I'm gonna be completely honest, I kind of suspected that might be the outcome when you brought it up." She scrunches her nose. "He just seems kind of…" Her voice trails off as she searches for an adequate adjective to describe the pre-med student.

"Boring," I reluctantly supply in place of her silence.

Her lips tremble as if she's trying to hold back a smile. "Just remember that you're the one who said it, girl. Not me."

With a resigned sigh, I deflate even further onto the chair and squeeze my eyelids tightly shut. "I know."

"Did he take it badly or something? Because honestly, I can't imagine that happening. He seems so mild mannered."

That question has my eyelids springing open. "I didn't get a chance to tell him. We were interrupted."

"Ohhh." Her eyes brighten as she marks her page and sets aside her book before slowly rubbing her palms together. "I have a feeling we just got to the good part."

"If you want to call Ryder McAdams the good part, then sure," I grumble, annoyed all over again.

She contemplates my comment before saying, "Actually yes, I'd definitely call him the good part. More like the delicious part." Her eyes go a little dreamy. "Blond hair, blue eyes and muscles for days."

"You left out how full of himself he is."

"Who doesn't love a self-assured man?"

"How about womanizing manwhore? Do you love those as well?"

She flashes an easy grin. "I've yet to hear any complaints from the ladies on this campus. In fact, from what I've heard—"

I throw up a hand to halt her in her verbal tracks. "I'm not interested in the urban legends and myths that surround Ryder McAdams' sex life."

"Trust me, there are plenty, but we've deviated from the topic. Tell me what he did to piss you off this time."

This time.

"Half the hockey team walked past while Aaron and I were in the middle of…you know." I shift on the chair as my cheeks heat.

Her brow lifts. "Kissing?"

"Yup, that would be it."

"One last-ditch effort to see if there was any chemistry between you two, huh?"

I jerk my head into a tight nod. The girl knows me well. She's not my bestie for nothing.

"Come on, don't leave me hanging here. Now I'm invested in the story."

"Just as you thought. Zilch. Nada. Nothing."

She presses her lips together and nods. "Well, you tried, girl. No shame in that."

"I really did," I admit. "That elusive spark just isn't there."

I refuse to acknowledge the combustible electricity that sizzles through the air anytime Ryder is in the vicinity.

How ironic is it that there's no chemistry whatsoever with the one person I actually have a lot in common with, and there's a veritable lightshow with the guy I can't stand? The one who crawls under my skin like a stubborn rash that's steroid resistant.

"Sounds more like you owe Ryder a solid for interrupting."

I snort. "Do you really think that's going to happen?"

Her shoulders shake as a few chuckles escape from her. "Nope. I can't even picture it in my head."

Me neither.

"All the guys walked past except Ryder. He just stood there and glared at Aaron."

"Please tell me the poor kid didn't piss himself."

"Practically," I mutter.

"Yeah, Ryder is...*massive*. In a couple different areas, so I hear."

"Anyway," I say, ignoring the last comment. "Aaron pretty much took off down the hall to get away from us. The next time I see him, I'll have to let him know that a romantic relationship isn't in the cards for us."

"Probably for the best," Carina says, agreeing with my assessment.

Just as I open my mouth to tell her how much I'm not looking forward to the conversation, music is cranked up from the apartment next door. It's so loud that the wall we share with Ford, Wolf, and Madden practically vibrates.

"Looks like the guys are having another get-together," Carina says, flicking a glance at the wall as if she can see through it. "Maybe we should head over and be social. I could definitely use a cocktail."

"Hard pass." I nix the idea and rise from the chair in one swift movement. "Since I'm home early, might as well hit the books and get ahead in bio stats."

Carina shakes her head. "You realize that you're going to burn yourself out before you even get accepted to med school, right?"

Probably, but what other choice is there?

Western is an academically rigorous school, and the pre-med program is even more so. The department is known for weeding out students who aren't able to hack it. And that's always been my biggest fear.

Failure.

The last thing I want to do is let my parents down.

Or myself.

"You know, it's okay to loosen up and have a little bit of fun every once in a while. Ever since we met freshman year, your nose has been buried in a book. And not the fun kind where you learn a new sexual position or how to give a better blowie."

A gurgle of laughter escapes from me. "There are actually books for that?"

"Oh, yeah." She wiggles her brows. "I have a whole shelf of them. I'm going to find one for you to borrow. It's senior year, for goodness' sake. Your last chance to cut loose and have some fun before the real world encroaches. You need to take advantage of the freedom before it's too late. Trust me, in a couple years, you'll regret that you spent so much time at the library instead of cutting loose."

I give her a placating smile. If I don't, she'll only continue to hammer home her point. "You're absolutely right. I'll give it some thought." I jerk a thumb toward my bedroom. "After I study for bio stats."

Carina rolls her blue-gray hazel eyes as I make my escape before she gets it in her mind to drag me next door. After what happened in the hallway with Ryder, he's the last person I want to spend time with. And I have zero desire to see all the puck bunnies that will inevitably be clinging to him. I get enough of that when we run into each other on campus.

If that thought leaves a sour taste in my mouth, I ignore it before grabbing my tome of a bio stats book and delving in. There's something that settles my nerves about focusing my attention on schoolwork. It's safe. Kind of like wrapping myself in a warm, cozy blanket. After twenty minutes, I roll to the side and yank open the nightstand drawer to grab a highlighter. The pink one. As I bring the tip to my mouth to pull off the chewed-up cap, I notice a folded-up square stuck under the small plastic bar.

Unsure what it is, I tug it free and open it. When it's spread out across the page of my book, my gaze scans the crinkled paper.

BUCKET LIST for College
1. Make out at the library
2. Skinny dip
3. Karaoke
4. Get drunk at a party
5. Romantic date
6. Orgasm (with another person)
7. Dance at a club
8. Sex in a public place
9. Skip class
10. Fall in love

TALK about a blast from the past. It's the list I made after high school graduation when I was sitting home while all of my classmates partied their proverbial asses off. Including the guy in the apartment next to us.

I know this because I was spying from my bedroom window and watched him get dropped off by a couple of girls in a convertible before stumbling to his front door. Then, I continued to stare as Lindy Mavis climbed his body like a tree and made out with him.

In that moment, I'd felt like the world's biggest loser for working so hard and earning the distinction as valedictorian for our graduating class. I'd vowed that college would be different and came up with a list of experiences I'd have during the next four years.

My gaze roams over the paper for a second time.

I'd almost forgotten about this list. In fact, I thought I'd chucked it after sophomore year when I'd moved out of the dorms.

The last three years have sped by and now, all of the sudden, I'll be graduating in the spring. An odd sort of discontentment steals over me. Don't get me wrong, I'm happy to be moving on with my life, but I had assumed I'd do more than study at the library. I'd thought there would be parties, activities, and boys...

You know, collegy things.

Fun things.

It's not like I couldn't have been going out on dates and getting to know more people, but I focused on my classes in an effort to make sure I could get into my choice of med schools. I'm graduating with a near perfect GPA. Honors up the ass. Every Greek organization that looked good on a resume—other than the social ones—I joined and presided over.

There's something to be said about setting yourself up for future success, isn't there?

But still...it's hard to believe that absolutely nothing has been ticked off this list.

Other than studying, what else did I do with my time?

I've been to a handful of parties but never drank more than a cup of beer. And even that was a struggle. I mean, it's not like it tastes very good.

My gaze gets snagged by number six, and I huff out a breath.

I've attempted to cross that one off my list several times.

With a couple different guys.

Most of whom didn't seem too concerned if I got off or not. In fact, one actually tried to tell me when I mentioned my lack of...*release*, that girls don't come as often as guys and that's just the way it was.

Yeah, right. Keep telling yourself that, buddy.

Especially when I have no problem achieving the big O on my own.

Self-absorbed jerk.

I almost hate to think about it, but Carina and I have lived together for three years, and I've heard her get it on with guys on more than one occasion. The walls in the apartments we've shared have been, unfortunately, paper thin. If the moaning that kept me up a few times could be believed, she was able to get off with no problem.

Or she's one hell of an actress.

Trust me, the last thing I'm trying to do is eavesdrop on a private moment, but that girl can be loud as fuck. I had a difficult time looking either of them in the eye the next morning without feeling like my cheeks had been set on fire.

Can you say awkward?

Exactly.

My brows draw together as I refocus my attention on the list. It seems kind of pathetic that I've been at college, living on my own, for the past three years and have barely experienced anything life has to offer.

But there's no way I'm going to do these things now.

I'm mean, come on.

Skinny dip?

Karaoke?

Sex in a public place?

No way.

I've got more important things to focus on—like my future.

It's carefully that I fold up the worn piece of paper and set it on my nightstand before delving back into my studies.

CHAPTER 4

RYDER

"*W*hat the hell are you doing, McAdams? Learn to play defense or get the hell off my ice!"

I lock my jaw and clench my teeth until it feels like my molars are being ground to dust.

His ice?

Not a fucking chance. This has always been *my* ice.

This guy is the interloper.

Not me.

I'm the one who belongs here.

It's so damn tempting to fire back, but I keep my trap firmly shut.

Are you kidding me?

Of course I do. I'd actually like to get some play time during our next game. With the way things are looking, that might not happen.

Can you even fucking imagine it?

Me riding the pine while everyone else is on the ice?

Even the thought is enough to twist my gut into a series of painful little knots, which only sets my nerves further on edge and makes me question every damn move I make. It's a vicious cycle that's never ending.

If I'd known Coach K would leave us high and dry, I would have skipped this bullshit and gone straight to play for Chicago, since they picked me up during the draft after my sophomore season. No contracts were signed, so I was still eligible to play the next two years for Western. At the end of my junior season, I had a convo with Brody McKinnon and my parents. We discussed the pros and cons of making a move to the next level. In the end, we all agreed that one more year dominating in college would do me good. It would allow me time to sharpen my skills and build more muscle, so I'd be a force to be reckoned with in the pros.

Every time you level up—be it from house to travel, travel to college or juniors, college to the NHL—it's a transition and there's a learning curve. You have to work harder because the competition is that much better.

The game moves at a faster pace.

Some guys thrive on the challenge, while others get chewed up and spit out, never to be heard from again. They end up coaching a high school team in bumfuck nowhere. I don't plan on being dropkicked into the latter category. I've been working toward the NHL my entire life.

So, to have this prick come along in the final hours and fuck with my mojo as well as my dreams?

No. Not going to happen.

I refocus my attention on Garret Akeman as he skates toward me with the puck. Behind the cage, his lips spread into a slow smile. If there's one guy who is enjoying my fall from grace, it's him.

Asshole.

We came in together as freshmen and have not so quietly been competing for the past three years. And since Coach K preferred me over him, it wasn't a contest.

Not really.

Wouldn't you know that the new guy thinks Akeman can do no wrong?

"Looks like your position is up for grabs, McAdams. Who would have guessed that you'd peak before the end of college? Sucks to be you."

I don't bother with a response. Instead, I knock into his shoulder and skate past.

The rest of practice only goes downhill from there. Every little thing I do, Philips is there with a complaint.

I need to work on my positioning. I'm giving my opponent too much space to make a play.

I'm not getting my stick in the passing lanes.

I'm not taking the body when I have the chance.

My decision-making needs work.

By the time I hop off the ice, my muscles ache and I want to smash my fist into something.

Preferably Akeman's smug face.

I swear, every time Coach bellowed at me, Garret was right there with a shit-eating grin plastered across his mug. I don't know how I'll get through an entire season of this.

I seriously don't.

That thought is enough to send me mentally spiraling.

Every time I step onto the ice for practice, I tell myself that this will be the one where I turn it around.

That has yet to happen. Only now am I beginning to wonder if it ever will.

I shove my way into the locker room and throw my stick in the rack near the door before stalking inside and dropping onto the bench as if the weight of the world is resting on my shoulders. Sweat rolls down the back of my neck as I unsnap my helmet and yank it off my head.

Ford does the same before shaking out his hair. "That guy really has it out for you."

I glare. "Gee, what gave you that idea? The fact that he gives me a colonoscopy every damn time I'm on the ice?"

He snorts. "Nice image."

With a shrug, I jerk the practice jersey over my head and rip away the straps on the shoulder pads. Everything that happened during the two-hour practice circles viciously through my brain as I get to work on my skates. Every fuckup. Every time he yelled my name. It plays on a constant loop.

All around me, there's laughter and chatter as boisterous voices fill the space. Convos turn to the parties that are happening around campus. A few of the guys talk about heading to Slap Shotz, a local sports bar where the hockey team likes to congregate. The place is something of an institution at Western.

After the reaming I've just been treated to, I'm not in the mood for either option.

I'm too fucking pissed.

At myself.

But mostly at Philips for coming along and not only fucking with my season but my confidence as well.

"Sounds like everyone's heading over to your house after this," Ford says, interrupting the churn of my thoughts.

Awesome. Just what I wanted. Sulking in private is no longer an option unless I want to hole up in my room for the rest of the night.

I drag a hand over my face and consider the option.

"Dude, you need to chill out and just relax. A little pussy will help with that," Ford continues when I remain silent.

When the hell was the last time I got laid?

A couple weeks ago?

I rack my brain for an answer.

Christ. Could it actually be longer than that?

As soon as Philips tanked everything on the ice for me, my mojo with the ladies pretty much nosedived as well. For all I know, it could be months. I just haven't been interested.

Maybe Ford's right.

Maybe I need to sink inside a nice soft female.

Sure, it won't solve my issues on the ice, but it might help me forget about them for a couple of hours.

At this point, I'll take anything I can get.

CHAPTER 5

JULIETTE

"*J*f there aren't any further questions on the material, you're all dismissed. See you next week."

As soon as the word *dismissed* falls from Dr. Bell's lips, everyone explodes into action. Books and computers are shoved into bags before students flee the classroom like rats from a burning building.

It's kind of comical.

And maybe I'd even appreciate the humor in it if I weren't one of those people trying to scurry from the room. Unlike a good number of my classmates, it's not because I don't enjoy the professor or his lecture. On the contrary, bio stats is one of my favorite courses.

I'm pretty sure that makes me a nerd.

Can I help it if I find the concepts and information fascinating?

I love using different tools and techniques to collect data before summarizing, analyzing, and interpreting it. The kind of information you can learn and then use to assist the general population has the potential to be life altering. We're talking about curing diseases and helping people live longer, healthier lives.

What could be more exciting than that?

My reason for wanting to make a hasty getaway has more to do with Aaron being a student in this class. There's no doubt in my mind that I need to pull up my big girl panties and tell him that he's been friend zoned. But does that necessarily mean it has to be today?

That convo could take place tomorrow.

Or even next week.

If I'm lucky, Aaron will lose interest by then and I won't have to deal with the situation at all. We can go back to being study buddies and forget about our failed attempts at a romantic relationship.

Just as I cross over the threshold, a sigh of relief escapes from me and my muscles loosen. Looks like I made—

"Hey Juliette, wait up!"

Like a coward, I duck my head and pick up my pace, weaving through the throng of people that now fill the congested corridor.

"Juliette!"

By the time it registers how close his voice is, fingers are wrapping around my bicep to halt my movements.

A bright smile gets pasted on my face as I force myself to meet his gaze. "Hey, Aaron. How are you?"

"Good. I've been calling your name." He scratches the side of his head. "You must not have heard me."

I wince as the lie slips a little too easily from my lips. "Oh, sorry about that. I was thinking about the lab for inorganic chem we have coming up."

He nods in complete understanding as we make our way toward the exit of the building and push out into the bright sunshine. "Yeah, I could see why you'd be preoccupied with that."

A chilly breeze slides over my cheeks as my belly constricts with the knowledge of what I have to do. It's like a Band-Aid that needs to be ripped off quickly to cause the least amount of pain.

Before I can open my mouth and force out the words, he clears his throat. "I just wanted to reemphasize that I had a really good time the other night."

I nod. "Yeah, me too. It was fun."

A relieved smile breaks out across his face and his narrow shoulders lose some of their rigidity. "Good. I kind of thought we were on the same page about this."

Do it now.

Tell him.

Just get it over with.

"Aaron." I steel myself to push out the rest. "As much as—"

"Since we're both in agreement," he says, cutting me off. "I thought we could make it official."

My voice dies a quick death as I stare at him with wide eyes. "Oh."

Yeah...

That's all I've got.

A zip of electricity skitters down my spine and across my arms. I lift my hands to ward off the strange sensation before glancing around at the crowded pathway. As soon as I do, my eyes collide with Ryder's blue ones. Even from the distance that separates us, I feel the sheer force of their intensity drilling into me. The way he continues to stare makes it feel like my skin has grown too tight for the confines of my body. Any moment, I'll self-combust.

"Juliette?"

I blink back to the conversation with Aaron. Even though my attention is no longer locked on Ryder, I'm still aware of his heated gaze burning into my flesh, singeing me from the inside out. It's like a physical caress that's impossible to ignore. It's only when he disappears through the sea of students, veering away from the ice arena on campus that I'm able to breathe again.

"So, what do you say? Are we Western's newest power couple?"

It takes a second or two for his words to penetrate the thick mental fog that has descended.

My teeth scrape across my lower lip before pushing out the words. "I'm really sorry, Aaron. I think it would be best if we remained friends instead."

His brows snap together, and I brace myself for an argument.

"Really?"

"Yeah." I tack on hastily, "I like you a lot but just not...romantically. I hope you understand."

"Oh." He glances down at his loafers. "I, um, guess we're not on the same page after all."

"No, I don't think we are. I'm really sorry for any confusion."

"Well, that's certainly disappointing," he mumbles, kicking a pebble with the toe of his shoe. "It's just that we have so much in common. Us being together seemed like a no brainer."

"You're right, we do have a ton of stuff in common. But there's just not a, you know, spark."

Not like when Ryder and I are together.

As soon as that insidious thought pops into my brain, I shove it away before it can take root and do permanent damage.

With a tilt of his head, he licks his chapped lips. "There isn't any scientific evidence to back up your assertion that chemical attraction even exists. Couples are successful because they have a rock-solid foundation regarding shared interests, morals, and values."

"Maybe attraction can't be qualitatively measured, but it exists." How else can you explain the physical reaction I have to Ryder McAdams? It's *all* chemical attraction. We have absolutely nothing in common. Hell, we don't even like each other and yet…

Fireworks explode when we're together.

His expression turns quizzical. "But if it can't be proven, how can you be so sure?"

"Because I've felt it, and I've seen relationships with chemistry that have stood the test of time. I believe in it, and that's what I want for myself."

Just not with Ryder.

Someone more like Aaron who I have shared interests with.

"Fair enough." His expression turns thoughtful as we continue walking. "I can't say that I'm not disappointed by this turn of events. You're missing out on something great."

I force a smile. "You're right, and I'm the one who'll have to live with that decision."

With nothing more to say on the subject, Aaron hitches his thumb over his shoulder. "I should probably get to the library. I need to study. Any chance you want to join me?"

"Maybe next time. I have an appointment with my advisor in ten minutes and then I'm off to my lab."

He nods before giving me a wave and disappearing.

Tension leaks from my muscles as we part ways.

As friends.

The rest of the day turns out to be a whirlwind. By the time I walk through the door of our apartment at seven o'clock that evening, my ass is dragging, and my brain is fried. I'm looking forward to hitting the sheets and sacking out.

"Hello?" I call out when I don't immediately spot Carina curled up on the couch in the living room, wrapped up in a book. Several lights are on, and music is playing, so I know she's around.

I peek my head inside her room. It's an explosion of clothes, books, colorful pillows, and makeup. Dance posters and photographs of friends and family decorate almost the entire wall space. Carina's room is a direct reflection of her personality—bursting at the seams with vibrant energy.

Our gazes meet in the full-length mirror before she spins around. "I'm so glad you're here!"

"Oh?" Her overly enthusiastic greeting has alarm bells going off in my head.

With narrowed eyes, I take her in. Her leggings and comfy sweat-shirt, which is what she'd usually wear if we're hunkering down for the night, has been replaced by a creamy low-cut sweater, short tan corduroy skirt, and rich, nutbrown suede boots. Her blonde hair has been left all long and loose to float around her shoulders and her make up is on point with a smoky eye.

"You did all this for me?" I wave a hand. "You shouldn't have."

Ignoring the comment, she says instead, "We're going out." Her gaze slides down my length before bouncing back to my face. "And you need to change into something a little more party appropriate."

The thought of rallying just to hit some off-campus rager makes me even more tired than I already am.

"Hard pass. I was going to spend an hour reading and then turn in early." I point a finger in her direction. "But you have fun tonight. Be sure to tell me all about it mañana."

When I attempt to back out of her room, she springs forward with a surprising amount of speed. Kind of like a snake intent on striking. Her fingers lock around my wrist before she drags me further inside her space. "No way! You're coming with."

When I open my mouth, she says in a rush, "Before you argue, just know that I'm pulling the best friends card tonight."

My eyes widen. "Seriously?"

"Yup." She pops the P at the end of the word. "I'm doing it for your own good. You've been working way too hard and need to loosen up and have a little fun." She tilts her head and studies me. "You do remember what fun is, right?"

I take a moment to search my memory. "Um, I think so."

She grins. "Excellent."

I point to my outfit. "Can I wear this?"

The way her eyes widen is answer enough, but just in case I'm slow on the uptake she snaps, "Absolutely not."

I cross my arms over my chest. "I don't have anything more party appropriate than this."

She presses her lips together. "That's so sad. I'm glad we're in agreement that your wardrobe lacks the necessary style we're looking for this evening. FYI—I took the liberty of rummaging through your closet and drawers. Nice vibe, by the way. Super cute. Love the pink and black aesthetic. And it's so small, you could literally pop it right into your purse."

I groan as heat scorches my cheeks. "You're a horrible person for bringing that up."

"What? I'm complimenting you on your taste in vibes. What's wrong with that?"

"Stop saying vibe," I mutter. Even though Carina and I are close, this isn't a topic I want to discuss with her. Or anyone else, for that matter.

"You prefer vibrator? Or perhaps personal pleasure tool? Self-love helper?"

"I'd prefer to pretend that we never had this convo in the first place." My brows pinch together. "And why the hell would I pack it in my purse?"

She shrugs. "I don't know. It's a horny day and you'll need to use it while out?"

"Where? The public restroom?"

"You say that like it's not a thing."

"Oh my god, Carina. It's not! No one masturbates in the bathroom at school."

She cocks a brow. "You sure about that?"

I press my lips together. "I think we're done with this convo."

She throws her hands up and rolls her eyes. "You're the one who started it." Before I can argue the point, she waves an arm all Vanna White-like at the bed. "Anyway, I pulled this fit from my closet."

My attention zeros in on a short red skirt and soft black cashmere sweater that her mother bought her for Christmas last year.

"How amazing would those black boots you just picked up on sale look with this?"

Actually…pretty damn amazing.

Carina might be a dance major, but she has an amazing eye for fashion.

Sure, I could argue, but I already know how the evening will end, and that's with me attending this party with my roomie.

And she's right. It's been a while since we've gotten dressed up and gone out together, which is what it means when she pulls the best friends card. She doesn't do it often. So when she does, I usually just roll with it. All right…maybe that's not one hundred percent true. Normally, I put up a little bit of a fight before gracefully giving in. Tonight, I'm not even going to bother.

"Okay, fine."

"What?" She blinks as if I've totally thrown her off.

"You heard me. I'll go, and I'll even wear the outfit you picked out."

"Wow," she mutters. "I wasn't expecting you to give in so easily." Her eyes narrow. "Wait a minute, is this some sort of sly bit of trickery on your part? Are you attempting to lull me into a false state of contentedness, so I'll lower my guard?"

My lips tremble. "Nope. I've been thinking about what you said the other day and you're right."

"Of course I'm right. What am I right about?"

"You said that this was our last year in college, and I should enjoy it." Lord knows medical school will be even more challenging than this. And then there'll be my residency. So...

I need to stop every once in a while, take a deep breath, and enjoy myself.

And that starts tonight.

Her face transforms into a grin before she jumps up and down, clapping her hands together. "Yay! I'm so excited. We're going to have so much fun!"

"Me, too." It's almost a surprise to realize that I actually mean it.

No matter what we do, Carina and I always have a good time. Even if that means we're just hanging at the apartment. We're opposites in every sense of the word, but she's turned out to be an incredible friend. We met during the first semester of freshman year in English 102 and have been besties ever since. Sophomore year, we decided to live together in the dorms and then the following one, we rented an apartment off campus.

I'm going to miss her next year.

No matter what we end up doing, it won't be together.

Thirty minutes later and I've been poured into Carina's outfit. And when I say poured, I mean it. Since she's a dancer, her build is longer and leaner than mine. And she certainly doesn't have D cups either. I'm almost afraid I'll stretch out her sweater. Although, it still has the tag on it, so I'm not sure she'd care. I have what my mom calls an hourglass figure. Neither of us knows where it came from, since she's slender like Carina.

The skirt is gorgeous, but here's hoping I don't drop anything, because there's no way I'll be able to bend over without flashing my panties.

Or, more accurately—thong.

Not only did that bitch go through my underwear drawer and find my vibe, she pulled out a teeny tiny thong and matching bra. I shift and resist the urge to pick the dental floss out of my ass.

With a frown, I meet her gaze in the mirror. "This thong is uncomfortable."

She waves away the concern. "Don't worry, you'll get used to it."

"Yeah, that's the problem. I don't want to get used to it. There's a reason why I buried it at the back of the drawer."

"I know. I had to really dig around, but don't worry, I still found it."

When I glare, she says with a smile, "They'll make you feel sexy."

How does that even make sense?

"Why would a string wedged up the crack of my ass make me feel sexy?"

She rolls her eyes and huffs out a breath before heading back to her desk slash vanity to grab a tube of mascara and lipstick. It takes another twenty minutes to do my hair and makeup.

A lot of days, I wear it up in a messy bun or ponytail because it's quick and easy. Much like hers, I have curls that float around my shoulders. And she's given me a smoky eye to go along with it.

I didn't even recognize myself when she swiveled me around to the mirror and said, "Ta-da."

I look...sexy.

"You certainly know how to work magic," I say, turning one way and then another to get a better look at myself. It's an odd sensation to stare at your own reflection and feel like you're looking at a stranger.

"It was hardly magic. You're gorgeous with amazing cheekbones and ridiculously long lashes. I just added a few curls and a little mascara to make your eyes pop. The sweater and skirt hugs your curves like nobody's business." She gives me a pleased smile. "Makes a world of difference, doesn't it?"

"But I like jeans and T-shirts." Or better yet, cozy sweatshirts and leggings.

A long-suffering sigh escapes from her. "Yeah, I know. I've been doing my damnedest to break you of that habit before the end of senior year."

My lips quirk. "It hasn't worked."

"No, it doesn't appear that it has."

She adds a few more finishing touches and voilà, we're ready to go. Even though it's chilly outside, we forego jackets and grab our purses before taking off. One step into the hallway and I nearly run into our neighbors.

"Hey, Jules," Ford says, gaze flicking over me. "You guys heading out for the night?"

Carina slams the door closed behind her and swings around. The smile falls off her face when she finds her ex-stepbrother standing on the other side of the threshold.

"Oh." Her voice turns monotone as her eyes darken. "It's you."

The smile he'd just flashed at me widens when he catches a glimpse of her. I almost expect him to rub his hands together with barely suppressed glee.

"You always know how to make a guy feel special. It must be your sparkling personality that has all the dudes on campus beating down your door. Or is it because they enjoy the way you beat them off?" His expression turns thoughtful as he taps his chin. "I've never been able to figure it out."

"There's something I've been meaning to give you." She makes a big show of digging through her purse. "Here it is." She pulls out her hand with a solitary finger raised and a scowl. "As if I'm interested in making you feel anything other than unwanted."

He crowds her personal space and whispers something I can't quite make out in her ear. Her eyes widen as she quickly shoves him back a step.

"You're such a perv," she growls.

He chuckles in response.

Wolf catches my eye before nodding toward the elevator. "Should we give these two crazy kids their privacy so they can hash out their issues?"

I glance at Carina and Ford. She looks on the verge of ripping him to shreds.

"That would probably be for the best. Who knows how long they're going to snipe at one another."

"True story," Madden adds with a roll of his eyes.

Once upon a time, Carina and Ford were step-siblings. I can't remember if it was her mother and his father or the other way around. The marriage lasted a handful of years before they parted ways. Even though the two are no longer related, they're constantly at each other's throats. It's been that way for as long as I've known them.

It probably would have been a good idea to live as far apart as they could get from each other, but Ford's father knows the property manager of the building and got a great deal on the rent, so here we are.

Neighbors with Ford.

Wolf and Madden are pretty decent guys.

For hockey players.

I don't know Wolf that well. He keeps to himself more than the rest of the guys. Plus, he's kind of intimidating with the shaved head and tattoos. He towers over me, and the breadth of his shoulders is impressive. He's always been nice, but still...

There's an intensity to him that I find unnerving. The way he stares leaves me feeling stripped bare. And not in a sexual way. More in an *I know all your secrets* kind of way.

Madden seems like a nice guy. He has dark hair that's cut short with mocha-colored eyes to match. He's quick to smile and has muscles for days. From what I know, he spends a lot of time working out. While he's not one of those athletes that hooks up with a different girl every weekend, I've never seen him seriously date, either. And he could. There are more than enough girls vying for his attention. Maverick mentioned that he was in a pretty serious relationship during high school, and they broke up freshman year of college.

Once we reach the elevator, I stab the button and pray it comes quickly. I can still hear Carina and Ford exchanging pointed barbs from down the hall.

"Those two need to have sex and get it over with already," Wolf mutters.

"What?" My head whips toward him as my brows shoot up. There's no way I heard him correctly.

He raises a dark brow as if daring me to argue. "They need to sleep

34

together so they can get each other out of their systems. Their constant bickering was cute at first. Now, it's just annoying."

Carina and Ford?

No way. He's totally misreading the situation.

I shake my head in disagreement. "That's not what's going on."

Wolf smirks. "Seriously? With them, all this arguing and taking shots at each other is foreplay. Enough already. Let's get to the main event so we can all move on with our lives."

My mouth falls open as I flick a glance at Madden to get his take on the matter.

He jerks his shoulders before nodding. "I have to agree with Westerville on this one, little McKinnon."

I'm so shocked that I don't even take offense to the *little McKinnon* comment.

It's with fresh eyes that I turn my attention back to Carina and Ford. He's standing entirely too close, invading her personal space, and her face is all flushed. Only now do I realize how much sexual energy is buzzing in the air between them.

Well, I'll be damned.

Maybe Wolf and Madden are right.

Maybe them getting it on is *exactly* what needs to happen.

Then peace can once again reign in the kingdom.

CHAPTER 6

RYDER

By the time I shower, change, and get the hell out of the athletic center, my mood has improved.

Somewhat.

Maybe Ford is right, and I just need to chill out for the night. Have a couple of drinks and find a girl to take my mind off the situation. Everything inside me loosens as I tip the beer bottle to my lips and take a long swig.

As I do, my gaze wanders over the packed room before getting snagged by Larsa Middleton. The moment our eyes lock, she lifts her hand in a wave. As soon as I reciprocate the greeting with a chin lift, she breaks away from the group of girls she's standing with before cutting a direct path to me.

Larsa isn't a girl who likes to play games. And that I can appreciate.

Her wide green eyes remain locked on mine as she weaves through the sea of students who are crammed into the first floor of the house.

"Hey, Ryder," she purrs.

"Hey, yourself. How's it going?" I take another drink.

The blonde presses her palms against my chest before slowly stroking them upward. "Much better now that I've found you."

I've known Larsa since freshman year. Every once in a while, we have a few classes together. From what I've seen, she's a smart little cookie with a weakness for hockey players. Preferably the ones who get lots of ice time.

Know what I like best about Larsa?

She understands that a couple hours spent rolling around between the sheets is exactly that. There's nothing worse than screwing someone and the moment you pull out, they want to know when they can see you again. Extracting yourself from those situations can be tricky. Sometimes you get an object chucked at your head. Other times, there's water works.

So…yeah.

Thank god for girls like Larsa who get it.

Maybe I didn't realize it before, but she's exactly what I need. A little TLC from the Wildcats' number one fan. This girl is like the energizer bunny in the sack. She'll strangle the life out of my cock until there's nothing more to give.

She presses close enough for me to feel the pebbled tips of her breasts through my T-shirt.

"Bro, have you seen McKinnon's little sis?"

I rip my attention away from the girl smiling slyly up at me with eyes that hold all sorts of wicked promises to stare at one of the freshmen players whose sole job at this party is to man the door.

"Huh?"

"Mav's little sis," he repeats. "She's here and damn, that girl is a total smoke show."

"Mav doesn't have a little sister." I pause for a second or two. "Are you talking about Juliette?" Just wrapping my lips around her name is enough to have me crashing back to earth with a painful thump. All those good vibes rushing through me dissipate as if they'd been a figment of my imagination.

His eyes slice to Larsa, where they stay ensnared. When he doesn't respond to the question, I snap my fingers in front of his face to reclaim his distracted attention.

"Um, yeah," he mumbles, still entranced by the blonde stroking her hands over me. "Juliette. She's a real hottie."

There's no damn way I heard him correctly. The guy is obviously shitfaced. These freshmen should only be allowed a couple drinks or shots before getting cut off for the night. They have no idea how to party responsibly.

"Hey, eyes on me." When he refocuses his attention, I clarify, "Are you saying that Juliette McKinnon is here?" I point at the wood floor beneath my feet. "At this party."

"Yup. She just walked in with Ford, Wolf, Madden, and Ford's sister."

With a frown, I rub my shadowed jaw and scan the vicinity, looking for the dark-haired girl.

When was the last time I saw Juliette at a party?

I'm not even talking about a hockey party but just a regular, off campus party.

Maybe a couple times freshman and sophomore year?

That girl is too busy getting straight As to actually have a social life.

If she's here, then my guess is that Carina twisted her arm and forced her into it. There's no way in hell she'd show up of her own volition. A rowdy hockey party where all sorts of shit goes down isn't exactly Juliette's scene.

Sensing a disturbance in the force, Larsa curls her acrylics into my chest.

When my gaze reluctantly snaps to hers, she gives me a full-on pout with pink-slicked lips. "I'm ready to get out of here. Aren't you?"

Hell yeah I am.

The sultry promise in her eyes tells me exactly what's in store for the evening, and I am definitely here for it. With any luck, a little time spent with the blonde beauty will help me to reset and I can hit the ice tomorrow with a fresh perspective. What I need is for Larsa to help soothe all the raging emotions inside me that I haven't been able to do for myself.

Dismissing the freshman, I say to her instead, "Yeah, baby. Let's go."

Her mouth curls as she reaches up on the tips of her toes and presses a kiss against my lips. She snags my lower one before tugging it with sharp teeth and then releasing it with a soft pop.

That sexy little maneuver just solidified my decision to take her upstairs.

I glance at the freshman, who hasn't moved a muscle. His eyes are unfocused as he stares at Larsa with a slack jaw. If I looked down, he'd probably be giving her a full-fledged salute.

Certainly can't blame the guy for that.

With a grin, I clap him on the shoulder. "See what you have to look forward to if you play your cards right?"

His Adam's apple bobs as he swallows and nods. The look on his face is one of pure envy.

Just as I wrap an arm around Larsa's slender shoulders, I catch sight of a dark head from the corner of my eye. Since it's crowded, that shouldn't be enough to give me pause and have me rubbernecking, but that's exactly what happens. Awareness prickles at the bottom of my gut as my eyes zero in on the girl who's caught my attention.

That's all it takes for my brows to snap together as my steps slow. Larsa shoots me a frown when I grind to a halt.

Wait just a second...

That can't be Juliette.

No.

Fucking.

Way.

I squint, trying to get a better look at the girl in question.

I mean...

It sure as hell looks like her. And the freshie's right. This girl is a total smoke show. My cock twitches in agreement. Actually, it does a hell of a lot more than that. The longer I stare, the harder it becomes.

Larsa brushes her fingers against my junk. "Mmm, so big. Let's go somewhere private and put that to good use."

Yes. That's exactly what I should do.

Except...

My feet don't budge.

I'm incapable of movement.

Especially when the girl turns just a bit and I get a better look at her face.

That first glimpse is like a punch to the gut.

Juliette flashes a smile to the guy standing next to her.

My gaze shifts to the douche at her side.

Wolf.

What the hell is going on around here?

"Ryder?" Larsa's fingers wrap around mine before giving them a gentle squeeze.

When a couple people move, giving me a direct line of sight, I get an eyeful of the black sweater that hugs her curves like it was made specifically for her. My gaze drops to the short red skirt that barely covers her ass and the tall black boots that showcase her legs.

If I was hard before, I'm like steel now.

My gaze lifts to her face for a second time to make sure it's really her.

Damn.

It's definitely her.

I've never seen Juliette in an outfit like this.

Never.

And I've known her since my family moved next door to the McKinnons' when I was in kindergarten. I suck my lower lip between my teeth and chew it. How the hell am I going to go upstairs and enjoy myself knowing that Juliette is down here looking like *that.* Every dick in the place will try shooting their shot with her.

I flick narrowed eyes at Wolf. He's someone I consider a good friend. If I thought for one damn second that he'd lay hands on her, I'd fucking rip him apart.

And I wouldn't even feel bad about it.

Christ.

This is the last thing I need.

I drag a hand down my face.

"Ryder, baby. I'm horny." That last word comes out sounding more like *hooooornnnney.*

I force my gaze away from Juliette to stare at the hottie in my arms.

Shit.

That's when I realize the mind-blowing sex I'd been anticipating is no longer on the agenda. In a last-ditch effort to salvage my plans, I glance around for Mav. There's no way he'd be good with his sister at a hockey party looking like that. Juliette might be a year older, but he's protective.

Unfortunately, he's nowhere to be found.

Figures.

"I'm, ah, sorry. There's something I need to take care of, but maybe later?"

Her eyes go from heavy-lidded and full of promise to wide and filled with disbelief in less than two seconds flat.

"Are you being serious?"

By the displeasure that fills her voice, later will not be an option.

For me, anyway.

"Yeah, I am. Sorry about that."

"You're missing out," she snaps, untangling herself from me.

Don't I know it. I'd been looking forward to all the little tricks she's got up her sleeve. The girl is like a one-woman circus act with stunts that are meant to shock and awe.

And, well, make you come.

I shrug.

Once she realizes that my decision is final, she swings around and stalks away. With the hot blonde forgotten, I refocus on Juliette. My brows snap together when I find that Wolf has disappeared.

In his place is none other than Garret Akeman.

Garret fucking Akeman.

And that, my friends, is all the incentive I need to haul ass.

CHAPTER 7

JULIETTE

"How about a shot?" the muscular hockey player asks.

"No, I'm kind of a lightweight. I'll probably just stick to beer."

He steps a bit closer and amps up the wattage of his smile. "All the more reason to have a couple. Let's get you loose."

Yeah...I don't think so.

I'm more than aware of Garret Akeman's manwhore rep on campus. I'm not looking to be added to his long list of conquests. Plus, I've always made a point to steer clear of the hockey players. Actually, I try to avoid most of the athletes at Western. I don't need any gossip getting back to Mav.

From the corner of my eye, I catch sight of a brawny figure shoving his way through the crowd. My head swivels in that direction, only to find Ryder. Most people are smart enough to scurry out of his way. The guy is like a locomotive barreling down the tracks. His eyes are narrowed, and his lips are pressed together in a thin slash as a muscle in his tightly clenched jaw tics a mad rhythm.

Smoke practically billows from his ears.

Huh.

What's his deal?

Before I can open my mouth to ask what the issue is, he snakes an arm around my shoulders and hauls me against him. A squeak of surprise escapes from me as I'm pressed against all that chiseled strength. My heart flip flops painfully in my chest, and my mouth turns cottony.

The beachy scent of his cologne is almost enough to weaken my knees.

When was the last time I stood this close to Ryder?

I rack my brain for a second or two but come up empty.

Probably never.

It's tempting to turn my face and inhale a giant breath of him. Shaking those disturbing thoughts loose takes effort. I glance at Ryder, only to find him glaring at Garret.

The other guy cocks a brow. "Is there something you needed, McAdams?"

Ryder's arm tightens, pressing me even closer. "You know this is McKinnon's sister, right?"

The other guy keeps his gaze steadily trained on his teammate as he brings a bottle of beer to his lips before saying, "I'm aware of who she is."

The flirty tone he'd been using is now long gone, and I get the feeling these two don't like each other very much.

"Then why don't you do us both a favor and stop hitting on her?" Ryder growls.

"Who the fuck are you? Her protector?" His gaze slices to mine before it drops, crawling down my length before flicking upward again. "She looks old enough to make her own decisions, don't you think?"

Even though the people surrounding us are all laughing and drinking, the tension between these two has ratcheted up, turning thick and oppressive. It wouldn't take much for it to explode.

"I'm a friend, and what she doesn't need is to get tangled up with you. Or any of the guys on the team," he adds, expression turning fierce. "Understand, Akeman?"

Instead of responding, Garret dismisses him before turning his attention to me. His voice softens, once again becoming seductive. "How about we get out of here and go somewhere quiet where we can get to know each other better?" A slow smile slides across his handsome face. "Would you like that, sweetheart?"

My brows shoot up.

Sweetheart?

Um, no thanks.

What's become apparent from our five-minute interaction is that Garret Akeman knows how to turn on and off the charm. He also doesn't follow bro code. None of Mav's friends or teammates have ever hit on me. The fact that he has no problem doing it says a lot about the type of guy he is.

Just as I open my mouth to tell him I'm not interested, Ryder beats me to the punch.

"No, she wouldn't. Now get lost."

The other guy straightens to his full height, which is still a couple inches shorter than Ryder's six-three.

Garret's voice turns steely as his upper lip curls. "Did I fucking ask you?"

Oh shit.

I seem to be trapped in the middle of their pissing match, and it's the last place I want to be.

Before the situation can escalate and erupt into a fight, which isn't unheard of at a hockey party, I slip from beneath Ryder's muscular arm and take a step in retreat before locking my fingers around his wrist.

"Can I have a word with you in private?"

Air stalls in my lungs as Ryder's deep blue depths lock on mine, pinning them in place. There's so much emotion roiling within them, but I have no idea if it's anger aimed at Garret or something more. That one look is all it takes for awareness to prickle along my skin. I couldn't be more cognizant of the way my fingertips press against the flesh of his wrist and how my heart flutters in response.

This unwanted attraction feels more like a curse. It's one of the reasons I've always been careful to keep my distance. Thankfully,

Western is a large university. It's been so much easier to avoid him in college than it was in high school.

When he fails to respond, I drop my voice. "Please?"

He jerks his head into a tight nod, and the fist gripping my heart loosens just a bit. At least enough for me to breathe.

I glance at Garret and force a smile. "I'll be back in a minute."

"I'll be right here waiting," he says easily.

Ryder glowers as I drag him through the dining area and into the kitchen. I glance around for a quiet corner where we can have a bit of privacy, but it's wall-to-wall people.

My gaze lands on the back hallway before I tow him in that direction. With my fingers still wrapped around his wrist, I shove through the door and stalk outside into the chilled night air. It feels so much colder than when we arrived earlier this evening.

It's only after the door slams shut that I drop his hand and whirl around to face him. "What are you doing?"

His broody gaze locks on mine, and just like before, arousal explodes in my belly.

All right, so maybe it explodes a little lower. I quickly douse the flames, unwilling to allow them to burn out of control.

He jerks a brow. "I think a better question would be—what are *you* doing?"

I straighten to my full height, which is a good eight inches shorter than him as my hands settle on my hips. "Excuse me? What does that mean?"

When he takes a step toward me, I have to lift my chin to hold his gaze. "You know exactly what it means."

"I was having a conversation with a friend." I'm using the term loosely, since we aren't, but I'll be damned if I admit it to Ryder. It's none of his business.

I'm none of his business.

"You know what he was looking for, right?" He takes another step closer, swallowing up some of the space between us as his voice dips several octaves. "I'll give you a hint—it wasn't to talk about your major or plans after college. The guy is looking to get laid."

Heat slams into my cheeks as his gaze pins mine in place. As tempting as it is to break eye contact, I don't allow it to fall.

When I remain silent, he growls, "What happened? Did you turn into a bunny when I wasn't looking?"

My eyes widen as the air gets knocked from my lungs.

"No!"

"Then do us both a favor and stay away from Garret. He's bad news." There's a beat of silence as he bristles, sounding irritated. "What are you even doing here? You never attend parties."

"Yes, I do." *Lie.* "They're just not the same ones as you."

From the dubious expression that settles on his face, it's clear he doesn't believe me. "You should go home and stick your nose back in a book where it belongs. A party like this is above your paygrade."

Fury ignites deep inside my chest. Unlike Ryder, I've never been prone to anger or outbursts. I don't throw punches or get in people's faces. In all honesty, it takes a lot to rile me up.

But right now?

Rage rushes through my veins like molten lava.

How dare he say that!

This time, I'm the one who eats up the remaining distance between us before stabbing a finger into his rock-hard pectoral. "I'll do whatever the hell I want, and you're not going to stop me! I'm old enough to make my own decisions along with my own mistakes. You aren't my brother, and you're certainly not my keeper. So stay out of my business!"

He presses his lips into a thin, tight line until they turn bloodless. Emotion sparks in his eyes.

When Ryder fails to respond, I give him another poke for good measure before swinging around and stalking to the back door. As I yank it open and step over the threshold, his deep voice halts me in my tracks.

"Your brother doesn't want you messing around with his teammates."

My spine stiffens in response as I escape into the house, slamming the door shut with such force that it rattles on its hinges. I glare through the dirty glass pane and twist the lock.

Now that I'm in the house, music and voices vibrate inside my head. I shove my way through the sea of students in search of Carina. On the way past the makeshift bar, I grab a red Solo cup full of beer.

I'm still seething that Ryder had the audacity to say that to me. As if I'd ever mess around with any of my brother's teammates. That's not a position I'd want to put Maverick in. And I sure as shit don't need a manwhore like Ryder McAdams to tell me that.

I bring the rim to my lips and suck down the contents in one thirsty gulp before slamming it on the bar and wiping the back of my hand across my mouth.

Ryder McAdams can go screw himself.

CHAPTER 8

RYDER

*W*ell…that conversation certainly didn't go as planned.

For a long moment, I stare at the last place I'd seen Juliette before she slipped inside the house and slammed the door. I'm pretty sure she locked the damn thing. A potent concoction of anger and lust swirls through me.

I've always been so careful to shove my feelings for her down until they were buried so deep, I could almost forget they existed. That's no longer possible. It feels like everywhere I go, there she is. Whether it's at her apartment, on campus, or at a party.

I drag a frustrated hand through my hair and tip my head back to stare at the stars that litter the dark night sky.

Nothing in my life is easy anymore.

Had I been smart, I would have allowed Larsa to lead me up the staircase to my bedroom. At this very moment, I could be buried balls deep in her soft pussy. Instead, I'm standing in the cold, more than likely locked out of my own damn house.

How's that for a kick in the ass?

And Juliette is inside, doing god knows what.

If anything, I've only made the situation worse.

For a handful of seconds, I consider heading back inside to find

Larsa. If anyone can erase the last twenty minutes from my brain, it's her. The things she can do with her mouth are borderline criminal.

And more than likely, illegal in half a dozen states.

Instead of the blonde beauty popping into my brain, an image of Juliette does. The sexy black sweater had clung to every single curve while the short red skirt barely skimmed her thighs. The tall, black boots had given her just a bit of extra height, making her legs look even longer. The way her dark hair fell around her shoulders in soft waves—waves I'd wanted to bury my fingers in before tipping her head back until she was forced to meet my gaze while I took her mouth—is enough to set my blood on fire. It had taken every ounce of self-restraint not to lay my hands on her.

So…there's no way I can hook up with another girl while Juliette is walking around our house looking like sex on a stick.

I don't even bother to check the back door. Instead, I stalk around the side of the house. As soon as I hit the front lawn, I find a dozen or so people milling around, finishing off their drinks.

What the hell?

I glare before grabbing their cups and dumping the beer onto the lawn.

"Hey, I wasn't done with that!" a drunk guy grumbles.

"What did you do that for?" a girl protests, slurring her words.

It only takes one dark look aimed in their direction for their complaints to die away.

One of the freshman players is supposed to be manning the door at all times. No one leaves the house with open containers.

Are these asshats trying to get us busted?

Like we need that.

As I stomp up the porch stairs, a female calls out my name. That alone isn't enough to make me turn, except I recognize this particular voice.

"Ryder!"

I swing around and find my cousin, Brooke, with a wide smile on her face. Her boyfriend, Crosby Rhodes, is steadfast at her side. He's a football player at Western.

As soon as I'm within striking distance, Brooke throws her arms around my neck before squeezing me tight. With her held against me, I meet Crosby's eyes over her shoulder. It wasn't so long ago that I gave him a shiner and busted his lip open for breaking her heart.

And what did the asshole do?

Just stood there while a crowd of onlookers surrounded us in the middle of campus while taking every punch I slammed into his face. I should have realized at that point how much he loved her.

When he gives me a chin lift in greeting, I do the same.

Brooke untangles herself and pulls away just enough to search my face. "I haven't seen you for a while. Everything good?"

I shrug. There's no damn way I'm telling her about Coach and how it feels like my last year playing college hockey is circling the drain.

Brooke tilts her head and scrutinizes me more carefully in the darkness. Her voice softens. "Are you sure that you're all right? There's a strange expression on your face."

"Kind of like someone has your nuts in a vise," Crosby adds, as if the thought brings him genuine pleasure.

Dickhead.

Crosby and I are friendlier than we used to be, but there's still a natural rivalry between us since he's part of the football program and I'm a hockey player. It's all about who has the most fans, brings home the most championship titles, gets the most funding, has the better facilities, yada, yada, yada.

As far as I'm concerned, the football players are a bunch of prima donnas who enjoy their ice baths, after-practice smoothies, and massage therapists a little too much.

Come lace up a pair of Bauers and we'll show you who gets knocked around more.

I shoot him a glare before refocusing my attention on Brooke. We've always been close. She's more like a sister, and there's nothing I wouldn't do for her. That includes beating Crosby to a bloody pulp if he's stupid enough to hurt her for a second time.

Although, by the way he stares at her, it's doubtful that will happen.

And the pics they post online?

They're enough to nauseate me. We're talking matching charcoal face masks. Who would have ever thought the guy would turn into such a simp?

And by the looks of it, he's enjoying every minute.

"It's all good," I tell her more firmly.

"So, what are you doing outside then?" she asks.

I blink before holding up the plastic cups I've taken away from the dumbasses on the front lawn. "Making sure we don't get busted by the cops."

She nods. "Smart. You ready to head back inside?"

"Yup."

I take away a few more bottles and cans before the three of us head up the porch steps and walk right in. Whoever is supposed to be manning the front door has gone MIA. Once inside, I set the containers on a small table in the entryway. The place is even more packed than it was twenty minutes ago. This is what happens when you don't have crowd control. I'm going to kick some freshman ass the next time we're on the ice.

My gaze combs over the sea of students. Space has been cleared in the living room and people are busting out their best dance moves.

It's not a pretty sight.

"Hey, isn't that Juliette?" Brooke asks, raising her voice to be heard over the thumping beat that reverberates off the walls.

My narrowed gaze coasts over the throng with more care until it lands on her dark head. I try to keep my voice tempered in order not to give too much away. My matchmaking cousin has always suspected my feelings for Juliette run deeper than I've been willing to acknowledge. If I'm barely able to own up to it privately, there's no way in hell I'll admit it to someone else.

Not even Brooke.

"Yup."

"I'm going to say hello."

She doesn't take more than two steps before Crosby reaches out and drags her back for a long kiss.

By the time he sets her free, her cheeks are stained with color as her gaze flickers between us. "You two play nice while I'm gone."

When I crack my knuckles, she narrows her eyes.

"Very funny."

"Who's joking around?" I ask with a popped brow.

Crosby straightens before muttering from the side of his mouth, "Go ahead and try it, McAdams. This time, I'll give as good as I get."

My lips slide into a grin as I clap him on the back.

Hard.

"Don't tempt me, Rhodes. I'd love nothing better than to have a second go at you."

He snorts.

My gaze settles on Juliette as my cousin taps her shoulder. When she spins around, her face lights up before the two girls throw their arms around each other and embrace tightly. Their genuine affection is apparent. As a kid, Brooke spent a lot of time at our house and the two girls became fast friends. I'd chill with Maverick while they'd disappear into Juliette's room or, during the summer, hang out by the pool in the back.

It was always sweet torture I couldn't get enough of.

Crosby folds his arms across his broad chest. "So...we're just gonna stand here and watch them dance?"

I shrug and give him a bit of side eye. "You got a better plan?"

Because there's no damn way I'm leaving. Barely can I take my eyes off Juliette. The way her body sways to the beat has my dick stiffening right up.

Again.

When Clint Peters, the freshman from earlier, walks by, I shout his name to get his attention. The guy looks completely shitfaced. He glances at me with bleary eyes, and I raise two fingers. With a quick nod, he stumbles off toward the kitchen. A couple minutes later, he returns with two frosty bottles of beer.

I grab one while Crosby does the same.

And then we do the only thing we can and settle in for the duration.

CHAPTER 9

JULIETTE

*B*est. *Night. Ever.*

I seriously can't believe how much fun I'm having. We've been dancing for what feels like hours. At first it was Carina and a couple of girls I recognized from our floor sophomore year when we lived in the dorms, and then Brooke showed up. I haven't seen her in ages.

The continuous flow of drinks certainly hasn't hurt either. I suspect that might be part of the reason I'm flying high. Who knew alcohol could make you feel so good?

Every time Ryder scowls at me from the edge of the dance area, I raise my plastic cup toward him before taking a healthy swallow. It's become something of a game. One he doesn't realize is happening because he's been wearing a permanent glower since he caught sight of me tonight.

That guy can take a flying leap, for all I care.

Even though my back is turned, the heat of his glare burns a hole through my skin. I don't think I've ever been more hyperaware of another human being than I am of Ryder McAdams.

I hate it almost as much as I love it.

Which is…confusing.

All I know is that my brain isn't racing a mile a minute with everything that needs to be completed for school, and I'm no longer focused on what life might look like a year down the road.

My mind is centered on the here and now.

The fun I'm having with Carina, Brooke, and the other girls.

It's surprisingly freeing.

When was the last time I smiled or laughed this much?

I rack my brain but can't remember.

With my arms lifted toward the ceiling, my head falls back, and I close my eyes, allowing the music to wash over me before it pulses through my body. One song bleeds into another and then a third until I lose count.

When I crack my eyes open again, I'm surprised to find Crosby pressed against Brooke's spine, his large hands wrapped around her waist as he buries his face in the crook of her neck.

A little pang of longing blooms in the pit of my belly as I stare at them. Brooke and I have been friends for years and I adore her. She's so sweet and a genuinely nice person. If there's anyone who deserves all the happiness in the world, it's Brooke.

I can't help but wish that I had someone who cared about me as much as Crosby cares about her. All you have to do is look at the guy to see how totally in love he is.

At the end of the day, isn't that all we really want?

To find someone who loves us for the person we are?

Someone who will stick by us through thick and thin?

As that thought circles through my head, I bring the cup to my lips only to find that it's empty.

Hmmm.

Looks like it's time for another refill to keep these good vibes flowing.

I get Brooke's attention and point to the kitchen, jiggling the red plastic cup. Honestly, I've lost count of how many I've had tonight. All I know is that I've never drank this much in my life.

With a nod, she burrows closer to Crosby as I slip through the sea of students cutting loose on a Friday night. I glance around, searching for my roomie only to find that she's MIA. Less than thirty minutes ago, we were just dancing together.

I also ran into Maverick earlier. He took one look at me and frowned. Honestly, it reminded me of Ryder, which was a total buzzkill. So, I gave him a little wave and took off. I haven't seen him since, which is probably for the best.

As I wind my way through the crowd, I catch sight of Ryder from the corner of my eye. It would be impossible to miss him. He's taller and more muscular than a lot of the students we go to school with, looking more like a grown man rather than a twenty-two-year-old guy in college.

For the first time since he decided to shadow my every move, he's busy talking to another teammate, making it easier to slip into the kitchen. The last thing I want or need is him up my ass.

The kid manning the keg gives me the once over before his gaze returns to mine. With his babyface, my guess is that he's a freshman.

"What can I get for you, sexy girl?" he asks.

My lips tremble around the corners and it's tempting to roll my eyes.

Sexy girl?

Please...

He looks young enough to need a babysitter.

"Just a beer. Thanks."

He raises a brow suggestively. "Are you sure that's all you need?"

"Yup. I'm sure."

Before he can say anything else, Ryder slaps him upside the head. The guy winces and rubs his scalp before turning to glare at Ryder, who's appeared out of nowhere.

"What the—" His voice trails off when he finds the older teammate glowering at him. "Oh. Hey, McAdams."

"Are you hitting on this girl?"

The kid throws an uneasy glance my way. "Um, no?" He clears his throat. "I was just being friendly."

"Well, don't."

"Sorry, man." He drops his voice. "I didn't realize this little honey belonged to you."

Excuse me?

"I'm sorry, did you just say I," I make air quotes with my fingers, "*belonged* to him?" Before the younger player can respond, I continue, "I'm a grown-ass woman and don't *belong* to anyone." I jerk my thumb toward Ryder. "Least of all him."

When they both turn and stare—the freshman in surprise, Ryder in aggravation—I pluck the cup from the kid's hand and stalk away. With any luck, I'll leave Ryder behind in my dust. Normally, we give each other a wide berth. I don't understand why that's changed and he's suddenly all up in my business.

If he's trying to kill my mood, he's doing an excellent job.

Just as I bring the cup to my lips, a deep voice entirely too close for comfort asks, "Haven't you had enough already?"

I grind to a halt before whirling around to face him. As I do, the room spins. Kind of like I'm on a Tilt-A-Whirl. Ryder's hands snap out to steady me before I can crash into the people pressing in at the edges. Through the cashmere of my sweater, I feel the heat of his large palms singeing my skin. It wouldn't surprise me in the least to find his handprints permanently tattooed on my upper arms. In that moment, our gazes stay locked. Air gets clogged in my lungs as his blue depths stay fastened onto mine.

"You've had more than enough, Juliette," he says quietly. "I think it's time for you to head home."

A potent concoction of hurt and anger blooms inside me. He's been on a mission to get me out of here all night, and I'm tired of it. The fact that he doesn't want me around shouldn't have the power to wound me.

In order to stop the tears from pricking the backs of my eyes, I wrench free of him before lifting the plastic to my lips and draining every last drop.

"Go away, Ryder. I don't need you watching over me."

I shove out of his arms before spinning around and stalking through the sea of students. One more shitty comment from him and I'll probably fall apart. That's the last thing I want to happen.

He's done enough damage to my ego for one night.

CHAPTER 10

RYDER

Go away?

Yeah, that's not going to happen anytime soon.

This entire night has turned out to be one giant clusterfuck.

Everything I say just pisses her off even more.

In all the years we've been neighbors, I've never seen this side of Juliette. One where she cuts loose and allows herself to live in the moment. She's always had tunnel vision when it comes to her academic goals. She probably took every AP course our high school offered. I'd be lying through my teeth if I didn't admit that her intelligence is sexy as fuck.

Almost as much as watching her dance with her friends.

If anyone deserves to have fun, it's her.

What I didn't like were all the assholes standing around and ogling her.

It was tempting to bare my teeth and growl.

Actually, that's exactly what I did.

Even though I was preoccupied, it didn't take long to notice a number of douchebags loitering in the vicinity, staring at her and Brooke while they danced. Crosby must have realized the same thing because he threw away his bottle of beer before stalking out there and pulling her close to stake his claim.

It was tempting to do the same with Juliette, except I know exactly how that would have ended...

And that's with a swift kick to my nuts.

I might be a lot of things, but stupid isn't one of them.

Usually.

I blow out a steady breath. What's become apparent is that I won't be able to talk her into taking off anytime soon. Which means that I'll be shadowing her for the remainder of the night.

It'll be over my dead and buried body that she goes home with another dude.

I continue watching from a distance as she heads back to the cluster of people writhing to the beat in the living room. Brooke is exactly where Juliette left her, dancing with Crosby. I search the area for Carina but don't see her blonde head anywhere. Much to Ford's displeasure, there's usually half a dozen guys vying for her attention. Ford might think he's being all super stealthy, but I'm pretty sure he's got the hots for her.

My attention refastens on Juliette as the irritation drains from her expression and she smiles at Brooke. It's only when my gaze licks over her body that I remember she used to take dance lessons. On more than one occasion, I was dragged to her recitals.

I have no idea why she quit.

Dance was always something she loved.

It's a real pleasure to watch her now as she shakes off our previous conversation and gets back into the music. Unable to help myself, my gaze stays pinned to her. I'm transfixed by the graceful way she rolls her hips. Her arms rise above her head and her back arches. It only makes her tits stand out more than they already do.

Fuck.

My cock throbs with painful awareness. With a quick look around, I adjust myself and hope no one notices.

The next time I slip my phone from my pocket and glance at the time, it's after one o'clock in the morning. I thought once Brooke and

Crosby took off, she'd decide she had more than enough, but nope. She's still going strong.

I'll give her fifteen more minutes to shake her ass.

Then, we're calling it a night.

Whether I have to carry her out of here kicking and screaming, it's time to go.

I've been more than patient.

Once time is up, I cut a path directly to her. People shift and scurry out of my way as I move through the press of bodies. I'm like Moses parting the Red Sea. Her arms are still lifted above her head. Even in the dim lighting, I see the thick sweep of lashes lying against her skin as a smile tips the corners of her mouth.

With her unaware of my presence, I'm able to look my fill. I might watch her from across a distance, but very rarely do I get an opportunity to be this up close and personal. I want to etch every dip and curve into my memory, because I know damn well that it won't come around for a second time.

My gaze drops to the generous bow shape of her pink slicked lips, and I chew my lower one as a burst of arousal arrows straight through me before settling in my dick. I've spent my entire life tamping down my lust for this girl, and it would seem like it's hellbent on breaking loose this evening.

After a while, her eyelids feather open, and our gazes collide. In that moment of intense connection, the music and people pushing in at the edges fade to the background until it's just the two of us.

Until she's all I'm cognizant of.

Instead of giving in to the harsh need that pumps through my system, I say in a tone that comes out sounding far gruffer than intended, "It's time to go."

She blinks before glancing around with a frown as if reluctantly waking from a dream. "I don't know where Carina is."

Instead of looking for her roommate, my attention stays pinned to her. "I haven't seen her for an hour or so."

"We caught a ride here with Wolf, Ford, and Madden."

"I'll drive you home. You can't walk alone at this hour."

When her brows slant together as if trying to come up with an alternative solution for the predicament she now finds herself in, I wrap my fingers around her wrist and tow her through the crowd.

"Did you bring a jacket?" There's a thick stack of them in the living room on an armchair.

"No."

I shoot her a scowl. "It's cold out. You should have brought one."

Irritation flickers across her face. "I'm not a child. Stop treating me like one."

No, she certainly isn't.

"You can wear one of mine," I grumble. Once we reach the entryway, I stop and point a finger. "Don't move a single muscle. I'll be right back."

She rolls her eyes.

Since that's probably the only response I'm going to get, I jog up the staircase to the second floor before turning down the hall. With a quick flick of my wrist, I throw open the bedroom door and grab the midweight jacket I pulled out a couple weeks ago when the weather turned colder. With the navy coat in hand, I retrace my steps. For all I know, Juliette could have ducked out once I disappeared up the stairs. She's stubborn that way and clearly doesn't want me telling her what to do.

Everything inside me settles when I catch sight of her in the entryway. As soon as my feet hit the last tread, I slip the thick material around her shoulders before carefully maneuvering her arms through the sleeves. The coat is ridiculously big on her. Her fingers don't even peek out of the cuffs. If I didn't already realize how much smaller she is than me, I sure as hell do now.

I can't deny the deep sense of satisfaction that fills me at the sight of her wearing something of mine. I want all the assholes who've been staring at her to understand that she belongs to me.

Even though that's not necessarily true.

I shove those disturbing thoughts away. "Ready?"

She nods before stifling a yawn.

With my arm wrapped around her shoulders, I steer her through the front door and down the porch steps to the cement walkway that cuts a path through the swath of lawn. My truck is parked a couple houses down the street. I click the locks before wrapping my fingers around the handle and popping it open. Juliette slides inside before burrowing into the jacket.

"It's cold," she whispers, teeth chattering.

"Yup." It's only one of the reasons she isn't walking her ass home tonight.

I jog around the hood before settling next to her and starting up the engine. When she doesn't make a move to click her seatbelt into place, I lean over and stretch the fabric strap across her chest. Her sleepy gaze fastens onto mine. I'm close enough to hear the hitch in her breathing. With our faces scant inches apart, it wouldn't take much to close the distance and crush my mouth against hers.

For a second or two, I consider doing exactly that.

What would the slide of her plush lips feel like beneath mine?

An internal war erupts in my brain. Deep down, I know it's a shit idea. I've secretly wanted this girl for years. Probably a decade, if I'm being completely honest with myself. It's the reason I've always been so adamant about keeping my distance and not spending time around her.

No matter how much I craved it.

A couple months ago, I'd actually congratulated myself on making it this far without crumbling under the crushing need I feel for her. Now, we're a little more than a semester away from graduating and going our separate ways.

Instead of closing the distance between us the way every instinct is demanding that I do, I force myself to retreat. Then, I turn away and stare out the windshield before pulling onto the dark, tree-lined street. My thoughts continue to churn as we head to her apartment.

I can't believe I came so close to kissing her.

This is exactly what happens when I don't throw up a wall between us. I can't trust myself to be alone with this girl for five damn minutes.

Even though I tell myself to stare straight ahead, I can't stop my gaze from flickering in her direction and soaking in the sight of her next to me. Especially now that her eyelids have feathered closed.

It doesn't take long before I'm pulling into the lot and parking near the entrance. I cut the engine and swivel on the black leather seat, simply content to watch her sleep. Her head is tilted just a bit, and her mouth is slightly parted.

It's funny...

Or maybe not.

Most of the time, when Juliette stares at me, there's a scowl twisting her pretty lips. Tension will vibrate from her in suffocating waves. Right now, the lines of her face are smoothed as if she doesn't have a care in the world.

The softness makes her look younger.

Heartbreakingly beautiful.

My hand rises to the curve of her cheek before stalling. It's so damn tempting to stroke my fingers over her bare skin, but I'm afraid to wake her. Or worse, it'll unleash the monster that lives deep inside me where she's concerned. It's taken effort on my part to battle it back all these years and pretend it doesn't exist.

One touch and...

It would all go up in a burst of flames and smoke.

My hand trembles as I force it to her shoulder before giving her a gentle shake.

"Juliette." My voice comes out sounding raspier than intended. Almost as if it's been roughed up with sandpaper.

It takes a moment or two before her eyelids flutter open and her gaze locks on mine. A slight smile tips her lips upward and a softness fills her expression that I never imagined would be aimed in my direction.

"We're at your apartment."

She blinks away the sleepiness and breaks eye contact to stare at the building that looms in front of us.

"Oh. Thanks," she mumbles, sounding as if she's still half asleep.

My attention gets snagged by a couple of guys jostling one another as they head inside the front entrance. By their obnoxious laughter and slurred voices, it's obvious they've been out partying.

There's no way I can send her inside on her own.

She fumbles for the door handle, and I exit the vehicle before coming around to the passenger side and popping it open. When she stumbles, I scoop her up into my arms before pressing her against my chest.

Her eyes widen as she squeaks. "What are you doing?"

"Making sure you don't break your damn neck," I say with a grunt. The weight and warmth of her feels so damn good.

After her combativeness tonight, I expect nothing less than an argument. Instead, she cuddles against me.

"I'm tired," she murmurs around a yawn.

"Not a surprise considering how much you were dancing."

"I don't remember the last time I had so much fun. I'll have to thank Carina when I see her."

Fucking Carina. I knew she was to blame for this.

With Juliette tucked safely in my arms, I stride up the walkway. Once we arrive at the glass door, I carefully shift her around so I can reach out and key in the code. I've been here enough times to have it memorized.

I pull open the door and slip inside the lobby before pressing the button for the third floor.

Just when I think she's fallen back to sleep, she mumbles, "Now I can check something off my list."

When the elevator arrives, I step inside. A second or two later, the metal doors slide shut and I press her warm body closer to mine, wishing the jacket wasn't between us. I want to feel the softness of her curves.

"What list?"

The car arrives at the third floor and the doors open with a rumble. I head to her apartment, passing by a couple people chilling in the hallway as loud music pours out from within. Unwilling to get sucked into a conversation, I avoid all eye contact.

Once we reach her door, I say, "Where's your key?"

She slips her hand beneath the jacket to the small purse tucked against her side before producing a keyring and dropping it into my palm.

As I shove open the door and carry her inside, I prompt, "Tell me more about this list."

I've been to their place a couple times with Ford and Mav, so I know exactly which room is Juliette's. One step over the threshold and the scent of her perfume slyly wraps itself around me, teasing my senses. I beeline for the queen-sized bed and set her carefully down in the middle of the mattress before straightening to my full height.

I should probably get the hell out of here before anything else happens.

"I made a list of all the things I wanted to do before graduating college." She shrugs out of my jacket. "And getting drunk at a party was one of them." Her lips tug down at the corners. "But I don't remember the number."

Juliette has a bucket list?

Now I'm curious.

What else is on this list?

I glance around the room.

My gaze is drawn back to her when she grips the hem of the sweater. "Carina made me wear this."

"You look good." Way better than that, actually.

More like fucking fantastic.

I've been salivating over her all night. Like a starving wolf that has a plump rabbit locked in its sights.

She shoots me a frown. "That's probably the nicest thing you've ever said to me."

Well, shit.

"You've always been such a jerk," she adds.

Guilt pricks at me. I know exactly how I've treated her. It was a deliberate move on my part to keep her firmly at arm's length. I just never realized she'd noticed.

Or cared.

With a scoot to the edge of the bed, she leans forward to unzip the tall black boots that hit right below her knee. The sound of the zipper being drawn down is enough to have my mouth going bone dry. That probably shouldn't be so sexy, but tell that to my dick. The damn thing is already twitching with interest.

I clear my throat. This would be an excellent time to take off. I've made sure that she got home safely. There's no other reason for me to stay.

"So, where's this list you keep talking about?"

Without glancing at me, she waves toward the nightstand. There's a glass lamp with a white fuzzy shade, paperback, pen, and lip balm. Everything on the small table is neat and orderly.

Just like Juliette.

God but it's tempting to mess it up.

Mess her up.

I immediately quash the idea.

There will be absolutely none of that.

As that thought circles through my head, I spot a folded square of paper before snapping it up and opening it. From the corner of my eye, I watch as she drops the boots near the closet. I'm about to turn my head when the first item on the list catches my attention.

BUCKET LIST for College

#1 Make out at the library

Make out at the library?

That is such a girly thing to write down.

#2 Skinny dip

My brows rise.

I can't even imagine that scenario…

Never mind. I can *definitely* imagine Juliette swimming around naked.

I drop down onto the mattress and continue reading.

#3 Karaoke

That's pretty tame.

#4 Get drunk at a party

Yup, she'll be checking off that one in the morning.

#5 Romantic Date

All right, that one's a little bit surprising. No one's ever taken Juliette out on a romantic date? If she were my girl, it would be romantic dates all the damn time.

Those thoughts empty from my brain as the next item on the list jumps out and grabs my attention.

#6 Orgasm (with another person)

My fingers tighten around the paper, crinkling the edges.

Orgasm?

The girl is twenty-two years old and hasn't experienced an orgasm with someone else?

That's…*surprising.* As much as I hate to admit it, there's a part of me that's secretly glad no other man has given her the big O.

Wait a minute…

Is she going to start ticking off these items?

Is that what tonight was about?

Working on this damn list?

The idea of another guy laying his hands on her, touching her, fucking her…*no.*

That can't be allowed to happen.

If Juliette wants to experience her first orgasm, I'll be the one who gives it to her.

That realization is like a punch to the gut and knocks the air from my lungs. Once that thought takes up residence inside my brain, there's absolutely no shaking it loose.

My gaze flickers to her, only to realize that she's stripped off both the sweater and skirt. She's standing in nothing more than a bra and—

Holy fuck.

A thong.

The girl is wearing a ridiculous excuse for a thong. It's nothing more than a thin scrap of material that does absolutely nothing to cover her backside. Those rounded cheeks are out there, begging to be stared at.

What would it be like to sink my teeth into that juicy peach of an ass?

This time, my cock doesn't just stir with interest, it stiffens right up like a bird dog spotting fresh quarry. I'm so damn hard that I could easily punch a hole through the wall.

As much as I know I should look away, I can't bring myself to do it.

Are you kidding me?

Of course I can't.

I'm barely breathing at this point.

My eyes slide back up her body before settling on her breasts. They're fucking perfect. I've seen her in a bikini but certainly nothing this skimpy. The lace of her bra is damn near see through.

Scratch that—I can definitely see the rosy hue of her nipples poking through the material.

I don't realize that I've risen to my feet until I take a step in her direction. That's when I force myself to stop.

Exactly what the hell am I going to do?

Touch her?

My breathing turns ragged as she reaches around and unsnaps the undergarment. The silky straps slide in slow motion down her arms before the cups fall away from her chest. From this angle, I'm just able to make out the curve of one pink-tipped breast.

A groan rumbles up from deep in my chest as I clench my hand until the knuckles turn bone white.

She's more than a handful. Even for someone like me who has large hands. I can't even imagine what it would be like to cup her titties and feel the soft, warm flesh against my palms.

As soon as the material drops to the carpet, she lifts her arms overhead, arches her spine, and stretches. There's nothing seductive or sly about the movement. She's not attempting to be sexy.

She just is.

Unaware of my intense perusal, she stumbles to her dresser and yanks out a drawer before digging through the contents until she finds a hot pink tank top and yanks it over her head, pulling it down to cover her breasts. It's so damn tempting to rip the flimsy material off her body so that she's wearing nothing more than the thong.

Fuck.

Instead of doing exactly that, I drag a rough hand through my hair.

When was the last time I was this worked up?

Have I *ever* been this turned on?

Doubtful.

I blink when she picks up a brush from the top of the dresser and yanks it through her hair. I can't help but wince as it makes a ripping sound. Before I realize my intention, I pluck it from her fingers and steer her toward the desk chair.

"Sit down and I'll do it for you. At the rate you're going, you'll pull out every last strand," I rasp, barely able to recognize the sound of my own voice.

And that would be a damn shame, because Juliette has gorgeous hair. It's long and thick.

Have I imagined it wrapped around my hand a time or two?

Guilty.

She turns to meet my eyes. There's a flicker of surprise in them as I nudge her toward the chair. "Oh. I forgot you were here."

I shake my head. Typical Juliette response. Any other girl would be falling to her knees and opening her mouth wide.

But not this one.

"I get that a lot."

With a snort, she meets my gaze in the mirror before settling at the vanity that doubles as a desk. "We both know that's a lie."

I arch a brow and gently run the brush from the top of her head to the tips of her dark, silky strands.

After a few strokes, her eyelids feather shut and a soft sigh escapes from her parted lips. "That feels really nice."

I don't understand how it's possible, but I'm more turned on now than before. All I'm doing is brushing this girl's hair. It doesn't make a damn bit of sense, but then again, nothing with Juliette has ever made sense. I came to a place of acceptance regarding that fact a long time ago.

After a couple of silent minutes, she tips her head back, leaning further into my touch.

"This reminds me of when Mom would brush my hair when I was a kid." Her voice turns wistful. "I miss that."

"I remember."

Surprise fills her coffee-colored eyes. "You do?"

"Yeah. Sometimes she'd do it in the kitchen before braiding your hair."

The way her lips lift into a smile is like a junk punch. I'd do just about anything to have her look at me like that all the damn time.

Silence settles over us again as those disturbing thoughts circle through my head.

When she stifles a yawn, I drag the brush through her thick strands one final time before reluctantly setting it on the vanity.

She blinks back to awareness. "I'm tired."

"It's pretty late. You should hit the sack."

Her hair floats around her shoulders as she beelines to the bed and tosses back the covers before slipping beneath them.

This girl is going to have one hell of a hangover tomorrow morning.

I clear my throat. "Do you have some painkillers around here?"

"On the counter in the bathroom," she says around another yawn.

"All right. I'll be right back."

I swing away, disappearing into the small room off the hallway before tapping out two pills and then heading to the kitchen to grab a bottle of water. Once I return to the bedroom, I give her the medication and she guzzles down half of the chilled liquid.

After resettling beneath the covers, her gaze locks on mine as her brow furrows. "You're being weirdly nice."

It's like there's an invisible string stretched taut between us that continues to draw me closer against my will. In a matter of seconds, I find myself at the edge of the mattress, staring down at the pretty picture she makes.

How tempting would it be to slide between the sheets with her?

Instead of admitting that she's right, I pick up the paperback on

70

her nightstand and turn it over to see what she's been reading. It's a surprise to find a bare-chested man on the cover. No matter what I was expecting, this wasn't it.

I take a closer look.

Exactly how many abs does this dude have?

There's no damn way this image isn't photoshopped.

Sure, I've got abdominals, but not eight of them. And I spend hours a day working out, keeping myself in tip-top condition.

I glance at her. "I didn't peg you for the romance novel type."

A smile quirks her lips. "It belongs to Carina. She claims there's a lot of stuff I can learn from it."

Interest piqued, I skim a few pages. "Oh yeah? Like what?"

She cups her hands around her mouth and drops her voice to a loud whisper as if someone might overhear her. "Sexy stuff."

I raise a brow. "And have you?"

Color blooms in her cheeks as her gaze flickers away. "Yes."

Before I can delve deeper into this interesting convo and ferret out specifics, her eyelids drift shut. Within a matter of seconds, she's snoring softly.

I glance from her to the paperback still clutched in my hand before turning it over and reading the blurb on the back. It's a college romance about a hockey player and the girl who falls for him.

Interesting.

I slip my phone from my back pocket and snap a pic of the list and then the book before settling in the papasan chair crammed in the corner of her room and stretching out my legs.

How can I leave Juliette alone when her roommate is still out partying?

What if she throws up or something?

Guess I'll just stay and wait. Once Carina returns, I'll head back to the house.

And while I'm here, might as well take a peek at all the sexy stuff she's been reading.

CHAPTER 11

JULIETTE

*I*t's the bright sunlight slanting through the window and penetrating the delicate skin of my eyelids that has me reluctantly surfacing from a deep slumber. Unwilling to give in just yet, I roll over and groan when the throbbing in my head picks up tempo, thudding an insistent beat that refuses to be silenced.

Oh god.

With my eyes squeezed tightly closed, I raise my arm, bringing my fingers to my forehead to rub gently. It feels like there are tiny men inside my brain gleefully hammering away. I've never been a person prone to migraines, but if I were, this is exactly what I imagine one would feel like.

I don't understand...

What the hell happened last night?

Another tortured groan escapes from me as an image of belting back a cup of beer at the party flashes through my brain.

And then another.

And probably a couple more after that.

Argh. My roommate might have twisted my arm to attend, but she certainly didn't force me to drink to excess.

Exactly how many did I have?

Three?

Four?

Good lord...*five?*

How do people party like this every weekend?

Here's what I know—I'm never drinking again.

Ever.

One and done.

Painkillers and water.

That's exactly what I need.

Unfortunately, that requires me to open both eyes and vacate the comfort of my bed. For a minute or two, I consider staying put, but the pressure building in my bladder tells me that won't be an option for long.

I release a slow breath and come to grips with the fact that I'll have to be vertical for a short period of time before nose diving back into bed.

Possibly for the rest of the day.

It takes at least thirty seconds before I'm able to pry my eyelids open. It feels like they're cemented shut.

Sure, I had a good time last night...

I think.

More memories slowly continue to surface.

Although, it certainly wasn't good enough to endure this kind of fresh hell.

I glance around the bedroom and draw in another deep breath. My belly feels like it's on a roller coaster.

And if there's one thing I hate, it's roller coasters.

My parents talked me into riding one when I was twelve years old. I was so sick afterward that I threw up in the garbage can as soon as I staggered off the ride. To this day, Mav enjoys bringing it up. Of course, Ryder was there to bear witness to my utter humiliation. The guy always seems to be around when I'm at my lowest.

That's exactly what the roiling in my gut reminds me of. I really hope I don't toss my cookies. Talk about a cherry on top of an already shit sundae.

It takes effort to heave myself into a seated position and tentatively swing my legs over the side of the mattress. Just as I'm about to sprint to the bathroom, I catch sight of a large figure sprawled out in the chair tucked in the corner and freeze.

What the...

I lift my hands to rub my eyes.

Oh god...am I hallucinating?

Did I actually drink that much?

Because there is no way Ryder McAdams is passed out in my room.

What the hell is he doing here?

My brows pinch together as I continue to stare, willing the image in front of me to melt away.

Wait a minute...did he drive me home from the party last night?

I try to tease the answer from my brain. For some reason, I distinctly remember Ryder shoving my arms through the sleeves of an oversized jacket and helping me to his pickup truck.

More memories roll through my head. I recall snuggling up against his hard chest. Did he carry me inside the building and up to the apartment?

A fresh wave of mortification crashes over me because yeah...

I'm pretty sure he did. The realization is actually more mortifying than when he stood off to the side and watched me hurl after that horrible ride.

That couldn't be helped.

This, unfortunately, is completely my own fault.

I could deal with anyone *other* than Ryder seeing me in that condition.

I drag a hand over my face and creep closer. His chest continues to steadily rise and fall. The soft fabric of his T-shirt is stretched taut across hard pectorals and the short sleeves are wrapped snugly around thick biceps. Even in his relaxed state, the muscles bulge.

What the heck size shirt is he wearing?

A smedium?

My mouth turns cottony, and I know damn well that it has

74

nothing to do with the headache or persistent roiling that fills my belly and everything to do with the hot man sacked out in my room.

I wince at that internal thought.

As my gaze licks over every inch of him, I realize that I've spent the last eight years tricking myself into believing that I felt zilch for this guy when nothing could be further from the truth.

Unable to help myself from inspecting him while he's unaware of my intense perusal, I sneak closer. Other than pouring over the photographs that appear online in the school or local paper, I've never gotten the opportunity to stare at him so openly.

In sleep, he appears younger. The tiny lines bracketing his eyes have magically disappeared. Lately, the grooves seem to be deeper, as if the weight of the world rests upon his broad shoulders.

There've been a few times when I've been tempted to reach out and smooth them away with my fingers.

Did I?

Of course not.

Are you kidding me?

The guy would probably think I'd lost my mind. That's definitely not the kind of relationship we have.

It's only when my attention resettles on his impressive chest that I notice the book splayed open against it.

What the hell?

My eyes widen until it's possible they'll fall out of my head and roll around on the carpet.

Was he actually reading the novel Carina gave me last night?

I'm vaguely aware of telling him about the sexy times in that particular book.

A tortured gurgle of embarrassment escapes from me.

When he stirs, shifting on the chair, I clap a hand over my mouth so that I don't make another noise. I should retreat to the relative safety on the other side of the room. The last thing I want is for him to open his eyes and find me hovering like one of the many groupies who stalk him around campus.

Except...

It's much too late for that.

His ridiculously long lashes flicker open before settling on me.

My muscles tense, making movement impossible. If I were hoping to employ some sort of invisibility shield as a last resort, it fails epically.

The moment his gaze collides with mine, I feel the zip of electricity straight down to my toes. For a second or two, there's confusion in his sleepy blue eyes, and the edges of his lips bow up into a lazy smile. The expression hits me like a punch to the gut, nearly stealing my breath away.

No man should look this good so early in the morning.

Especially when I feel like roadkill.

And when he stares at me with that sexy look as if he's happy to see me, it weakens my knees. It takes every ounce of strength I have to keep myself upright so that I don't melt into a gooey puddle at his feet.

"Hey." He stretches, raising his arms overhead before making a growling noise deep in his throat. The cotton of his shirt slowly rides up his abdominals, revealing a perfectly chiseled six-pack.

My lady parts twitch in appreciation.

All right, fine...they do way more than just twitch. Riverdance might be taking place down there. From here on out, I will no longer be able to feel superior regarding the girls on campus who moon over this man.

And make no mistake, he's all man. While I've been doing my best to pretend Ryder McAdams doesn't exist, he's filled out to be a perfect specimen of one. Who needs to stare at the cover of a romance novel when you have the real thing in front of you?

"Umm, hi." I shift from one foot to another as embarrassment licks at me. The laundry list of reasons why is at least a mile long, and I will never—not in a million years—be able to live them down.

His drowsy gaze slips from my face before settling on my breasts. I feel the heat of it as if it's a physical caress. That's all it takes for my nipples to tighten into hard little peaks at the silent scrutiny. A quick glance down has me realizing that they're poking through the thin fabric of the tank top. My face goes up in flames as I cross my arms over my chest in an attempt to cover them.

I clear my throat, hoping to draw his attention away from my breasts. "What are you doing here?"

He blinks and jerks his gaze to mine. His expression becomes shuttered as he drags a hand over his face. This is exactly the kind of reaction I've come to expect from Ryder, and a little prick of sadness blooms inside me at the wall that has slammed down between us.

I've never understood what his problem was with me and have spent years telling myself that I didn't care. He could be besties with Mav if he wanted, all the while barely acknowledging my presence.

It's yet another lie I spent years trying to convince myself of.

"I drove you back to the apartment last night. Carina wasn't home and I didn't want to leave you alone after you'd been drinking." He shrugs his massive shoulders. "So, I crashed here."

When he stretches again, the book on his chest tumbles to the floor. I immediately bend over to pick it up. He does the same. Our movements stall as our hands brush and our gazes collide across the inches of space that separate us. Air gets trapped in my lungs for a second time in a matter of minutes. Heat sizzles in the air between us before his attention drops to my chest. His eyes darken and I realize that he can probably see my bare breasts as the tank gapes in front.

I snatch the book from the carpet and stumble back a few paces.

Silence settles over us as Ryder continues to stare. Hunger grows in his eyes, darkening them. The black of his pupil swallows up the ocean blue. It's not a look I've ever seen directed my way.

It's as thrilling as it is scary.

I hold up the book and blurt, "Were you reading this?"

The intensity of his stare sets my nerves on edge. My skin feels hot. Tight. As if I'll burst out of it any second.

"Yeah." His voice is shades deeper than it was only a few moments ago. "I got about halfway through it."

Before I can find my tongue, he adds. "Last night, you mentioned that it was pretty sexy."

My eyes widen. "What?"

His heated gaze pins mine in place, making it impossible to breathe. "You told me that you'd learned some stuff and I was interested in what it was."

Heat slams into my cheeks. "I...*did?*"

Someone needs to put me out of my misery before this gets any worse.

He nods. "I thought I'd check it out and read a chapter or two. The next thing I know, a couple hours had slipped by." There's a pause. "I must have fallen asleep after that."

"So...did you learn anything interesting?" The question is out of my mouth before I can shove it back inside where it belongs.

A slow smile curves his lips. It's so predatory in nature that my pulse trips.

Instead of responding, he tosses that loaded question right back at me. "Have *you?*"

My teeth scrape across my lower lip. "It's definitely given me some ideas."

"Well, we can agree on that."

My insides contract at the idea of him trying out different scenes from the book with another girl. As soon as that thought pops into my brain, I shove it away. A heavy silence blankets us as he rises to his feet and prowls closer.

Nerves shoot to the surface of my skin, and I blurt, "Don't you have practice this morning?"

His expression falters and his eyes lose some of their intensity as he slides the phone from his pocket and glances at the screen. His brows knit together. "Yeah. In thirty minutes."

Thick tension ratchets up between us until it feels combustible. It's as if we're teetering on the precipice of something explosive.

When his gaze resettles on mine, the moment fades.

For all I know, it was never there to begin with.

"I should probably get moving," he mutters.

As he swings toward the bedroom door, I can't resist asking, "Do you want to borrow the book so you can read the rest?"

It's a joke, of course.

There's no way Ryder would actually read a romance novel.

He tosses a glance over his shoulder. "Nah, I'll buy the e-book and finish it."

Not expecting that response, my jaw crashes open.

"Oh, and make sure you cross drinking at a college party off your list. You were definitely lit up last night."

A strangled sound escapes from me as I echo the word. *"List?"*

He yanks open the bedroom door and grinds to a halt before swinging toward me and pointing to the nightstand. Humor sparks to life in his eyes as a smile simmers around the edges of his lips. "Yeah, you showed it to me. Don't you remember?"

Oh, the humiliation.

It's official. I'm never drinking again.

"Can you just..." My voice trails off as I clench my hands. My fingers curl around the paperback. With a painful gulp, I force myself to continue. "Forget about that?"

The same heat filling his eyes earlier ignites in them again. But there's something else there too.

Something darker.

"Nope."

That one word sucks all the oxygen from my lungs, making it impossible to breathe.

With that, he saunters out of the room.

It's only when he disappears from sight and I hear the faint click of the door in a distant part of the apartment that my knees weaken, and I nearly collapse on the floor.

CHAPTER 12

RYDER

I sweep my stick across the ice as Garret Akeman races toward me with the puck. We're scrimmaging, and even though he's playing defense for the other team, he's rushing for the net. Skating backward, I lower my center of gravity and watch his hips to see which direction he'll move.

It's just like Shakira said—the hips don't lie.

The game of hockey has always come naturally. It's not something I had to overthink. I instinctively knew what would happen. I was able to anticipate how a player was going to move. The play would unfold in my head seconds before it did on the ice. Kind of like a sixth sense.

That's no longer the case.

My ability to read the situation has been disabled.

Unlike football or baseball, hockey is fast paced. It's constant action. You get a second or two to make a decision and commit. As soon as doubt creeps in at the edges, it's like a snowball rolling down-hill, picking up momentum. A heartbeat or two can feel like a lifetime that's over within the blink of an eye. There are no second chances, and then you live with the consequences of your decision.

I've never understood just how paralyzing that knowledge can be.

Until now.

Even during practice, I'm a mess of nerves.

My gaze lifts to Garret's face.

Goddamn motherfucker.

In that moment of distraction, he pivots. Even though I take off after him, I'm a beat too late and he manages to fly past me. As a last resort, I extend my stick and attempt to catch him, but he manages to pull out of reach.

Fuck.

Fuck.

Fuck.

He drives toward the net and fires off a shot. Wolf slides to the left before falling to his knees. Just when I think he's caught it in his glove, the puck whizzes past and hits the net.

"Better luck next time, Westerville," Garret laughs, circling around the back of the net before skating toward me.

A smirk twists his lips.

God, but he's loving this.

Loving my fall from grace.

My fingers clench in my gloves with the temptation to punch him in the face as he continues to glide closer like a lazy shark. Already, I know he's going to make a smartass comment. He's been full of them lately.

"McKinnon's sister looked good enough to eat at that party. Think she's smart enough to know what to do with that pretty little mouth of hers?"

There's a taunting edge to his voice as if he understands that she's a weakness.

Instead of ignoring him the way every instinct is screaming at me to do, I snap, "Stay the fuck away from her."

He skates closer as a satisfied chuckle escapes from him. "And if I don't?" He notches his chin higher. "What are you going to do about it?"

Fucking beat him until he's nothing more than a bloodspot on the ice.

My jaw is clenched so tight that it feels like my teeth will crack and shatter.

His grin widens as his voice drops so low that only I can hear. "Ever wonder just how soft her pussy is? Well, I plan to find out."

That's all it takes for my brain to click off and for me to leap at him. We tumble to the ice in a wild tangle of limbs as I slam my gloved fist into his helmet. It doesn't take long before he's fighting back. Hayes and Bridger are the first to arrive on the scene. A shower of ice is sprayed as they come to a quick stop, reaching down to rip us apart.

It's only when I'm pulled away bucking and frothing at the mouth that the shrill sound of the whistle penetrates the roar of the ocean that fills my ears, blinding me to everything else but Garret.

"What the fuck are you doing, man?" Bridger growls, continuing to shove me back a couple of steps.

I crane my neck in order to look past him. My gaze stays pinned to Garret.

"Nothing."

Fucking cock sucker.

The same smile Akeman had been sporting earlier stays plastered to his lips. Only now, it's wider.

"McAdams!" Coach bellows. "Get the fuck off my ice right now! You're done!"

"Good job, dumbass," Hayes mutters. "I'm sure we'll be skating suicides for the rest of practice."

A couple of players help Garret to his feet. It's so damn tempting to knock him back to the ice where he belongs. Hayes and Bridger must have psychic ability, because their grip tightens around me.

"Now, McAdams!" Coach shouts, his sharp voice echoing off the cavernous arena walls.

Garret lifts his hand in a wave. "Sounds like you gotta go buh-bye, McAdams. Better get moving."

With a growl, I surge forward. Hayes and Bridger continue to restrain me. If they weren't...

I don't know what I'd do.

Actually, that's not true.

I know *exactly* what I'd do.

And it would be such a pleasure.

"Shut the fuck up, Akeman," Hayes snaps.

"Stop being a douche," Colby McNichols adds.

There aren't many guys on the team who like Garret. For some reason, he's under the misguided impression that he's a more talented player than he actually is.

His expression turns sullen as I swing around and head toward the bench.

"I'll catch you later," Garret calls after me.

"Count on it."

As much as I want to avoid our coach, my gaze reluctantly lifts to his. There's a mixture of anger, irritation, and disappointment swimming around within his eyes.

Even though I don't like Reed Philips, and he clearly has nothing for me, it's the disappointment that chafes my ass most. Like he expected better, and I let him down. My gaze flickers to the other coaches who are shaking their heads and whispering as I step onto the rubber mat and stalk away.

"If something like that ever happens again, there won't be a place for you on my team," Coach Philips says gruffly.

I pause as my shoulders stiffen.

It wasn't all that long ago this had been *my* team.

Mine.

"Do you understand?"

"Yeah, I got it."

I slam into the locker room before jamming my stick into the holder and dropping onto the bench. It's only now that I'm alone in the quiet of the echoing space that I realize how hard I'm breathing and how fast my heart is racing. The way it slams into my ribcage makes it feel like it'll burst from my chest.

I unsnap the strap and rip off my helmet in one smooth movement. It's tempting to hurl it across the room, but I manage to hang onto my temper by a thread. I suck in a deep breath before holding it hostage in my lungs. Only when it feels like they're on the verge of exploding do I slowly release it back into the atmosphere. I repeat the exercise a handful of times until my muscles loosen and the red haze filling my vision finally clears.

Sweat drips down the back of my neck and clings to my forehead.

I shouldn't have reacted to what Akeman said. This is our fourth year playing together. From the very beginning, we've rubbed each other the wrong way. The guy has always been a shit talker. I should be used to it by now. Under normal circumstances, I'd let him run his mouth without missing a single beat. I'd block out his taunting barbs and focus on the scrimmage at hand.

But I wasn't able to do that today.

Not when he brought up Juliette.

Not when she's been front and center in my mind lately.

Filling both my thoughts and dreams.

Yesterday morning, I woke up with a raging boner. I keep thinking about the way she'd stripped off her clothing the night I took her home and the curve of her bare breast. Not to mention, the way she filled out that thong. Even now, as pissed off as I am, my body reacts to the mental image. I'm like one of Pavlov's dogs, salivating at the ringing of a bell.

No longer am I able to keep Juliette neatly locked away in the back of my brain like I've always done. And certainly not after catching a glimpse of the list she wrote.

I get hard just thinking about it.

And that book...

Who fucking knew a romance novel could be filled with such spicy stuff?

Certainly not me.

Have I learned a few things?

You better believe it.

It makes me horny as hell to know that what she read turned her on. In a weird way, it feels like getting a peek behind the curtain into the kinds of things girls want.

What they find sexy.

Did I already plow my way through the damn thing and pick up the next one in the series?

Sure did.

I almost shake my head as these thoughts swirl through my brain.

What the hell am I doing?

Juliette isn't a distraction I can afford right now. Not when my season is going down the shitter and Coach is looking for an excuse to toss me off the team.

But...

There's no damn way I'll allow another guy to touch her.

I drag a hand over my face.

So where does that leave me?

CHAPTER 13

JULIETTE

*I*t's official—inorganic chem will be the death of me.

Aaron and I usually study together, but he's been a little distant since I told him that we were never going to reach power couple status. It only reconfirms that I shouldn't date guys from my classes.

I expel a deep breath, ready to delve back into my tomb of a textbook when someone yanks out the chair across from me and drops down onto it. My head jerks up and my eyes widen at the sight of Ryder. I've done my best to avoid him since he woke up in my bedroom Saturday morning.

Snippets of our conversation flash through my head until it's tempting to crawl beneath the table to avoid the intensity of his stare.

When he remains silent, I straighten my shoulders and raise my brows.

"Is there something you wanted?"

"I'll do it."

When he fails to elaborate, I ask carefully, "Do what?" Did I somehow miss the first part of this conversation? "What *exactly* are you going to do?"

He shifts closer before resting his hands against the table. My gaze drops to them. His sweatshirt sleeves have been shoved up and the crinkly hair of his forearms is clearly on display.

That shouldn't be so sexy.

Except…it is.

Horrified by the direction my brain has turned, I mentally shake the thought away and force myself to meet his gaze. A spark of heat fills his eyes as if he knows exactly what I'm thinking.

Ugh.

Why does he affect me this way?

When he's near, everything inside me sits up and takes notice.

He presses closer to the table. "I'm going to help with your list."

Huh?

"I…don't understand." Is it possible that Ryder has taken one too many slap shots to the noggin?

How sad.

His blue eyes grow darker, more vibrant. Heat snaps from them, nearly singeing me alive from the distance that separates us. "Sure, you do."

Actually, I don't, and that's part of the problem.

When I remain silent, he pulls out his phone and taps the screen. Everything inside me loosens now that his gaze is no longer pinning me in place. With a frown, I crane my neck, trying to catch a glimpse of what he's so focused on.

"Look, I have a lot of work to do." I point toward the staircase that leads to the first floor. "So, if you wouldn't mind exiting stage left, I'd greatly appreciate it."

"Number one—make out in the library. Number two—skinny dip. Number three—karaoke. Number four—get drunk at a party." He glances up. "I assume you checked that one off after Friday night?"

My jaw crashes into the table as a shocked screech escapes from me. Students seated in the vicinity whip around and stare. A few shoot dirty looks our way before shushing us.

I clap a hand over my mouth as my eyes grow wider.

Ryder raises a brow at a table of guys, and they quickly glance away.

It's only when I've tamped down the urge to scream that I lower my hand and strain forward. *"How did you get that?"*

He turns his phone around and flashes the screen. "I took a picture."

I hiss out a shocked breath. "I can't believe you did that!"

"Why not?" He shrugs as his brow furrows. "You're the one who showed it to me."

"I was drunk." My voice escalates with each bitten-out syllable.

A smirk lifts his lips as he nods in agreement. "Yes, you certainly were. After I drove you home, I carried you up to your apartment. I was afraid you'd break your neck if I allowed you to walk by yourself."

Maybe it would have been better if I had.

This humiliation is almost unbearable.

It's tempting to leap across the table and strangle the life out of him. Or, at the very least, wrestle away his phone and delete the image.

He glances at the screen as his finger drifts over the smooth surface. "You never answered the question."

"What question?"

"Did you check off number four?"

I cross my arms protectively against my chest and glare, hoping he'll drop the topic.

Instead, he cocks his head and holds my gaze impatiently. "Well, did you?"

"Yes," I ground out, unable to believe we're actually engaging in this conversation.

Did it feel good to finally check something off that list?

Stupid as it sounds—yeah, it did.

He glances at the phone. "So, only nine more to go. See? Aren't you glad I'm going to help you with this?"

"Not really."

"Oh, come on. It'll be fun."

I force a hoarse laugh. "That's doubtful." I lift a hand to rub my forehead and force out the question. "Why?"

He raises a brow as if he doesn't understand what I'm asking.

"Why are you so interested in helping me with this?"

CHAPTER 14

RYDER

hy do I want to help her?
Excellent question.

I'm fairly confident that telling her the truth would go over like a lead balloon.

That her first orgasm belongs to me.

I've already claimed it.

Instead, I volley the question back to her and attempt to play it cool. "Why not?"

She narrows her eyes. "That's not an answer."

I should have realized that she wouldn't be on board with the plan. Most of the girls on this campus would be thrilled with the notion of spending a little one-on-one time with me. Even if it's to check items off a list.

Juliette, on the other hand, is not one of those girls.

She's never been one of those girls.

"Because we're friends."

Sort of.

"No, we're not. Our families are friends. You're friends with Mav." She waggles a finger between us. "The two of us have never been friends."

I sweep my tongue slowly across my teeth. "Did you ever think it might be time to rectify that situation?" Before she can shoot down the question with a resounding no, I add, "Plus, you're going to need help tackling that bucket list, which is where I come in." I eat up as much distance as I can between us until the thick edge of the table bites into my chest before dropping my voice several octaves. Even the thought of her wanting another guy pisses me off.

"Is there someone else you have in mind for the job?"

Her gaze never falters as she draws her lower lip between her teeth. She chews the plump flesh for a long, drawn-out moment that makes my heart thump harder before shaking her head.

My muscles loosen in response.

Unable to help myself, my attention gets snagged by her mouth and my cock stirs against my boxers. Ever since Friday night, I've spent a fair share of time fantasizing about what it would be like to crush her lips to mine. To sweep my tongue inside her mouth and have her surrender to my dominance.

I've spent so many years forcing Juliette to the back of my brain. Now that the door has been cracked open, there's no way to slam it shut again. For better or worse, those monsters have been unleashed.

"It's just..." Her voice trails off as she glances away.

The color that blooms in her cheeks only amps me up more. The girls I normally screw around with are skilled and know how to manipulate a situation. Every flip of their hair, bite of their lip, coy look aimed in a guy's direction is a practiced and calculated move on their part. At the end of the day, it's all a game. And they sure as shit don't blush when thinking or discussing sex.

It only reinforces how different and special she truly is.

"What?" It's so damn tempting to shove the table aside in order to get my hands on her.

Instead, I release a steady breath and force my muscles to loosen. If I come on too strong, it'll only scare her away, and that's the last thing I want to do.

"There's something on the list that's..."

"Come on, spit it out." Nerves prickle at the bottom of my belly.

"Sexual."

That one word is all it takes to turn my cock to stone. I'm so fucking hard that it's painful.

I lift a brow and try to remain casual when all I want to do is lock her down tight. "And?"

Her gaze slices to mine as she shifts restlessly on the chair. Any moment, she's going to go up in flames.

And I'll probably go up with her.

"We can't," she whispers.

"Why not?"

Her eyes dart away. "Because you're not attracted to me."

Is she out of her mind?

How does she not see through the thin veneer I've kept in place all these years?

Instead of responding to that comment, I jerk to my feet.

Her eyes widen as I stalk around the table, swallowing up the distance between us. She squeaks when I wrap my hand around her smaller one and haul her from the chair. There isn't time for questions as I tow her through the maze of bookshelves until we're buried deep in the back corner, away from prying eyes. She hastens her step to keep pace with me.

Just when she opens her mouth, I grind to a halt. Her smaller body crashes into mine before I wrap my fingers around her shoulders and force her backward until her spine hits a shelf filled with dusty periodicals.

Our faces are inches apart.

Other than the night I carried Juliette to her apartment, have I ever stood close enough to see the golden flecks that make up the inner ring of her irises?

Only now do I realize how mesmerizing they are in their vibrancy. It wouldn't surprise me if I ended up drowning within their amber depths. Hell, it might be a more preferable way to go.

When I press my thick erection into the softness of her belly, her mouth forms a shocked little O.

"Does it really feel like I'm not attracted to you?" I growl.

With a gulp, she shakes her head.

"Now tell me—do I turn you on?" The question escapes from me before I can stop it.

When she remains silent, I flex my hips for a second time. My hands are still wrapped around the tops of her shoulders as I lower my head until my mouth can ghost over hers. That's all it takes for the air to stir around us, turning electric.

There's no damn way this attraction is one sided.

It can't be.

"Well?" Unable to help myself, I thrust against her again. "Do I?"

My muscles coil tight as that question hangs in the charged atmosphere. Intensity ratchets up between us until there's a good possibility it'll explode, blowing us both to smithereens.

"Yes."

I don't realize how tightly strung I've become until the whispered word escapes from her. My body turns slack as my lungs empty in relief.

I rub the tip of my nose against hers and nip at the plump flesh of her bottom lip before tugging it with my teeth and drawing it into my mouth. In the silence of the library, her shaky inhalation is as loud as a gunshot. It echoes throughout my brain until it's the only thing I'm cognizant of.

Unable to resist, I slant my mouth over hers. Back and forth I strum until the movement is nothing short of dizzying. Until the warmth of her breath can feather across my lips.

How many times have I fantasized about doing exactly this?

Too damn many to count.

The knowledge that this girl now belongs to me explodes in my chest. My need for her has never been something I've allowed myself to dwell on. I pushed it from my brain and told myself it didn't exist.

I tried my damnedest to pretend *she* didn't exist.

But it didn't work.

Not really.

Juliette was always there, hovering on the periphery, slyly fucking with my thoughts.

It's only when I've teased both of us that I give in to years of pent-up longing and allow my mouth to settle over hers. The velvety softness of my tongue dances across the seam of her lips. That's all it takes for her to open as a growl of need vibrates within my chest. I want to stake my claim so every fucking guy on this campus knows who she belongs to. Maybe this isn't a long-term situation, but for the time being, Juliette is mine.

When her sweetness explodes in my mouth, I find myself deepening the caress. It's so tempting to consume every single part of her. I want to eat her up in one tasty gulp. Need thrums through me as I press closer until every inch of my body is aligned with her soft curves. With a tilt of her head, she allows me greater access. My tongue lashes hers, tangling with it.

I'm so fucking turned on.

I have no idea how long we stand pressed against the stacks.

It could be minutes or hours.

What I do know is that it's not nearly enough.

It will never be enough.

If I don't rein in my desire while I still can, it'll burn completely out of control.

It takes effort to pull away. When I finally do, we're both breathing hard. Her hands are pressed against my chest, her fingers curled into the fabric of my hoodie. It's as if she's hanging on for dear life.

The dazed look filling her eyes sets fire to my blood.

"How many guys have you kissed?"

Juliette blinks as if she's incapable of wrapping her mind around the question. "Kissed?"

Unable to resist the temptation, I nip her plump bottom lip. "Yeah, tell me."

Her fingers rise before drifting over her mouth. "I don't know... maybe a dozen."

"And were any of them as good as that?"

She scrapes her teeth across her lower lip before giving her head a slight shake.

A slow smile spreads across my face. "All you need to know is that I do everything with just as much finesse."

Her eyes flare.

When she remains silent, I ask, "So, are we on?"

After that kiss, there's no way this *isn't* happening. I'll do whatever it takes to convince her that I'm the man for the job.

"Yeah." Her response comes out sounding shaky.

My muscles loosen at her easy capitulation. Then, I tackle the last obstacle standing in the way. "About number ten..." My voice trails off.

"What about it?"

"Let's take it off the table."

"That...makes sense."

"Good. Then we're both on the same page." I hold out my palm. "Give me your phone."

She blinks a few times before reaching into her back pocket and pulling out her cell. Once she opens the locked home screen, she hands it over. I quickly input my number and pass it back.

Even though I don't want to, I take a step in retreat. Then another. Her gaze clings to mine the entire time. Little does she know that every instinct within is demanding I grab hold of her until she's locked up tight in my arms for safekeeping.

"I'll catch you later," I force myself to say.

"Okay."

And then I swing around and take off before I can destroy all the painstaking progress I've made this afternoon.

CHAPTER 15

JULIETTE

"*H*ey, sweetheart! It's good to see you," Dad says, pulling me in for a warm embrace. "I've missed you."

Even though I roll my eyes, my lips bow up into a smile. "You just saw me last week."

"It doesn't matter. I always miss seeing my little girl's face."

For just a moment, I rest my head against his chest as he wraps an arm around me, and we settle in the bleachers to wait for the game to get underway.

"Hey, baby," Mom says, leaning over to kiss my cheek.

"Hi."

"How are classes going?" she asks.

"They're pretty good." It won't be long before we're heading into finals, so I've been doing my best to stay on top of everything.

"Even inorganic chem?" she asks with a smile.

"It's fine. I'll drop in for office hours if I need to."

With a shake of her head, she glances at Dad. There's a twinkle in her mocha-colored eyes when she says, "I'm not sure where this one came from. She's too damn smart to be ours."

Dad grins before dropping a kiss on the crown of my head. "She's definitely all yours, Nat."

My gaze bounces between them and the smiles that simmer across their lips as they stare at one another. For just a moment or two, it feels as if the arena and all its noise fades to the background and it's just the two of them.

As soon as Mom turns away to talk with Ryder's parents, Cal and Sadie, who are seated on the other side of her, Dad leans closer and whispers, "All the plans are set for Mom's birthday at Taco Loco."

"She's going to be so surprised." It's hard to get anything past my mother. But I don't think she has a clue about what Dad's up to.

"Sure will. I threw her a surprise birthday dinner at a Mexican restaurant when we were in college. Did I ever tell you about that?"

"Yup." And it makes my heart melt every time he shares the story of how they fell in love. Back then, she refused to give him the time of day. According to Dad, she couldn't stand him. They're so in love now that it's hard to imagine. They actually pretended to date, one thing led to another, and she fell head over heels for him.

It's exactly the kind of relationship I've been searching for. I want someone who can make my heart skip a beat and my tummy tremble when our gazes lock from across a crowded room. I want someone who makes me forget my own name when we kiss.

Kind of like at the library with—

My phone vibrates with an incoming text, and I slip it from my pocket before glancing at the screen.

Don't make plans after the game. We're checking something off tonight.

My heart plummets to my toes as I stare at the message. It's been days since I ran into Ryder at the library. I'd almost thought he forgot about our agreement.

Looks like I was wrong.

I glance up just as the Western Wildcats take to the ice, circling around their half. Their opponents do the same on the opposite end. My gaze sweeps over the players until it lands on Ryder. Even though all the guys look similar in their uniforms, padding and helmets, I'd know him anywhere.

Number fifty-five.

His stick rests across his shoulders as he takes long strides to warm up his legs. His muscular arms hang over the length as he twists his torso back and forth. When he skates past our seats, his gaze locks on mine and electricity snaps and sizzles, lighting my nerve-endings up. My mouth turns cottony as I glance at the message for a second time and conjure up a mental image of the list, wondering which item he has in mind.

Number one (make out at the library) and four (get drunk at a party) have already been checked off. That leaves seven possibilities, since falling in love has been removed. My belly clenches at the idea of skinny dipping with Ryder or worse...

Him giving me an orgasm.

It's humiliating that he knows something so private about me. He must think I'm such a loser. Although, I'm pretty sure he thought I was a loser way before that. The list has only solidified it.

Ugh.

"Your brother looks good out there," Dad says, interrupting the whirl of my thoughts.

My gaze touches on Maverick momentarily before drifting back to Ryder. The tiny hairs at the nape of my neck rise when I find his attention still locked on me.

CHAPTER 16

RYDER

$\mathcal{I}$ press a hand against the tile wall and allow the hot pulse of water to beat down against my hair, neck, and back. Hooting and hollering surrounds me. Everyone is riding high off the win. It wasn't an easy one. We had to fight for every goal.

There's talk of heading out to the bars and getting loaded.

And laid.

Since those two usually go hand in hand.

Especially after a win.

People need to blow off steam.

But that's not what's circling through my brain.

All right, that's not altogether true.

But it's much too soon to consider having sex with Juliette. After our kiss in the library, it's been on my mind more and more. Now that I'm finally allowing myself to think about her after years of shutting those thoughts down, I can't stop. They're like a runaway train barreling down the tracks.

She's a temptation I can't wait to explore.

After the library, I actually went home and jacked off.

Can you believe that?

I haven't masturbated in years.

Not since I started getting laid on a regular basis.

When you have chicks constantly throwing themselves at you, willing to spread their legs or drop to their knees at your slightest whim, there's no need to take matters into your own hands, so to speak.

Could I have texted a girl that I've messed around with in the past to come over and alleviate matters?

Yup. There were a couple of puck bunnies hanging out at the house the other night that I could have hooked up with but...

I don't know. The idea of fucking one of them to douse the fire that Juliette stoked to life didn't do it for me. Here's a weird little twist —I actually like the slow build of anticipation.

That's not something I expected.

I've been screwing since sophomore year in high school. Once I started, there was no stopping. I've had straight-up, no-frills, missionary style sex and then swung to the other side and gotten freaky in bed with two chicks who had enough tricks to keep me there for a couple of hours until I'd thought there was an excellent chance my dick might fall off.

The point is, I've been there and done that.

Know what I haven't done?

Waited.

Anticipated.

Bided my sweet time while everything slowly built inside until it reached a fever pitch.

I've never contemplated someone for days on end and all the delicious ways I was going to run my hands over their body.

But with Juliette, that's exactly the way it is.

My cock twitches at the idea of sinking inside her delicious warmth.

Fuck, I bet she's tight.

She admitted to only kissing a dozen guys. I probably should have asked how many she's slept with, but I was afraid to push for more information in case she got cold feet and completely nixed the idea.

When my cock stiffens, I twist the handle of the shower head to cold and hiss out a breath when icy drops of water rain down on me. It does exactly what I need it to and kills the growing erection.

Especially since I'm showering with a bunch of naked dudes.

Hey, I have no problem if that's what turns your crank.

Go for it, man.

Just…not in the locker room.

Want to know what it feels like to have your junk duct taped to your thigh?

That would be the quickest way to find out.

From what I hear, it's painful.

So, no thanks.

It's only when I'm completely flaccid that I crank the silver handle and grab a towel to rub over my face before wrapping it around my waist. Once dried, I pull out my T-shirt and jeans from my locker. I throw on some pit sauce, then cologne before running my hands through my hair.

Good enough.

Ford quirks a brow. "Looks like someone wants to get laid tonight."

"Nah." That is most definitely *not* on the agenda.

"Since when?" he asks with growing interest. "You gone celibate on us? Taken a vow of chastity?"

I give him a bit of side eye. "Is Carina planning on making a cameo appearance tonight?"

That question is all it takes to have his eyes narrowing and lips flattening. "How the fuck should I know? Am I her keeper or something?"

Did the motherfucker really think he was going to poke at me?

Ha!

All I have to do is mention Carina's name and his disposition changes.

And not for the good.

There's definitely something there, and I'm curious to know what it is.

I shrug, delighted to have turned the tables on him with so little effort. I mean, it wasn't even a challenge.

"Maybe she'll bring her new boyfriend with," I toss out for shits and giggles.

He straightens and glares.

Screwing with him is almost too easy.

Although, still entirely satisfying.

"The fuck you say?"

"Guess you'll have to ask her about it."

"Damn right I will," he grumbles.

I need to get out of here before I bust out laughing and Ford figures out that I'm messing with him.

My guess is that he has the hots for his stepsister.

Or ex-stepsister.

Or whatever the hell they are to each other. I have no idea if their parents are married or not. It's kind of comical to watch him get all fired up about her and then try to pretend he has zero interest.

"Catch you later, man," I say, slamming my locker door shut.

He doesn't bother with a response. I'm sure he's in his head right now, trying to figure out what's going on with Carina.

My lips twitch as I head to the lobby where everyone has congregated while waiting for the players.

As I turn the corner, my gaze drifts over the crowd before settling on Juliette and slowly sweeping over the length of her. The girl is gorgeous with long, mahogany colored hair that falls like a rich curtain down her back and eyes that are just as deep and dark. She's all curves. I hadn't realized how stacked she was until the party last weekend.

And then when she'd shed her clothing...

Yeah.

Tonight, her outfit is casual. More like what it is when I run into her on campus. A black puffy jacket has been layered over a pink sweater that leaves everything to the imagination, and a pair of jeans hugs her heart-shaped ass. There's a black Wildcats knit hat on her head and matching scarf wrapped around her neck.

She turns and glances at me as if she can feel the heat of my stare. When our eyes collide, hers flare wide before color seeps into her cheeks and she rips them away.

A smile curls around the edges of my lips.

Are thoughts of the way I kissed her at the library rolling lazily through her head?

Or how about the way I flexed my hips while pinning her against the bookshelf?

My cock twitches at the memory.

As I join the group, Brody flashes me a smile. "Nice win out there."

"Thanks." Even though he doesn't bring it up, we both know that I didn't have a great game. Coach pulled me in the third period to sit my ass on the bench after I fumbled a pass.

"It's all right," Dad says, as if he can read my mind. "Everyone has an off game."

He knows just how much shit has been eating at me lately.

With a nod, my hand rises to the back of my neck. The last thing I want to discuss is the game and all the mistakes I made on the ice.

Already, there's a meeting set up with Coach for Monday at noon to go over game film. He'll point out every fucking mistake and I'll walk out of his office and wonder why the hell I bothered to lace up my skates in the first place.

Even though I'm no longer on the ice or in the locker room, it feels like I'm slowly being suffocated. I glance longingly toward the doors that lead out of the building. It feels like my lungs are starved for fresh air. What I need to do is get the hell out of here.

I refocus my attention on Juliette. She might be a distraction I don't need, especially right now, but I find that she's the only thing that takes my mind off hockey. Even if it's just for a few blissful hours.

She's going to shit a brick when she figures out what I've got in store for her. Pushing that girl out of her comfort zone will be an absolute pleasure.

"What are your plans tonight?" Mom asks. "Big party to celebrate?"

I shake my head as my gaze flickers to Juliette. "We're heading to the bars, right?"

For the second time in a matter of minutes, her eyes widen. Only this time, it's in surprise. "What?"

It's kind of enjoyable to knock her off balance.

I tilt my head as my gaze pins hers in place, silently daring her to argue. "Remember, we talked about it the other day? You agreed to hang out with the team tonight."

A frown morphs across Maverick's face. "Seriously?" Before she can respond, he fires off another question. "Since when do you party with the guys?"

"Umm..." Her mouth works a couple of times as panic flashes across her face. "I just thought..."

Watching her flounder has the corners of my lips lifting. This is a girl who usually has an answer for everything.

"We ran into each other at the library the other day, and I talked her into chilling with us after the game," I reply easily.

When she remains silent, I prompt, "Isn't that right?"

Her gaze remains pinned to mine as she swallows thickly. "Yes. We spoke at the library, and it sounded like fun."

Maverick's scowl deepens. "I don't like it."

Brody elbows his son in the ribs. "There's nothing wrong with your sister hanging out with you tonight. Just think of it as a little McKinnon sibling bonding time."

Maverick rolls his eyes. "What that really means is that I'll have to keep an eye on her so no one gets ideas."

"No need to worry about that," I cut in. "She'll be with me."

"Guess we know how your night is gonna turn out," he mutters under his breath.

The guy doesn't have a clue. And that's exactly the way it needs to stay. Mav would lose his shit if he found out what Juliette and I are up to.

"I guess we should take off then," Natalie says.

All the parents agree to head over to the McKinnons' for drinks.

In the chaos of the moment, Maverick pokes me in the chest. "You better keep a close eye on her. I don't want her hooking up with any of these assholes. You know what they're like."

Yup, I do. And if she were my sibling, I'd feel the same way.

"I think your sister is more than capable of taking care of herself, don't you?"

He grunts in answer before walking away.

Juliette hugs and kisses her parents, telling them that she'll see them soon.

And then, it's just the two of us.

She glances around the open space before her gaze reluctantly flickers to mine. It's as if she's trying to look everywhere but at me. Nervous energy radiates off her in thick, suffocating waves.

I'm not going to lie, it's a little intoxicating.

Kind of like waving a red scarf in front of a bull.

"You ready to get moving?" I ask, making a concerted effort not to reach out and drag her into my arms.

"Do you really think this is a good idea?"

Fuck yeah. In fact, it's the best damn one I've had in a while.

"Yup."

"Are you going to tell me what we're doing?"

"It's a surprise," I say with a slow smile. "You'll just have to wait and see."

Before she can fire off any more questions or attempt to back out, I give in to temptation and step closer, wrapping my arm around her shoulders before steering us toward the exit.

CHAPTER 17

JULIETTE

The bar is packed to the gills when we arrive. The mountain of muscle acting as a bouncer takes one look at Ryder and waves him through the back door without bothering to glance my way. One step over the threshold and the loud music and boisterous voices hit me.

It's standing room only.

After every game, the team heads over to Slap Shotz, a sports bar slash dive joint that caters to the Western Wildcats hockey team. I think the owner is an old player who apparently didn't want to stop reliving his glory days. So, there are team photos dating back to the eighties dotting the walls along with sticks, jerseys, framed photos, and signed pucks.

I've been here a time or two.

All I have to say is that it's not really my scene.

The music is cranked up way too loud and there are too many people crammed into a small space, making it feel borderline claustrophobic.

Not to mention, the floor beneath my shoes is sticky.

"Hey, Ryder," a pretty blonde in a skimpy shirt calls out with a wave and toothy smile.

She's exactly the kind of girl I'd expect Ryder to hook up with. I couldn't be more—

Whoa.

I stop those thoughts in their proverbial tracks. It doesn't matter what kind of girls Ryder normally takes home at the end of the night. All he's doing is helping me tick off items on my bucket list. I need to keep that in mind and not pretend this is an actual relationship.

Ryder's hand settles on my lower back as he steers me through the sea of people. More than half are decked out in team colors along with licensed shirts or jerseys. That's when I notice how many have Ryder's name and number proudly stamped across the front and back.

He presses closer before asking, "Want something to drink?"

A reluctant shiver dances down my spine as his warm breath feathers across my flesh.

Unable to help myself, I glance over my shoulder and meet his gaze. Even though there are fans trying to get his attention, the intensity of it is solely focused on me. Once his eyes capture mine, it feels like I'm ensnared in a trap.

I shake my head as air gets wedged in my throat, making it impossible to catch my breath. "Not after last weekend."

His lips quirk around the edges. "One or two won't get you shit-faced. More than that? Probably." His gaze slides down my body before rising to my face. "You're a lightweight."

Even though I told myself I was never going to drink again, a thick knot of anxiety has taken up residence at the bottom of my belly. Maybe just one beer would take the edge off and help me relax. Although, if Ryder would tell me what his plans are for the evening, that would go a long way to settle my nerves.

"Okay," I relent. "Just one."

His white teeth flash in the dim lighting of the bar. "All right, stay right here. I'll grab us something and be back in a sec."

I give him a nod and he takes off, plowing his way through the throng. Honestly, shoving isn't required. People scurry out of his way. Ryder probably towers a couple inches over six feet. On the ice, he's even taller and broader with the skates and padding. He's always been a force to be reckoned with.

That thought has my mind tumbling back to the game.

I've watched Ryder play hockey since he was a mini mite, and he's not playing with the same level of confidence. I know their old coach left abruptly at the beginning of the year and a new one has taken his place. But as tempting as it is to ask him about it, there's no way I'd bring it up. It's not like we're close and talk about our personal stuff.

I only realized it was an issue when I overheard Mom and Dad discussing the situation. Dad owns a sports agency that represents professional athletes. There are a lot of hockey players since he played in the NHL for more than a decade before retiring and taking over my grandfather's management company. Mom also works for the family business. I assume Maverick will end up doing the same. Mav entered the NHL draft last year and was picked up by Boston. Just like Ryder, Dad thought it would be best for him to play this season before signing his contract with them.

My gaze stays locked on Ryder as a female bartender catches sight of him and beelines in his direction. Even from here, I can see the cleavage baring shirt she wears with the name of the establishment stamped across her breasts. She grabs two brown bottles before setting them on the long stretch of bar and leaning against it so that Ryder has an unobstructed view of the goods.

They chat for a minute or so before he shoves away from the counter and swings back toward me. The woman stares after him with a besotted look on her face before turning to the next customer.

I almost shake my head.

I've attended elementary, middle, high school, and now college with Ryder. I've watched this exact scene play out with hundreds of different girls.

This is what's known as the Ryder McAdams effect.

The man doesn't even have to turn on the charm to have the fairer sex falling at his feet. His handsome face and athletic build do the job for him. Girls have always been putty in his hands.

A little zip of awareness scuddles down my spine as his gaze fastens on me. And just like before, the crowd parts as people clap him on the shoulder and tell him what a good game he had.

Once he's a foot or so away, he extends a bottle to me. Only now do I realize how parched my throat is. I bring the glass container to my lips and take a small sip. The icy cold liquid feels surprisingly good going down.

Ryder continues to stare before lifting his own and taking a long swallow. My gaze drops to his throat and the way his muscles constrict.

Something like that shouldn't be so sexy.

But I'll be damned if it's not.

I force my gaze away before he notices my reaction.

"Let's head to the table," he says, his deep voice startling me from my thoughts.

When his arm slips around my waist, I turn and collide with his chest. I tip my face up only to find him staring down at me. He's close enough for his breath to drift over my lips. That's all it takes for his nearness to scatter my thoughts, making it impossible to think straight.

"Okay." My answer comes out sounding ridiculously breathy.

What the hell is wrong with me?

Just like when we left the arena and walked into the bar, he draws me close and maneuvers us through the press of bodies until we arrive at a long table in the back. My guess is that two or even three of them have been shoved together to make room for about twenty people. A good number of Ryder's teammates are already settled on chairs. Girls are either perched on their laps or are buzzing around like drunken bees trying to find a guy.

Since every seat is occupied, Ryder pulls up alongside a sophomore player and jerks his thumb over his shoulder. "Up."

The younger guy's eyes widen before he scrambles out of the chair without a word of protest. When I glance at Ryder, he smirks before dropping down. It's almost a relief when his hand falls away from my body. Being touched by him does funny things to my insides. Like there's a high-wire trapeze act taking place within the confines of my belly.

I don't like it.

I'm a person who likes to be in control, and Ryder's touch makes me feel the exact opposite.

When I continue to stand awkwardly beside him, he taps his thigh with the flat of his hand.

My brows slam together as I shake my head.

Is he crazy?

I'm not going to sit on his lap like some kind of puck bunny. That would give off the wrong impression. Especially to my brother, who's sitting at the opposite end of the table. He looks to be in deep conversation with another teammate. A few girls circle, stroking their hands over his arms and shoulders.

Gross.

Not exactly the kind of image a sister wants singed into her brain for all eternity.

When I don't budge, Ryder leans closer. "Do you see any alternatives?"

I chew my lip and glance around. He's right. Although, he cleared a seat for himself, so…

"Can't you move one of these guys?"

His gaze never falters from mine. "Nope." He taps his thigh for a second time. "This is your seat for the night. Take it or leave it."

My mouth turns cottony at the thought of being perched on his lap while he holds court. To buy a little time, I lift the bottle to my lips and take another pull. The alcohol does nothing to settle the nerves tingling at the bottom of my gut. I fidget for another moment or two before sucking in a deep breath and forcing myself to step closer. Satisfaction flickers in his eyes as his hands wrap around the curve of my hips, helping me settle tentatively on his lap. Just as a puff of air escapes from me, he drags my body closer until I can feel the steeliness of his chest pressed against my stiff spine.

"Isn't this more comfortable than a hard chair?" he whispers against my ear.

"No."

A soft chuckle slips free from him, and the sound of it scampers across my skin, making the tiny hairs on my arms prickle with newfound awareness. One hand curls around my thigh as the other slips beneath my sweater and settles at my waist. The feel of his calloused palms against my sensitive skin sends arousal spiraling through me, and I can't help but shift.

"Keep wiggling around like that and you'll find something hard poking your ass," he growls.

I gulp and immediately still my movements. The longer I remain frozen in place, the more tempting it is to squirm as need pools in my core like warmed honey. My teeth sink into my lower lip in an effort to keep the moan gathering in my chest trapped inside where it can't see the light of day.

His thumb strums my flesh above the waistband of my jeans where no one is the wiser. The way he touches me turns my insides to mush. What I don't know is if it's because I've never had anyone arouse me like this, or it's specific to Ryder.

My greatest fear is that it has everything to do with him.

I clear my throat and attempt to distract myself from the dangerous thoughts circling around in my brain like hungry sharks. "When are you going to tell me what we're doing?"

Before he can respond, the music stops as an older man hefts himself up onto the small stage I didn't realize was on the far side of the bar.

He brings the microphone to his mouth. "The Wildcats brought home a win tonight, and you know what that means!"

Actually, I have no idea what it means.

But I seem to be the only one.

I glance around as everyone in the bar yells back in response, "Karaoke!"

"You got it!"

Oh no.

My head whips toward Ryder so fast that I nearly give myself whiplash. A slow smile spreads across his face as our gazes collide.

"Figure it out yet?"

CHAPTER 18

RYDER

*H*er eyes widen to the point where they look like they might fall out of her head.

"No, I can't," she whispers in a voice that sounds like she's being strangled from the inside out.

My gaze stays pinned to her face as I relax against the chair. "It's on your list, isn't it?"

She presses her lips together until they turn bloodless as every muscle goes taut. I'm kind of wishing that I hadn't brought it up. I was enjoying the feel of her curvy little body against mine. The soft weight in my arms as my fingers stroked the bare skin beneath her sweater. It only makes me eager to explore more of her. And if she were any other girl, that's exactly what I'd be doing.

Although, that's not going to happen in front of Maverick. He'd have no problem getting in my face and asking what the hell I'm doing with his sister. Even though I'm a year older than Mav, we've always been friends. And teammates, because Mav played up in hockey.

The last thing I want to do is lie to him. But I also know if he discovers that I'm messing around with Juliette, it'll probably be the end of our friendship.

That alone should be enough to give me pause.

It doesn't.

"Yes," she says grudgingly. "I never should have written it down."

"But you did."

"Yeah…"

I pop a brow. "And you want to check it off, don't you?"

She draws in a deep breath through her nose before forcing it out between her lips. "I do."

"The course of action seems pretty cut and dry, doesn't it?"

"Stop asking questions that only dig my grave deeper," she grumbles.

I can't help but grin. "Why not? Those are the best kind."

Fear flickers in her coffee-colored eyes as she glances toward the stage. Already, a couple of girls are climbing onto it and grinning at the crowd. For some of the groupies, getting up and singing their little hearts out—especially if it's a sexy song—will clinch who they go home with at the end of the night.

The girls glance at the screen with the lyrics as the intro to the song begins. It doesn't take long before they're prancing around and grinding against one another. My gaze flickers to the guys at the table. Most are riveted to the performance.

Juliette's mouth falls open as her eyes widen. "There's no way I'm doing that."

And there's no damn way I'd allow it.

I'm not looking to throw fists tonight, which is exactly what would happen.

"You just have to sing. That's it."

She rips her attention away from the stage long enough to glance at the hockey players, some of whom are hooting, hollering, and whistling for an encore performance. Her body stiffens even more. "They don't want to watch someone sing. They want a burlesque show. There's no way I'm getting up there and making a fool out of myself."

Once the song ends, the girls take a bow before hopping off the stage. A couple guys lumber up and belt out 'I Want it That Way' by the Backstreet Boys. Honestly, they're not bad.

Another girl does 'I Wanna Dance with Somebody.'

Damn. She sounds more like a professional. If I had to guess, I'd say she was probably in the music program at Western.

Juliette swivels on my lap and pleads, "Please don't make me get up there. How am I supposed to follow that?" She points to the girl who just killed it. Her vocal range was pretty impressive.

"No one expects you to top that. Just have fun."

"Fun," she mutters. "Ha! Pissing myself in front of a bar full of drunk hockey players isn't exactly what I'd consider a good time."

I snort. "That's not going to happen."

"Wanna bet?"

Her gaze pins mine in place and that's all it takes for me to get lost in her eyes for a heartbeat or two. There are times when it feels like I could drown in her dark depths.

Honestly?

It wouldn't be a bad way to go.

"Want me to come up there with you?"

Relief floods her expression. "You'd do that?"

It hadn't been my original intention but...

"Yeah, sure."

She blows out a steady breath as her gaze cuts back to the stage. "Okay."

A couple more people make their way up there and belt out their lungs. Some are good. And others...

Not so much.

More like cats in heat.

"Final act of the night," Sully announces. He's the owner of this fine establishment and played hockey for Western way back in the day. When we do team fundraisers, he's usually one of our biggest sponsors. So, we try to give back by bringing our business here. It's certainly not a hardship. The beer and shots are cheap, the music is loud, and hockey games are playing on every television mounted behind the bar.

I press closer until my face is buried in the thick strands of her hair. "You ready to do this?"

Her muscles tense before she jerks her head into a reluctant nod. "As I'll ever be."

My grip tightens around her waist as she rises to her feet. It lingers for a second or two before falling away. I've spent years wanting to lay my hands on her. Now that I can, I'm loath to set her free.

Which is exactly why I straighten to my full height and snag her fingers, towing her through the thick press of bodies to the stage. From the corner of my eye, I catch sight of Maverick. A frown tugs at his lips as he follows the path we cut. I can practically feel the way his narrowed gaze beats into my back as questions churn through his head.

Juliette shoots me an anxious look as she climbs onto the stage. I give her a nod of encouragement before flipping through the list of songs. One in particular jumps out and I queue it up. She wraps her hand around a microphone and pulls it closer. Guilt pricks at me when I notice the way her hand trembles and her face pales as she silently surveys the drunken crowd. She looks moments away from hurling all over the place.

A few of the guys from the team whistle and clap.

"Serenade us, McAdams!" one loudmouth yells.

I shake my head and give whoever keeps catcalling me the finger.

When the first notes of Evanescence's 'Bring Me to Life' plays, her gaze flickers to mine in surprise. It used to be one of her favorites. She'd listen to it on repeat until I could recite the lyrics word for word. And I didn't even like the damn song.

She squeezes her eyes tightly closed for a second or two before bringing the microphone to her lips. Her voice is soft and thready as her gaze bounces from the lyrics on the screen to the crowd. The rowdy bunch falls silent as they gradually become entranced by her performance. Even if she sucked major ass, guys would still stop and pay attention. Juliette has no idea how strikingly beautiful she is. Maybe she's able to move through her everyday life by keeping her head down and hiding out in the library with her nose buried in a book, but up here on stage?

That's no longer possible. Her presence commands their attention. I can see by the surprised expressions that transform their faces that it's like they're seeing her for the first time. When a few of my team-mates whistle, her confidence grows and her voice becomes stronger.

And then I come in.

Her gaze slices to mine as a smile curves her lips, making her look even prettier than before, because contrary to what she expected, she's actually enjoying herself. Our gazes stay locked as we belt out the lyrics. The instruments hit hard as our voices rise above it, harmonizing together. There's a back and forth to the song as I continually jump in.

By the end, Juliette's vocals soar over the audience, filling the bar. I'm so intent on watching her get lost in the music that I almost miss a lyric. That's when I remember she took four years of choir in high school and knows how to project her voice while hitting all the notes on key.

Is she as good as the other girl? The one who's probably a music major?

Nah. But she's damn close. Definitely second best of the evening, and that's saying something.

By the time the last note reverberates and fades, everyone has jumped to their feet. The applause that follows is thunderous. Juliette looks a little shellshocked as she beams, taking a little bow before jumping off the stage. I follow quickly behind her. My hand settles at the small of her back as I guide her to the table. At this point, I'll take any excuse to touch her.

I drop down onto my chair as she settles next to me in an unoccupied one. She picks up her beer and drains the rest before slamming the bottle on the table. There's a brightness to her eyes that wasn't there before as she vibrates with the adrenalin of her performance. A few guys congratulate her and raise their arms for fist bumps.

"See? That wasn't so bad, was it?" I say, picking up my own drink.

A sheepish smile simmers around her lips. "Actually, it was kind of fun."

I nod toward the stage. "You really killed it up there. I forgot you could actually sing."

She shrugs off the compliment as if it makes her uncomfortable. "The song was perfect. As soon as the intro started, the words flooded back to me, and I got a little lost in the music." There's a moment of silence. "I used to love that song."

"Yeah, I remember."

She blinks, her gaze refocusing on me as her dark brows slide together. "You do?"

Now it's my turn to shrug, playing down the memory. "You'd always blast it up in your room."

"I did," she admits with a chuckle. "For months. It drove Mav crazy."

"It got to the point where I'd be humming it in the shower."

She tucks a stray lock of hair behind her ear. "I didn't think you noticed."

Unable to help myself, I shift closer as my gaze stays pinned to hers. "I noticed everything."

For just a heartbeat or two, the music blasting through the speakers and chaos around us fades to the background. It's so damn tempting to lean closer and—

She rips her gaze away and pops to her feet before pointing to the bar. "I'm, ah, going to get a bottle of water. After that, I'm super thirsty."

I force my muscles to relax against the chair. "Okay."

Mid-flight, she pauses. "Do you want another drink?"

I bring the bottle to my lips and take a sip. "Nope, I'm good."

"Okay. I'll be right back." With that, she takes off through the crowd.

"And I'll be here waiting," I mumble under my breath. My attention stays locked on her as more people offer their congratulations.

When I finally force my gaze away, it collides with Maverick's narrowed one.

There's not a single doubt in my mind that he'll have questions. Ones I don't necessarily want to answer.

CHAPTER 19

JULIETTE

*W*ith the back of my head resting against the cushion of Ryder's pickup, I close my eyes and hum 'Bring Me to Life' under my breath. Never in a million years would I have suspected that being on stage would be such a rush. Even now, hours later, adrenalin continues to pump wildly through my veins.

There's no way I would have been brave enough to attempt karaoke if Ryder hadn't forced me up there. After I'd stumbled onto the makeshift stage, my gaze had coasted over the drunken crowd, and for a second or two, I'd grown a little lightheaded and thought I might pass out.

How embarrassing would that have been?

I'd never be able to show my face around campus again.

The only thing that kept me frozen in place was the knowledge that I wasn't alone. That Ryder was up there with me. I figured everyone would stare at him anyway.

Especially the girls.

But the guys as well.

People just seem to naturally gravitate to him. He's always been popular. Even when he wasn't trying to be.

Once the familiar tune started to play, everything inside me loosened. At first, I'd watched the screen and the lyrics, but after about twenty seconds, it all came flooding back to me. It's surprising that Ryder would remember how much I loved that song and played it on repeat until even my parents wanted to stuff plugs in their ears.

I crack my eyelids open and glance at him as we drive back to my apartment. Soft music floods the dark space. His attention stays focused on the black ribbon of road stretched out beyond the windshield as pale moonlight illuminates the way. If you'd told me two weeks ago that I would willingly be spending time with Ryder McAdams and he'd be helping me tick off items on my bucket list, I would have laughed myself silly.

We've never spent time alone together.

He was always Maverick's friend.

And yet, here we are.

It's a little surreal. I've spent years going out of my way to avoid Ryder. Not because I had a problem with him, but because he seemed to have one with me. He wasn't a dick or anything like that. It's more that he didn't bother talking or interacting with me. We just kind of ignored each other and went about our lives. There were times, especially when we got older, when I'd feel the heat of his gaze, and it would make my insides feel funny. He'd stare until warmth flooded my cheeks.

"What?" he asks, flicking a glance at me.

"Hmm?" I blink, knocked from the thoughts circling through my brain.

"You've been staring."

He turns the steering wheel to the right and swings into the lot, parking near the front of the building before killing the engine and swiveling toward me.

When I remain silent, he says, "Are you going to tell me what you were thinking about?"

When my teeth sink into my lower lip, his gaze dips to the movement. Something subtle changes in his expression as his eyes sharpen.

"Well?" he adds gruffly.

It seems far safer to keep my private thoughts to myself. At least for the time being.

"I had a lot of fun tonight," I say instead. "Thank you."

He drags his gaze to mine. "Yeah, me too."

With a snort, I roll my eyes. The tension that had gathered in me gradually loosens. "Doubtful."

While getting up on stage and belting out a song will end up being the highlight of my month, it's nothing for Ryder. He glides onto the ice every week during the season to thousands of fans cheering his name.

"What's that supposed to mean?" He shifts and stretches his arm across the back of my leather seat.

"I'm sure what happened tonight was pretty tame by your standards." I glance at the digital clock on the dash. "This would be considered an early night for you. I'm willing to bet that most of your evenings end with someone sliding into your bed."

There's a moment of silence as the tension ratchets up between us. I wish I could steal the words from the air, but that's impossible. For better or worse, they're out there.

"Not always."

A kernel of longing blooms in the pit of my belly. Before I can inspect it more carefully, I stomp it out. Feeling anything other than friendship for Ryder would be dangerous.

Not to mention, foolish.

Especially since it would be all one sided.

I might be a lot of things, but stupid isn't one of them.

"And how do most of your nights end?" His fingers lightly strum my shoulder and a sizzle of awareness shoots through me. I hate to admit just how much my brain short circuits at his slightest touch.

"Studying," I whisper.

He nods as if unsurprised by my response. "Your nose has always been buried in a book."

I gulp. "I've wanted to be a doctor ever since Mom…" My voice trails off.

"Was diagnosed with breast cancer," he finishes softly.

"Yeah. I want to help women like her. It was terrible when we thought there was a possibility we could lose her. That's not something I can imagine." My heart clenches as I blink away the wetness that gathers in my eyes. Mom has always been my rock. And during that difficult period, I tried my damnedest to return the favor and be there for her. It's one of the reasons I chose to attend school at Western. I wanted to stick close to home.

His fingers curl around the top of my shoulder and squeeze gently. "But she's good now. She's been in remission for a couple of years."

I nod and try to clear the thick emotion that has gathered in my throat. It feels like a knot is wedged there, making it impossible to breathe.

"You've always been so driven."

"Is that a euphemism for boring?" I ask, attempting to lighten the heaviness that has descended.

One side of his mouth hitches. "No. You've always been focused on attaining your goals. There's nothing boring about that."

"The same could be said for you." Even when there weren't team practices, Ryder was at the arena with Maverick and Dad, working on stick skills and speed.

He glances away to stare out the windshield. Something I never thought I'd hear from him invades his voice.

Doubt.

"Yeah. Who knows if that'll happen or not." He gives me a bit of side eye before adding quietly, "I'm kind of screwed if it doesn't."

A frown tugs at my lips. "Why would you say that?" I've never known Ryder to be anything other than confident. I hate to admit just how attractive his self-assured attitude is.

Another weighty silence falls over us as he stares into the darkness that surrounds the vehicle.

"I don't know," he says with a sigh. "There's just been some shit going on, and it's been messing with my head."

"Like what?" I twist more toward him.

He drags a hand through his hair. "Just with this new coach. I guess you could say we're not gelling."

My mind tumbles back to the arena as I carefully comb over the game. Only now do I realize that he was benched during the third period. In all the years I've watched Ryder play, it's not something that's ever happened before. I didn't think much of it at the time but...

Coach Kaminski loved Ryder. I didn't realize there was an issue with the new one. I've heard Mav mention that he's tough and regimented but nothing more.

"I'm sorry. It sucks that Coach K left right before the start of your senior season."

He shrugs. "I can't really blame him for it. A coaching job in the NHL is a dream come true for him. But yeah, it was definitely shitty timing."

"Have you talked to my dad about it?"

He spears me with a glance before shaking his head. "Nah. I'm not gonna whine about it to Brody. I just need to work harder and stay focused."

I chew my lower lip before saying hesitantly, "I don't know, maybe he could give you some advice on how to work with the guy. Does Dad know him?"

"I think so. They probably played against each other in the pros."

My brows rise. "Interesting."

"As for working with him?" A mirthless laugh falls from his lips. "There's no way to do that. The man is a grade A dick. If I'd known Coach K was bailing, I would have done the same. Then this wouldn't be an issue. But there's nothing I can do about it now. I don't have any other choice but to stick out the season."

Impulse takes over and my hand drifts to his chiseled jawline.

If I'd paused for even a second to contemplate the gesture, there's no way I'd be bold enough to touch him so intimately. That's not the kind of relationship we have.

Just when I consider drawing away and pretending it never happened, his hand settles over mine. I release a steady puff of air as all of my reservations fall away, leaving a strange warmth in its place. Light stubble covers his jaw as if he hasn't used a razor in a day or so.

How many times have I wondered what the sculpted lines and planes of his face would feel like beneath my fingertips?

Too many to count.

Minutes tick by before I clear my throat. "I wish there was something I could do to help."

"I appreciate the offer, but there's not. This is something I need to work through on my own."

"Just know that I'm here if you want to talk."

"Thanks." His gaze stays locked on mine. "Answer something for me?"

"Maybe."

His lips quirk, but his voice remains soft. "How many guys have you slept with?"

My belly hollows out as I quip, "Just guys?"

When his eyes widen, I burst out laughing.

"Three. Okay? Just three," I confess.

"Would it be totally douchey if I admit that the image of you and another girl getting it on is totally hot?"

"One hundred percent."

He snorts and some of the heaviness that had descended during our conversation lifts. "Yeah, that's what I thought."

I shake my head. "Why is that a fantasy for so many guys?"

"Really?" He arches a brow. "Do you actually have to ask?"

I roll my eyes as a smile hovers around the corners of my lips. "I suppose not." There's a pause, and the question tumbles out of my mouth before I can think better of it. "I suppose that's something you've already done." I cringe, unsure if I want to know the answer.

He shrugs as his tone stays even. "Once or twice. It's definitely an experience but not something I'm into."

My hand falls away from his face before it finds my other one and twists together in my lap. "I must seem pretty inexperienced in comparison."

Dull.

The fingers wrapped around my shoulder rise before settling beneath my chin, lifting it until I have no other choice but to meet the intensity of his stare. Even in the darkness, it feels as if he's able to sift through my eyes and read my innermost thoughts.

Not only is it disconcerting, it leaves me feeling stripped bare. Vulnerable. No one has ever had the power to do that.

"I don't think that at all."

Heat stings my cheeks. "Right."

He inches closer until the warmth of his breath can feather across my lips. "The amount of experience you have is perfect. There's not a damn thing wrong with it."

His fingers continue to hold my chin in a firm grip. The feel of them singes my skin, making me even more hyperaware of the contact. "Just like you said, I've spent these last three years studying. Getting up on that stage tonight showed me just how much life I've missed out on."

"Isn't that the reason we're working on your list?"

Even in the darkness that presses in on us, the intensity in his blue eyes shines brightly. "Yeah."

When his mouth ghosts over mine, barely stirring the air around us, my eyelids feather closed.

"Maybe we'll even add a few things to it," he whispers.

Before I can ask what he has in mind, his tongue softly sweeps over the seam of my lips. It's not a conscious decision to open, it just happens. There's nothing rushed about his gentle exploration. It's as if we have all the time in the world. That's all it takes for my brain to click off as sensation explodes through me, rocking me to my very core.

I've spent days thinking about the kiss in the library. Wondering if it was as good as I remember. Honestly, I've tried like hell to convince myself that it wasn't.

If anything, this caress is even more devastating.

His fingers remain locked around my chin as he slants his mouth one way and then another, taking the kiss deeper. His other hand slips into my hair, wrapping around the back of my head as if to hold me firmly in place.

It's totally unnecessary.

There's nowhere else I'd rather be than here with him.

He breaks contact long enough to mutter, "Your mouth is so damn sweet."

Barely am I given a chance to suck in a lungful of air when he's back, assaulting my senses, pulling me under until it feels like I've been deprived of all oxygen.

And then, I'm drowning.

I don't realize that my arms have slipped around his neck until a growl escapes from him. Both hands drop to my waist as he drags me onto his lap. Once I'm straddling his thighs, he shifts me around and pulls me closer so that his hard length is nestled snugly against the V between my legs. The feel of his cock has arousal exploding in my core, and a whimper of need rises in my throat.

His fingers curl, biting into my waist before slipping beneath my sweater and stroking up my ribcage until they reach the elastic band of my bra. He strums the material as his gaze stays pinned to mine.

"Please," I whisper. My voice comes out sounding so guttural that I barely recognize it as my own.

Flames leap in his heavy-lidded eyes as his hands slide around to my front, settling over each breast. Another tortured sound is choked from me when he squeezes them, palming the soft flesh as if trying to learn their weight and shape.

It's funny—all right, maybe not funny. I've been out with a half a dozen guys. I've kissed them, had sex, but none have managed to turn me on quite like this. The way Ryder revs me up is almost an epiphany of sorts. I never realized I was capable of all this delicious sensation ricocheting through my body.

Any moment, I'll burst at the seams.

It reminds me of the romance novel I've been reading and the way the heroine got so turned on. The hero understood exactly what to do without her having to say a word. He knew her body and needs better than she did. That's the way it feels with Ryder. Somehow, he just understands what will feel good. He knows when to apply a little more pressure or tease until I'm on the cusp of falling apart.

Like now.

His fingers delve inside the silky cups, shoving them down until there's nothing to cover them except the soft sweater. The knitted fabric slides over my pebbled nipples, stirring even more sensation within me before his thumb and forefinger wrap around the stiff little buds, tugging at them in tandem.

He breaks eye contact long enough to glance around the dark parking lot before shoving the sweater up until the material bunches at my collarbone. His gaze slices to my bare breasts as his hands pluck at them before palming and squeezing the softness.

"You're so damn beautiful," he says with a groan.

My eyelids feather closed as I arch against the leather steering wheel as if I'm offering myself up as a sacrifice.

This girl...the wanton one in the front seat of his truck isn't me.

It's never been me.

I have no idea who she is or where she came from.

I just know that I like it. It's as if I'm attempting to break free of the protective shell that's been wrapped around me my entire life. Ryder makes me feel things I didn't know were possible, and I'm eager to explore it all.

I gasp when the warmth of his mouth closes over one nipple, drawing it deep inside before sucking it. The velvetiness of his tongue strokes over me, setting fire to my blood. My head lolls back as I press closer, greedy for more of the sensation that reverberates through my veins.

Just when I think I'll explode, he pops my nipple free and brings the other taut peak to his mouth, giving that one the same ardent attention as the first. My hands rise until the fingers can tunnel through his blond hair, holding him to my chest.

I can't help but grind against his thick length. By this point, my panties are completely drenched. I'm sure he can feel through the layers that separate us just how turned on I am.

From kissing...

Okay, maybe a little bit more than kissing.

He releases the other stiff bud and growls, "If you don't stop doing that, I'm gonna come in my jeans."

The thought of being able to provoke such a response from him turns me on more than I thought possible. I lift my head until our gazes can lock. He's stretched out on the seat and his head is pressed against the cushion. His eyelids are at half-mast and a tortured expression mars his face.

One I never thought would be directed at me.

It's an intoxicating sensation.

"Maybe I want you to come," I whisper.

His teeth sink into his lower lip, and I don't think I've ever seen anything as sexy as Ryder McAdams in this moment.

The way he's staring...

Like he's fighting the spiked need rampaging through him.

Need I stoked to life.

Me.

Unable to help myself, I flex my hips. His hands settle on them as if to anchor me in place. Another groan escapes from him as he arches to meet the movement. My eyes nearly roll back in my head as I ride him.

I lean forward, wanting to close the distance between us until my lips can press against the column of his throat. My teeth sink into the firm hollow before sucking the skin into my mouth. The muscles constrict as my tongue laves the abraded flesh.

The notion of marking him makes my core throb with new and painful awareness. It's a primitive need I've never experienced before. I've caught sight of other people with hickeys and thought it was gross and childish.

Only now do I get it.

I lick and nip my way up to his chin before sinking my teeth into the stubborn point, and then my lips are settling on his. When he opens, I slip inside so that our tongues can tangle.

His hands slide from my hips around to my back before crushing me against his hard chest.

"Juliette," he groans. "I'm not kidding. You need to stop right now."

Doesn't he realize that it's much too late for that?

The desperation filling his voice only spurs me on.

The harder I grind, the more sensation gathers in my core until there's nowhere left for it to go. Like an impending storm on the verge of a torrential downpour, dissipating and turning into nothingness is no longer an option. Maybe it never was. My muscles tighten as my tongue continues to dance with his.

That's all it takes for me to detonate. My pussy convulses as I moan out my release.

"Fuck."

And then, he's doing the same.

Air hisses from between his lips as he grinds against me. His jean-covered cock is at the perfect angle to bump my clit. Sensation bursts within me like fireworks, lighting me up from the inside out in a powerful symphony of explosions.

It takes a minute or so before I slowly float back to earth. Barely am I able to crack open my eyelids and meet his heavy-lidded gaze. There's a look in his eyes that I've never seen before, and I'm not entirely sure what it means.

My sweater is still shoved above my chest and my nipples are peaked from the cool air of the truck. I shift and tug the material over my breasts before glancing around.

How could I have forgotten that we're in the lot outside my building?

Have I totally lost my mind?

It's a relief to find the parking lot empty. Even though Ryder's windows are tinted, making it difficult to see inside the vehicle, it would be embarrassing to be caught in such a compromising situation.

Especially if one of his teammates found us together.

There's no way my brother wouldn't hear about it.

Ryder's hands are still splayed against my back, pressing me close.

Embarrassed by the force of my own arousal, I clear my throat and attempt to crack a joke. "Should I cross orgasm off the list?"

His gaze drops to my lips for just a moment before slanting upward again. "You'll cross that one off when I'm buried deep inside your pussy."

Even though I realized what would happen between us when I agreed to his assistance, hearing him say it so boldly has my belly hollowing out with an unexpected burst of nerves.

It also makes me realize just how much I'm looking forward to number six.

CHAPTER 20

RYDER

*T*he puck bounces with ease between the blade of my stick as the edge of my skate cuts into the ice. There's nothing like being in the arena bright and early in the morning. There's a snap to the air that invigorates my lungs. It's always been one of my favorite things. The best way to start a day. I can let my mind wander as instinct takes over.

No surprise who it meanders to.

Juliette.

And the way she'd ground against my dick.

Christ...

When was the last time I came all over myself like a prepubescent teen?

High school maybe?

Sophomore year more specifically?

I didn't think it was even possible to get that turned on. I mean, come on. I'm a twenty-two-year-old man who's been having regular sex since I was sixteen. And I've had a lot of it. There's never been a shortage of available pussy.

When she'd joked about being with another girl...

Now there's an image I'll have a tough time evicting from my brain. Then again, the idea of sharing her doesn't appeal to me. Even if it is with another chick. I want her all to myself. I want her attention solely focused on me when we're together.

That's the precise moment I realize—

That thought is knocked from my brain when someone trucks into me from the side and the puck gets knocked loose as I catch myself from landing on my ass.

Barely.

By the time I have my wits about me, Madden scoops up the small black disk and speeds off before I can even think about catching the fucker.

I turn and glare at the guy who's ground to a stop in front of me, spraying ice in my face.

Maverick.

I blink in surprise when he knocks a gloved fist into my chest.

"What the hell is up with you and my sister?"

I should have known this was coming. I saw the way he was watching us at the bar. Even before we stepped foot out of the arena the other night, I knew his antenna had been raised.

"Nothing." The lie pops out of my mouth before I can stop it.

What exactly am I supposed to say?

The truth?

Ha!

The guy would definitely give me a beatdown right here in the middle of the ice. And unlike some of these other guys, Maverick knows how to throw a punch. Brody had us both take boxing lessons while we were freshmen in high school for just this reason. He'd wanted us to know how to take a hit and give one in return. We're evenly matched in height and weight. We've spent hours sparring in their basement gym. Although, to be fair, Mav has righteous anger on his side.

That'll win out every time.

He narrows his eyes from behind his cage. "Didn't look like nothing to me." Before I can respond, he grits out, "She was sitting on your lap."

"There weren't any available chairs. You saw how packed the place was."

He presses his lips together. "And then you sang karaoke? Since when do you get up on stage and perform?"

I shrug and continue to lie my ass off. "She didn't want to do it alone. It was nothing. We're friends."

He lifts his chin, trying to poke holes through my excuses. "Since when? You two have never been friends." He knocks his glove into my chest again before reversing on his skates. His gaze stays locked on mine. "Do us both a favor and stay away from Juliette. She doesn't need you messing with her."

And then, he swings around and skates back to the other side of the ice.

Fuck.

Maverick is the last person I want to have issues with. We've always been solid. Friends and teammates since kindergarten. That's not a relationship I want to jeopardize.

If this were about any other girl, I'd back away without a second thought and wash my hands completely of the situation, but there's no way I can do that with Juliette. She's always been there, circling around in the back of my mind. I've stayed away because I thought it was best for both of us, but that's no longer possible.

Especially after the other night.

She's so damn responsive to my every touch.

It fucking turns me on.

Then again, everything about her has that effect.

It always has. Even when I didn't want it to.

And now that I've finally laid my hands on her?

Felt how soft her skin is?

Kissed her sweet mouth?

It's game over.

For better or worse, this is happening.

"Get your ass moving, McAdams," Coach shouts, snapping my attention back to the present.

With a wince, I skate to my position on the blue line. As I do,

Akeman snags my gaze. A slow smile spreads across his face from behind his cage.

"Thanks, man," he says as we pass one another. "You're making it easier and easier to snatch your position away."

I grit my teeth, refusing to rise to the bait.

Although, it's hard.

Really fucking hard.

CHAPTER 21

JULIETTE

*J*ust as I'm about to delve into bio stats, there's a knock on the apartment door.

Carina left thirty minutes ago to grab something to eat. So, unless she forgot her keys, it's probably not her. I pad to the door and peek through the peephole, surprised to find Ryder on the other side. We haven't seen each other since Thursday night when we messed around in the front seat of his truck.

Those memories are all it takes for heat to flood my cheeks.

Have I ever experienced something so hot in my life?

And we didn't even have sex.

Just made out.

I suck in a lungful of air before wrapping my fingers around the handle and pulling open the door.

"Hey." As soon as my gaze locks on his, awareness explodes inside me before scuttling down my spine. "What are you doing here?"

He shifts before shoving his hands into the pockets of his sweatpants. "I thought we could tick another item off your list."

I break eye contact and glance toward the small dining room table where my books and computer are spread out. "Oh. I was studying."

"Do you have a test or paper due tomorrow?"

"No. I was just trying to get ahead…"

"Then it sounds like the perfect time." He jerks his chin toward the apartment. "Grab your jacket and let's go."

When I chew my lower lip with indecision, he steps forward, swallowing up some of the distance between us. It becomes necessary to tip my head in order to hold his gaze. The scent of his beachy cologne hits me, and my belly hollows out.

His tone turns cajoling. "Come on, Juliette. Remember what you said in the truck the other night about feeling like you've missed out on experiences because your nose has been buried in a textbook? All I'm trying to do is rectify the situation."

That comment is all it takes for my shoulders to loosen. He's right. This is exactly the kind of opportunity I'm trying to seize.

But it's not easy to step outside my comfort zone.

"Okay. Let me grab my purse."

His lips quirk into a smile.

Five minutes later, we've slid into his truck and are heading toward campus. Alternative rock fills the silence between us. After what happened the last time we were together, the atmosphere is a little awkward. Or maybe it's just me. Maybe I'm the awkward one.

I clear my throat, needing to fill the silence. "Let me guess, you're not going to tell me what we're doing."

"Nope." His gaze flickers to me as he pops the P at the end of the word.

"I suppose I could figure it out by going through the list and eliminating what's already been ticked off."

"Sure, go for it," he says easily, a smile simmering around his lips.

"Obviously not going to get drunk at another party. Been there, done that."

"With flying colors," he tacks on.

I snort.

"And I've already made out at the library." I glance at him from the corner of my eye as his lips continue to bow up at the corners. That's when I realize just how much he's enjoying this. "So, we're not going there."

"Correctamundo."

"And you've already given me the big O in the truck…"

His head whips toward mine. "I told you that didn't count."

There's significantly less humor lacing his voice now as the low timbre of it scrapes at my insides.

"So you claimed."

I'm so attuned to the man next to me that I barely notice when he pulls into the parking lot of the athletic center and slides into a spot near the front entrance of the building before cutting the engine. He swivels toward me and slides his hand around the curve of my jaw.

"I told you the other night that you'll check off number six when I'm buried deep inside your pussy." His gaze searches mine carefully. "Understand?"

That's all it takes for arousal to explode in my core and air to catch at the back of my throat.

When I remain silent, his brows rise, and his grip tightens around my jaw. "Juliette?"

"I got it."

His gaze drops to the movement and a groan rumbles up from deep in his throat.

For a second or two, I wonder if he'll close the distance between us and kiss me again like he did the other night. I've dreamed about the way he took my mouth and what it felt like to grind on his thick erection.

Instead, his fingers loosen as he relaxes against the leather seat. My body trembles as I attempt to fight my way free of the thick haze that cocoons itself around me at his slightest touch.

I'm not sure it's possible.

Ryder McAdams has always had this kind of effect on me. All he has to do is lay hands on my body and my world gets turned upside down and inside out. It's as exhilarating as it is frightening.

I rip my gaze away in an attempt to regain my equilibrium. As I do, my attention falls on the athletic center.

My brows pinch together as I stare at the sprawling building. "What are we doing here?"

The smoldering look dissolves as secrets dance in his eyes. It's enough to steal my breath away, just as much as the hot look that had flashed across his face earlier.

"Haven't figured it out yet?"

I draw the corner of my lip into my mouth and chew it as I contemplate the situation. Without further explanation, Ryder exits the vehicle and walks around the hood before popping open the passenger side door.

"Come on, Miss smarty pants." He extends a hand for me to take. "Tell me what your theory is."

"I'm not sure," I mutter. For the first time in my life, my brain is failing me. It's not working properly. Although, I think that has more to do with the guy at my side than anything else. His nearness makes it impossible to think straight.

Ryder flashes a grin. "Good. I like keeping you on your toes."

Even though nerves gleefully eat away at my insides, I place my fingers in his and allow him to help me from the vehicle. The moment our hands touch, energy sizzles through the tips. I'm not sure if I'll ever get used to the sensation.

He clicks the locks on his truck as we head to the main entrance of the sprawling building. That's when I notice his vehicle is the only one parked in the lot.

"What are we doing here if the place is closed?"

Once we make it to the sidewalk, we swing to the right, walking around the massive brick structure to a plain metal door that's been propped open.

My brows skyrocket as Ryder meets my inquisitive stare. "A friend works here as a custodian. I told him that we wanted to borrow the facilities for a couple of hours."

"Why?" I ask, pitching my voice low as we slip through the door.

It takes a minute or two for my eyes to adjust to the murky darkness. Ryder turns on his phone flashlight before his other hand slips around mine to tow me down the long stretch of deserted corridor.

I've been inside the building a few times to work out with Carina, but it's weird to be here when the place is completely empty. The way our shoes echo off the concrete walls is creepy.

I tug on his hand. "Are you sure we should be here? What if someone catches us?"

He glances at me. "Then we run really fast."

Oh god.

I've never been in trouble. Not even so much as a tardy for being late to class in high school. I'd hate for that to change during my senior year of college. All I see are my hopes for a prestigious med school going up in a puff of smoke because of one bad decision.

"Ryder," I whisper hesitantly. "Maybe we—"

He stops and jerks my hand until I'm stumbling forward and crashing into his broad chest. Even in the darkness that surrounds us, his gaze pins mine in place.

"I won't let anything happen to you, all right?"

My lungs empty of air.

His hands settle on the tops of my shoulders as he presses me closer. "Do you trust me?"

I don't know...

Do I?

Do I trust Ryder McAdams?

I've known him forever.

Our families are best friends.

In all honesty, I don't think he'd do anything to deliberately cause me harm. As that thought circles through my brain, I jerk my head into a nod.

"I'll keep you safe."

The tension filling my muscles drains away as he releases his grip and retreats a step. And then we're once again moving along the corridor. We make a few turns. One left and then a right before heading down a flight of stairs. There's a labyrinth of twists before Ryder opens a heavy door. I wince as it squeaks on its hinges, unable to help myself from glancing around cautiously.

Didn't he mention that the custodial staff is here working?

The beam of his light slides over a row of black metal lockers as we wind our way around wooden benches. The soles of our shoes echo off the ceramic tile floor and walls as he shoves through yet another door into a cavernous space. I grind to a halt as the pungent scent of chlorine assaults my nostrils. The expansive area is surrounded on two sides by walls of glass, allowing bright moonlight to filter in and illuminate the tranquil surface.

"The pool?" I whisper in surprise. "What..." The question dies a quick death as I realize why he brought me here.

Number two.

My wide gaze swings to his.

"Figure it out yet?" he asks with a smirk, satisfaction sparking in his eyes.

"Skinny dipping." Barely am I able to push the response out.

"Yup."

My mind somersaults. Before I can say anything—like maybe this isn't such a great idea—he drags his thick sweatshirt up his torso and over his head before dropping it to the tile at his feet. The T-shirt that hugs his thickly corded biceps quickly follows suit until he's standing before me bare chested.

My mouth turns cottony as my gaze unconsciously licks over him. Even in the pale moonlight, I can make out the sculpted lines of his upper torso.

"I, ah, didn't bring a suit," I whisper thickly.

The whiteness of his teeth flashes in the darkness that presses in on us. "Yeah, that's how skinny-dipping works. No suits required."

"Oh. Right." I rip my gaze away long enough to glance at the crystal-clear water. "How can you be so sure no one will walk in on us?"

By the time my attention resettles on him, his gray sweatpants have been shoved down his legs and he's peeling them off along with his socks. He straightens to his full height. The only article of clothing still in place is a pair of dark gray boxer briefs that hug his trim waist and muscular thighs.

My teeth sink into my lower lip as my gaze roves hungrily over him for second time. He isn't even fully naked yet and my brain is malfunctioning.

No one should look this good.

He could be plastered across a billboard in Times Square.

He's that perfect.

Heck, when he's playing professional hockey, advertisers will clamor for him to endorse their products.

It's not like I haven't seen him in a pair of boardshorts during the summer by the pool or when our families have vacationed together, but it's been a couple of years. During that time, Ryder has completely filled out. He's no longer a boy but all man. One who is capable of turning a woman's insides to complete mush.

"My friend made sure to clean this area first. Plus, isn't that part of the experience? Getting caught swimming naked where you shouldn't be?"

In theory?

Sure.

In practice?

Probably not.

He tilts his head as his gaze holds mine captive. "You're not going to chicken out, are you?"

"No."

As soon as the response falls from my lips, he shoves the boxers down his thighs.

And then he's stripped completely bare.

Holy mother of...

Even though I should look away, doing so feels impossible. My gaze stays pinned to his cock.

And shaved balls.

I've watched some porn and a lot of those guys are clean shaven. I've just never seen it in real life...

Is it bad that I want to step closer and inspect him with more thoroughness?

That's exactly when I realize I've eaten up the distance between us. His dick stirs, the thick length hardening before my very eyes.

"You keep staring like that and more than number two will get checked off the list tonight."

My wide eyes slice to his smirking ones. Before I can respond, he swings around and dives into the deep end of the pool. My attention stays locked on him as he arrows gracefully through the water.

Ryder McAdams is absolutely gorgeous.

The perfect specimen.

I can understand why girls talk about him in dreamy tones.

When he finally surfaces in the middle of the rectangular shaped pool, he whips his head back and drags both hands through his long blonde strands, shoving them away from his face.

He glances around until his gaze can lock on mine. "You coming in or what?"

My heart jackhammers a mad beat as I shrug out of my black puffy jacket and toss it onto a wooden bench near the wall where a couple of towels are neatly stacked. My fingers shake as I unlace my Converse and toe off the white canvas. My socks are next to get stripped off. I glance at him from the corner of my eye as my fingers tighten nervously around the hem of my T-shirt.

Even though he remains in the same place treading water, I feel the heat of his stare pinned to me as I inhale a deep breath and yank the cotton over my head before tossing it on top of the jacket. The jeans are the next item to get shucked. I flick open the metal button and drag down the zipper before shoving the thick denim over my hips and thighs. A fine tremble racks my body as the sultry air of the room wafts over me. My arms drift to my sides. In this moment, it feels like they weigh a thousand pounds.

"Do you always wear matching sets?" he asks, voice low. The heavy weight of it sinks to the pit of my belly like a stone.

This one is turquoise hued with pretty lace covering the silky cups and a tiny black bow stitched into the fabric band that sits in the middle of my chest. A matching ribbon is sewn into the front of the panties.

"Yes, I like them." There's something about the garments that makes me feel pretty and sexy.

"Me, too." His gaze roves greedily over my nearly naked form. "Now take them off."

My nerves jump at the growled-out command. With a gulp, I reach around my ribcage and fumble with the clasp. On the third attempt, it springs apart. The stretchy straps slide down my shoulders and arms until the garment falls away from my breasts and drops to the tile.

"The next time we get naked, I'll be the one doing the honors," he says gruffly.

That's all it takes for arousal to flood my core like warmed honey.

A fresh round of nerves explodes in me as my fingers settle at the elastic band at my hips and I shove the scrap of material down my legs until I'm just as bare as he is. The way his gaze licks over every inch makes my skin feel both hot and tight. Like it's been baked in the sun and will burst any second.

It's so tempting to lift my arms and cover myself.

But I don't. I know he'll just tell me to lower them. I can almost hear the demand echoing in my ears.

"Do you have any idea how beautiful you are?" he asks softly, interrupting the churn of my thoughts.

I force the air from my lungs and give my head a barely perceptible shake.

Not once have I ever felt beautiful.

More like average.

Dark brown hair and wide eyes that match in shade. My brows are thick but not overly so, and my cheekbones certainly couldn't cut glass. My breasts are a little too generous. Definitely more than a handful. It's one of the reasons I quit dance in high school when I started to feel self-conscious in a leotard. All that cardio kept me toned, but that's no longer the case. My body is soft and curvy.

Heat fills my cheeks as self-doubt eats away at me.

"You are, Juliette. So fucking beautiful that it hurts to look at you sometimes."

My eyes widen at the compliment.

It's difficult to imagine him feeling that way about me. Not when he could have any girl that he wanted. The way they throw themselves at him is difficult to watch.

So I don't.

144

To hear him state otherwise blows my mind.

"Are you gonna get in on your own or do I need to come get you?" There's a beat of silence. "Because you know I will."

The gruff promise in his voice has my core clenching. It's carefully that I settle on the edge. A hiss of breath escapes from me when my ass hits the cool tile and I tentatively dip my toes in. Ryder's eyes stay locked on me as I lower myself into the pool. My arms and legs slice through the water. It feels so odd not to be wearing a suit.

And yet...

There's something strangely freeing about it.

I expect him to close the distance between us, but that's not what happens. He gives me both the time and space I need as he continues to tread water a dozen or so feet away. As the quiet settles around us, my muscles gradually loosen. Even when I dip beneath the surface and swim a few laps, I'm still ridiculously aware of Ryder's presence.

It's always been like this with him.

Even when we were children.

There was just something about him that drew me and held my attention captive.

Shoving that thought from my head, I say, "One more thing to check off." Even though I keep my voice pitched low, it still echoes off the cavernous walls.

"Yup. We're working our way down the list."

It doesn't matter where I swim, he turns, gaze staying pinned to me. I'm never out of his line of vision.

"Maybe I should have asked for your help a while ago."

"Why didn't you?"

It's not a question I need to think about. "Because we've never really been friends."

He closes the distance between us one lazy stroke at a time until there's no more than a foot of space to separate us. "We were always friends," he says quietly. "I would have helped you with anything."

Maybe.

"You've always been careful to keep your distance."

"So have you."

I lift my shoulders in acknowledgment. "It just seemed safer that way."

"Guess we're rectifying that situation."

His fingers snag mine before reeling me to him until I'm close enough for my breasts to press against the steeliness of his chest. Air gets trapped in my throat, making it impossible to breathe.

His eyes are a dark, cobalt blue. In the silvery moonlight that slants through the glass walls, I'm able to see the different flecks that make up the various shades. His eyes are as deep and vast as an ocean.

He nips at my lower lip, tugging it with sharp teeth as his arms slip around me, pulling my body closer until the thickness of his erection presses insistently against the V between my legs. A whimper of need escapes from me as both of his hands drift to my ass, cupping it before hoisting me against him until my legs can wrap around his waist and my pussy is splayed open against his abdominals.

Shock and need spiral through me at the intimate contact.

Not in a million years did I see this scenario playing out. Not even in my wildest fantasies.

"Fuck," he growls against my mouth.

I couldn't have summed it up any better myself.

My brain turns into a pile of mush as he takes my lips in a kiss meant to sear my very soul.

No one has ever made me forget my own name.

Or how to breathe.

But that's exactly the way it is with Ryder.

He's just...*too much.*

Too masculine.

Too cocky.

Larger than life.

I've always felt the magnetism that wafts off him like pheromones meant to drive girls crazy. To have it all directed at me is heady stuff.

The way his tongue tangles with mine makes me wonder if he's trying to devour me in one tasty gulp. Or maybe I'm the one intent on doing the devouring.

I'm no longer sure who is the aggressor.

I just know that I want more.

Everything he's willing to give.

I don't realize that he's walked us to the side of the pool until my back hits the scratchy surface of the wall. Before I can ask what he's intent upon doing, his hands tighten around my waist, and he hoists me from the water before setting me down on the tiled ledge. Water sluices from my body as he pushes my legs apart until he can shoulder his way between them.

My heartbeat kicks up several notches as I stare down at him. As much as I want to squeeze my legs together, I force them to remain open. Barely am I breathing as our gazes stay fastened. He breaks eye contact as he turns his head and brushes his lips against my inner thigh before sinking his teeth into the supple flesh.

I don't realize how tense I've grown until he whispers, "Relax."

As if that's possible.

Any moment, I'm going to keel over.

Naked.

In the athletic center pool at Western.

That's how hard my heart is hammering against my ribcage. It wouldn't take much for it to turn painful. It's so tempting to lift my hand and rub my chest in order to ease the growing ache inside.

His palms gently press against my knees, spreading them as his lips drift closer to the part of me that throbs insistently for him. He nips and licks his way to the apex of my thighs. That's all it takes for my breath to get wedged at the back of my throat as his gaze drops to my core. I don't think I've ever felt more on display or vulnerable than I do in this moment.

Never has a man stared at me quite so openly. In the past, when I've had sex, the lights have been turned off, plunging the room into darkness.

This...

Couldn't be more of a different experience.

"Fucking gorgeous," he murmurs before pressing his lips to the plump flesh of my mound.

Air escapes from my lungs in an agonizing rush until it feels like there's nothing left.

"I've always wondered what you'd taste like." He slants a look up at me before running the flat of his tongue along my slit. "Delicious."

That's all it takes for a wave of pleasure to crash over me as a groan is ripped from my lungs. As much as I'd like to keep it trapped inside, that's not possible. I brace my palms on the cool tile and lean back, allowing him greater access as he presses closer and nibbles at my clit.

"Totally addictive," he growls against me before spearing his tongue deep inside my softness.

The velvety stroke of him is enough to have every wall I've ever tried to hold firmly in place between us come tumbling down in an avalanche of sensation. I don't realize that I've widened my legs until both of his palms settle on my inner thighs, forcing them even further apart until I'm spread impossibly wide.

Until he can see every delicate inch.

And I don't care.

How could I possibly when there is so much need building deep within my core?

Every time he swipes at my clit, sucking it gently into his mouth, it feels like I'm dancing along the precipice. Any moment, I'll fall over the edge and crash to my death. My body unconsciously strains closer as he retreats, turning his attention elsewhere. I want to scream with the pent-up desire that rushes through me.

Every once in a while, he turns his face and scrapes his teeth against the sensitive flesh of my inner thigh. His warm breath drifts across me, intensifying the growing ache within.

In all of my twenty-two years, I've never experienced desire like this.

When he does it a handful of times more, I realize he's toying with me.

Deliberately setting fires only to let them smolder.

As much as I want to squeeze my eyelids closed and revel in the delicious sensation coursing through me, my gaze remains fixated on him. The image of Ryder's blond head between my spread thighs is so damn sexy.

Mesmerizing.

And the way he strokes me with his lips, teeth, and tongue…

It's deliciously maddening.

Two of my previous boyfriends went down on me, but it felt nothing like *this*. It's almost like they weren't even doing the same thing.

He continues to lick at my clit, stroking it gently with his tongue. The stubble covering his chiseled cheeks and jaw scrapes against my delicate flesh, only adding to the tempest that whips through me.

"You're teasing," I finally say on a groan.

He flicks heavy-lidded eyes up at me.

He pulls away just enough to admit, "That's exactly what I'm doing."

A tortured moan escapes from me as I arch, pressing closer, attempting to seek out more pleasure.

"Why?"

With a turn of his head, he sinks his teeth into my flesh again. "A better question would be—why not?"

Another wave of need crashes over me.

"What is it that you want, Juliette?" He spears his tongue deep inside my body. The velvety stroke makes my insides clench. "To come?"

"Yes." I'm so worked up that I can barely force out the response.

"Then beg for it."

My teeth scrape against my lower lip. As much as I don't want to, I can't stop the guttural word from tumbling free. "Please."

"Please what?" He takes another leisurely lap of my softness. "What do you want?"

"To come."

"How?"

Frustration spirals through me as a response explodes from my lips. "I want you to lick my pussy."

"All you had to do was ask, baby girl," he says with a growl.

I don't know if it's the endearment or the way he zeros in on my clit, but I splinter apart beneath his talented lips, arching into his touch, seeking out more of what only he can give me. My cries echo off the high ceiling and walls before ringing in my ears.

In that moment, I don't give a damn who hears me.

I wouldn't care if the stands were packed full of spectators watching us.

All I'm cognizant of is the sensation rolling through my body and the pleasure that has sparked to life in my nerve endings. It's almost too much euphoria to be contained within the confines of my skin.

The orgasm that ripples through me seems to last forever. It's only when I turn boneless, on the verge of slipping into the water and sinking to the bottom of the pool, that I crack open my eyelids and find him watching me as he wrings every last drop from my body.

He presses another kiss against my soaked flesh before drawing away and hoisting himself beside me. Rivers of water pour off him in a torrent as he wraps his arms around my exhausted body and drags me onto his lap so that his hard cock is pressed against my pussy and his mouth can take mine. He licks at the seam of my lips until I open before plunging inside. One hand tunnels through the tangled length of my hair, twisting the damp strands around his palm and drawing them taut until my spine bows. The possessive grip is enough to spark another round of arousal in my core.

He pulls away just enough to growl, "Can you taste your honey on my lips?"

The heated look in his eyes singes me alive. Any moment, I'll burst into flames, and not even the water of the pool will be enough to extinguish it.

"Yes," I whisper.

"One taste and I'm addicted."

He kisses me again, dragging me to the very bottom of the ocean where I'm unable to breathe.

Or think.

The only thing I can do is give myself over to the pleasure he's capable of.

"One lick of my lips and I'll be able to taste you there."

That's all it takes for him to strike a match and set the world on fire.

And I'll happily burn with it.

His arms tighten as he pulls me close enough to bury his face in the hollow of my neck. When his warm breath ghosts across my flesh, I realize how chilled my skin has become and a shiver dances down my spine.

He pulls away just enough to search my eyes. "Cold?"

"A little." Although, not nearly enough to stop what we're doing. I could stay here wet, naked, wrapped up in him all night long and not think twice about it.

Without further comment, his grip tightens around my waist, and he removes me from his lap as if I weigh nothing at all before popping to his feet. His fingers wrap around mine to hoist me up. After grabbing a towel from the bench, he drapes it around me. My body feels over sensitized against the scratchy white material. As soon as I'm taken care of, he grabs another and briskly dries himself off before tucking the towel around lean hips.

"Are you sure I can't check off two items from the list? That orgasm…" My voice trails off. It'll be a memory that I take out and relive for years.

His fingers lock around mine before he tugs me to him and presses a kiss against my lips. "What did I say about number six?"

"Technically speaking, you were inside me."

He smirks. "Still doesn't count. You need something thicker filling your sweet little pussy when we check that one off."

Even though I'm standing before him naked, and he just went down on me, his dirty words have the power to heat my cheeks.

"By the way," he says almost conversationally, "I finished that book."

My brows pinch together in confusion before I realize what he's talking about. "You did?"

"Yup." A slow smile simmers across his lips. "Have you?"

I shake my head. "No, I'm still working on it."

"Did you get to chapter nineteen?" He waggles his brows. "Some pretty interesting stuff in there."

When my mouth falls open, he flashes a full-on grin.

"I wouldn't mind reenacting that scene." With a chuckle, he smacks another kiss against my lips. "Now, let's get out of here. We've pressed our luck enough for one night."

CHAPTER 22

RYDER

"Surprise!" everyone yells on cue as Brody walks into the backroom at Taco Loco with his arm wrapped around his wife.

The slender, dark-haired woman lifts both hands to her mouth as she stares wide eyed at the crowd. As soon as they step over the threshold, Juliette rushes forward and throws herself at Natalie, hugging her tightly. Maverick follows closely behind his sister, slipping his arms around both women. Brody gets in on the action, holding his family close.

It's only when they're standing all together that I realize how much Juliette resembles her mother. They both have the same shiny, dark hair. Natalie's is cut in a sleek bob that sweeps her shoulders while her daughter's flows down her back like a thick curtain. My fingers clench as memories of the other night at the pool flood my mind and what it felt like to have those damp strands wrapped around my hand.

It takes effort to shake that recollection away before I pop wood.

Mav has the same build as his father paired with Natalie's dark hair.

My gaze meanders to Brody. Ever since our families became close, he's been a guiding presence in my life. His hockey career is the stuff legends are made of. He played Juniors before attending Whitmore University, a DI college, and then headed to the pros where he dominated for more than a decade.

Those thoughts lead me back to what will happen at the end of this season. Unwilling to contemplate the possibility of a derailed future, I hoist the beer to my lips and refocus my attention on Juliette.

As much as I can't afford to get distracted, she's become a welcome one.

Deep down in a place I'm afraid to inspect too closely, I know what's going on between us is way more than that.

Even now, days later, I can still taste her honey on my lips.

It's all I've been able to think about since I spread her legs wide on the tiled edge of the pool and tongued her pussy until she had no other choice but to moan out her pleasure. The throaty cries that echoed off the walls were almost enough to make me come.

Here's the funny part—I wasn't joking when I told her that I'd actually learned a thing or two from that romance novel. And it obviously worked, because by the end, she begged me for an orgasm.

Now, that's something I never expected to happen in this lifetime.

Have I downloaded the third book in the series?

Damn right I have.

When she glances at me from across the space that separates us, our gazes collide, making it obvious that I've been standing around and watching her. Normally, I'm a lot more subtle.

I have game.

At the moment, however?

I don't give a rat's ass if she realizes that I've been staring like a stalker. That's how far gone I am.

Once I've snagged her attention, dull color creeps into her cheeks.

And I love it.

Love that all it takes is one look and she's blushing, thinking about all the delicious things I've done to her body. Maybe even pondering what I'll do in the not-so-distant future.

Fuck.

I really need to shut down these thoughts before I get a full-fledged boner. It's doubtful anyone would appreciate me lusting after the host's daughter.

"Would you like another drink?"

I'm knocked out of those thoughts by the ebony-haired waitress who's been circulating around the room.

Lola.

We've had a class or two together throughout the years. Much like Juliette, she's not someone I see around at parties. From what I remember, her family owns the restaurant, and she works here part time. Since I'm no stranger to Taco Loco—hello, taco Tuesday—I've seen more than a few guys shoot their shot. I've also watched her annihilate them without the slightest bit of hesitation. Can't say it's not enjoyable.

I lift the bottle and give it a little wiggle. "Nope, still good. Thanks."

"Let me know if you need anything else," she says.

"Will do."

She moves on without so much as another look in my direction.

Juliette's grandfather, John McKinnon, and his second wife, Amber, are also here with their girls. Hailey and Stella. I know Stella pretty well. She and Riggs go way back and have been besties for a while. I give her a chin lift in greeting from across the room. She's a gorgeous girl with a killer body and long blonde hair. Riggs jokingly refers to her as a serial dater.

Or maybe not so jokingly.

She goes through guys the way some people go through sticks of chewing gum. Even though Riggs has never come out and said anything about Stella, I get the feeling there's more between them than he lets on.

Or maybe he just wishes there were.

Sometimes, I like to needle Riggs by telling him that I'm going to make a play for his bestie.

It always pisses him off.

I'm a little surprised my teammate isn't here. Most of the time, those two are joined at the hip.

When my gaze meanders back to Juliette, I realize there's a guy chatting her up. I lift the bottle to my lips again and take another swig as my brows pinch together. He looks to be around our age. Maybe a year or two older. His casual yet upscale look screams young professional. As does the short, perfectly styled hair. Not one damn strand is out of place. My guess is that he works in a bank or something. Definitely a desk job. He's with an older couple who look vaguely familiar.

My gaze shifts back to the guy. He's standing entirely too close to Juliette for my liking.

And the way he's smiling at her...

I know exactly what's going through his mind, because it goes through mine all the damn time.

It's tempting to stalk over and yank her into my arms so that this *Wolf of Wall Street* douche understands exactly who this girl belongs to.

Except...

Juliette doesn't actually belong to me.

I'm just the guy helping her tick items off a bucket list.

It's not like we'll continue hanging out after everything is said and done.

Why that thought pisses me off, I don't know.

Or maybe I do.

When he pulls her in for a hug, a red haze clouds my vision and I cut a direct path to her. It doesn't take long to reach the small circle of people and push my way to the center. My gaze flickers from Juliette and this asshole to her father. I force a smile and thrust out my hand, shaking Brody's before hugging Natalie.

Over the years, these people have become like second parents to me. I spent my childhood at their house, hanging on Brody's every word, staring at his jerseys that line the walls and all the memorabilia on display in his study and in the basement.

To have such unrestricted access to a sports legend as a kid was the stuff dreams were made of. He took an interest in me at a young age and helped nurture and develop my talent. This man is a big reason I've achieved as much as I have. He's been such a solid presence in my life. Especially now that he's taken me on as a client and is guiding my career.

Well, potential career.

My gaze resettles on Juliette, and I try to strike a low-key chord, not giving away too much. "Hey."

The way she tucks an errant lock of hair behind her ear has even more need gathering inside me. "Hi."

"Long time no see."

Her eyes widen. "Um, yeah. Thursday. The game."

I smirk.

Sure, we'll just go with that.

The guy at her side gives me a chin lift in greeting.

Juliette clears her throat as if only now remembering him. It's enough to assuage my pride. "Sawyer, this is Ryder. You've met before."

Sawyer.

Right.

Now that my memory has been jogged, I recall meeting him several times over the years when the McKinnons would host holiday or birthday parties. His parents are family friends or something like that.

"Good to see you, man," he says, sizing me up as he keeps an arm slung loosely around Juliette's shoulders as if trying to stake a claim.

I don't like it.

Not one damn bit.

"You, too. Been a couple years. I almost didn't recognize you."

He grins good naturedly before shrugging. "I'll take that as a compliment. I graduated two years ago and am working at an investment firm. All that sitting around at a desk ten hours a day wasn't doing me any favors, so I changed up my eating habits and started lifting." He pats his toned belly. "Now, I'm in the best shape of my life."

"You look good," I say grudgingly, because it's true.

"Thanks." He glances at Juliette. "I'm trying to convince Jules that we should go out." He gives her a little wink. "For old times' sake."

Jules?

157

Who the fuck does this guy think he is?

Is he really trying to swoop in and steal my girl?

I almost wince.

This situation is so much worse than I thought.

I lift my brows and flick a steely look at her. "Is that right?"

Juliette shifts before carefully extracting herself from his hold. "I, um, need to use the bathroom. I'll be right back."

There's no chance to respond before she disappears through the crowd and into the main restaurant area.

Silence falls over the pair of us before Sawyer clears his throat. "So...you play hockey at Western, huh?"

I rip my gaze away from the last place I saw Juliette before she vanished from sight. "Yeah."

"I was just mentioning to Brody that I'd like to check out a game and watch Mav play."

"Sounds like a plan."

Not.

He cocks his head and leans in a bit closer. "Juliette usually shows up for them, right?"

I narrow my eyes. "Yeah. Although, I think she might be seeing someone at the moment." That last sentence is out of my mouth before I can stop it.

He flicks a glance toward the entrance to the room as if he's impatient for her return. "Really? That's strange. She didn't mention anything."

Instead of responding, I lift my bottle and give it a shake. "Well, it was good talking to you. I need to grab a refill."

"Yeah, me too. I'll come—"

I walk away before he can finish that sentence. On my way out, I set the bottle on a table and head for the hallway where the restrooms are located. Instead of busting inside the small space, I fold my arms across my chest and lean against the wall, casual as fuck, which is the complete opposite of how I feel at the moment.

She doesn't keep me waiting long.

As soon as the door swings open and she steps over the threshold, her gaze collides with mine.

Surprise morphs across her expression. "Ryder." My name comes out sounding all breathy.

I glance behind her. "Anyone in there?"

"What?" Her brows slide together. "In the bathroom? No."

Excellent.

I shackle my fingers around her upper arm and force her into the cramped space before slamming the door shut behind us. Then, I twist the lock so she can't make a quick escape.

Her eyes widen. "What are you doing?"

I force her spine against the tile before aligning my bigger body to her softer one. "What's up with that guy?"

"Sawyer?"

We're so close that her warm breath is able to feather across my lips. It's nothing short of intoxicating. This girl has me all twisted up inside. "Yup. That would be the one."

"Nothing."

When her tongue darts out to moisten her lips, my gaze drops to the movement. Juliette has never been one to wear a lot of makeup. Today, her lips are stained pink. Unable to resist, I nip the plump flesh with sharp teeth. Her eyelids flutter as a whimper escapes from her.

Once I release the lower one, I growl, "You sure about that? It kind of seems like he was asking you out on a date."

"He did," she admits reluctantly. "I told him this semester was a little crazy and I'm bogged down with classes."

Her response only fuels my jealousy and possessiveness.

I push further into her space until my thick erection can press against the softness of her lower abdomen. That's all it takes for her pupils to dilate. The black circle swallows up the mahogany-colored flecks that dance around within their dark depths.

My hands tunnel through her hair to lock her in place. I want every bit of her attention focused on me.

At all times.

"Is that the only reason you're not interested in getting together with him?"

Her chest rises and falls in quick succession. "Maybe."

My lips drift over hers, never quite touching. It takes every ounce of self-control not to take her mouth. When it comes down to it, I'm torturing myself just as much as I'm tormenting her.

It's only when her lips part and a groan of need breaks free that I finally give in to temptation. Our tongues tangle as she opens under the firm pressure I exert and the taste of her floods my senses. It has the power to dissolve all the jealousy festering inside me, eating me alive. It's only when the beast within has been beaten back enough for rational thought to once again prevail that I pull away and lean my forehead against hers.

"Do you have plans after this?"

Her gaze stays locked on mine. "No."

"Now you do." Something within me settles at the notion that I'll have her all to myself tonight.

"I suppose you're going to keep it a secret?"

A slow smile curls the edges of my lips. "It wouldn't be fun otherwise."

Even though I don't want to, I force myself to take a step in retreat to give us both a bit of breathing room before heading to the door and twisting the lock.

Just as I move into the hallway, my gaze slices to Juliette. She's still pressed against the tiled wall. A dazed expression fills her eyes, and her hair is in slight disarray from my fingers tunneling through the thick strands.

I like it.

Like that I'm the one who mussed her up.

It's something I've been wanting to do for years.

The temptation to eat up the distance between us and steal another kiss thrums through me. The need pulsing through my veins is almost too much to resist.

Here's the problem—if I touch her again, it won't end with a simple caress of my lips. It'll go much further.

And I don't want that.

Not here.

For now, this will have to be enough to satiate me.

"Oh, and Juliette?"

She blinks away the mental fog before her gaze locks on mine.

"Stay the fuck away from Sawyer."

CHAPTER 23

JULIETTE

"*H*appy birthday, Mom! I really hope you enjoyed the party."

She wraps her arms around me and tugs me close. "I did, baby. Thanks so much for helping your father plan this."

With a shrug, I smile. "He did most of the legwork."

"Well, I still appreciate it. Did I ever mention that when we were in college, your dad threw me a surprise party just like this? That's when I realized I was falling for him."

To hear Dad tell it, he'd crushed on her for a while, but she wouldn't give him the time of day because he was a player.

Can you even imagine my dad being a womanizer?

It makes me laugh every time.

The man is such a smitten kitten when it comes to my mother.

My gaze reluctantly drifts to Ryder. As soon as our gazes collide, a shot of electricity zips through my veins and I force my attention away from him. Even though it's tempting to pretend that what we have is more than just physical, I've never been one to lie to myself.

Ryder has zero interest in settling down or being exclusive.

And why should he, when girls throw themselves at him everywhere he goes?

In fact, Aunt Hailey has been eating him up with her eyes since he walked in the door, which is a little weird given the fact that she's four years older than me.

Hailey and Stella are from my grandfather's second marriage to Amber. So, there's twenty years between my dad and his half-sister, Hailey. Then there's twenty-five years between him and Stella. Stella and I are actually the same age, born just a month a part. We grew up together and have always been close.

My gaze unconsciously returns to Ryder as all of these thoughts somersault through my head. Allowing myself to catch feelings for him would be foolish.

"Yup, he told me all about it," I say, picking up the thread of our previous conversation.

Mom's gaze settles on Dad. The love shining brightly from her eyes brings a thick lump of emotion to my throat. Especially when he glances at her as if he's able to feel her gaze.

The love they share is the real deal. Their marriage didn't crumble when their children left for college. Honestly, I think they're happy to finally have time all to themselves. Especially now that Mom is in remission.

When she was diagnosed, Dad took a leave from work and was steadfast by her side, taking her to chemo and staying with her. He took care of everything at home so she wouldn't have to. He wanted her attention solely focused on beating the disease that had snuck into our lives to wreak havoc. When there were complications with the insurance, he dealt with it. He hired someone to come in and prepare meals that were rich in carotenoids.

He researched everything. Medications, experimental treatments, and therapies. When her hair started falling out from radiation, he shaved his in solidarity. And when her scans finally came back clean, Dad took us all to the Bahamas to celebrate.

"Juliette?"

I shake away those thoughts and refocus on Mom. "Yeah, sorry. I spaced out for a minute. What did you say?"

Mom tilts her head and searches my eyes. "Just wondering how your date went the other week. Didn't you mention something about going out with a guy from one of your classes?"

"Oh. Yeah. Umm…we decided that we were better off as friends."

Her expression softens. "That's too bad."

I shrug. "Even though we had a lot in common, there just wasn't a spark between us."

When she loops her arm through mine, I lean my head against her shoulder. I really don't know what any of us would have done if we'd lost her. She's the very heart and soul of our family.

"It just takes time to find your person, but you will. You're an amazing woman with so much to offer."

I snort. "I think you might be a tiny bit biased."

With a slight twist of her head, she presses a kiss against the top of mine. "Not in the least."

A few guests make their goodbyes as the crowd begins to thin.

"Do you mind if I take off?" I ask.

"Not at all." She wiggles her brows. "Got some exciting plans tonight?"

There's no way I'm telling her about Ryder.

"Nah. I was going to check in with Carina and see what she's up to." Then I tack on, "Or, you know, maybe study."

A puff of air escapes from her. "You work way too hard, Jules. You need to enjoy your last year of college."

My shoulders collapse under the weight of her words. It's something I've been dwelling on a lot lately. "Believe it or not, I'm trying."

"Good."

When she releases my hand, I press another kiss against her cheek. "I'll see you on Thursday for the game."

"Perfect. Love you."

"Love you, too."

When I glance at Ryder, he gives me a barely perceptible nod before making his own goodbyes to both sets of parents.

Just as I grab my coat, Maverick throws an arm around my shoulders. "You leaving already?"

I glance at my watch. "That was the plan. It's after nine and the party seems to be winding down."

"I'm heading out as well. Need a ride back to your apartment?"

"No." I give him a bit of side eye before casually tacking on, "Ryder said he'd drop me off, but thanks for the offer."

His feet grind to a halt. "All right, what's going on?" There's a pause before he fires off another question. "Since when do you two spend so much time together?"

"It's just a ride home, Mav. Chill out." Guilt pricks at my conscience. I've never been one to lie to my family.

Not even my brother.

We've always been close. If he wasn't with Ryder or practicing hockey, he was with me. And then when Mom got sick, our bond became that much stronger. When you're faced with the possible death of a loved one, you quickly realize that family is all you have in this world, and holding them close takes on even more importance than before.

His fingers wrap around my upper arm until I'm forced to stop as he searches my eyes. "Are you sure about that?"

I straighten to my full height, which is still half a foot shorter than him. "Of course. We're friends."

Sort of.

Maybe.

"I don't like it," he says with a grunt.

"You don't have to."

His eyes narrow at my snappy response. "The guy is a good friend, probably the best I have, but he's still a player." There's a pause. "You understand that, right?"

Even though a little piece of my heart crumbles, I lift my chin and hold his gaze. "Why would that matter to me? We're not involved."

"Good. Keep it that way." His expression softens as his voice dips. "I just don't want to see you get hurt, Jules. That's all."

I force a smile in hopes that he'll drop the subject. "I appreciate your concern, but it's unnecessary. It's nothing more than a ride."

He jerks his head. "If you say so."

"I do." I press a quick kiss to his cheek before pulling away. "I'll see you soon, okay?"

"Yeah."

And then I'm hightailing it from the restaurant before he can get it into his head to follow me. As I rush through the glass doors and into the chilled night air, my brother's warnings churn unwantedly through my head. He's not telling me anything I don't already know.

Ryder is a self-admitted manwhore and can have any girl he wants. It's been that way since high school, and it won't change anytime soon. Especially if everything goes the way it's supposed to, and he plays for Chicago after college. Then there'll be even more women throwing themselves at him.

I spot Ryder's black truck idling outside the entrance near the sidewalk. As soon as I slide inside the vehicle, he takes off, pulling out of the parking lot and into traffic.

When I remain silent, lost in thought, he flicks a glance at me. "Everything all right?"

Not really.

The last thing I want to do is fall for him. It wouldn't be difficult. Already, I can feel myself teetering on the brink. Even though I've known Ryder my entire life, he hasn't turned out to be the guy I'd always assumed. I've seen a different facet to his personality. He's opened up and shared more with me these past weeks than during the entire time I've known him.

"Juliette?"

I force those thoughts to the back of my brain to mull over at a later date. "Yeah, it's fine."

That's when I realize we're not heading back to campus but driving in the opposite direction toward downtown. As we pull onto the main street that cuts through the heart of the city, I do a quick mental rundown of the list and what's already been eliminated.

It's a relief to shove those concerns from my head and focus on something else. "I think I know what we're doing tonight."

The smile that simmers around the edges of his lips arrows straight to my core before exploding on impact.

When we pull into the parking lot for Blue Vibe, a local club, I know I'm right.

Number seven.

Even though it's only half past nine, the parking lot is packed. Ryder pulls into a space in the back, and we leave our jackets in the vehicle before exiting. My pulse leaps with excitement. Lame as it sounds, I've never been to a nightclub before. Carina has attempted to drag me to a few, but I've always declined the invitation.

Ryder's arm snakes around my waist as he steers me toward the two-story red brick building. As we approach the door, he reaches around and grabs the handle before ushering me inside. After a couple of steps, his palm settles at the small of my back and I feel the heat of his touch through the fabric of my dress. He gives a chin lift to the bouncer.

"Haven't seen you in a while, McAdams."

"Been lying low," he responds with a grin. "You know how it is during the season."

"Sure do," the guy says with a snort before giving me the quick once over. "Have fun in there."

"Without a doubt. Catch you later, man."

Once he propels me inside the club, everything hits me all at once. It's like an assault on the senses. The techno beat pulses off the black walls as strobe lights cut through the darkness. There's a long stretch of glass bar at the far side of the room with booths and tables scattered around the perimeter. The dance floor is opposite. Just like the parking lot, the space is jampacked. There's a range of people from college-aged students to adults in their mid to late twenties. A DJ sits perched high above the crowd, mixing music.

My gaze flies around the sumptuous interior, trying to soak everything in all at once.

It's almost a surprise when he leans close enough to whisper, "You've really never been here before?"

I pull my attention away from the writhing bodies and shake my head.

"Do you want something to drink or—"

167

"No, I want to dance." Already the music is calling my name, and I feel the beat of it thrumming through my veins.

He flashes a grin. "Then lead the way."

My fingers lock around him as I wind my way through the sea of people talking and flirting with one another. Once we make it to the lit-up dance floor below the DJ booth, Ryder carves out a small space for us. He wraps his hands around my waist and draws me closer. Our gazes cling and everything around us falls away. There are times when we're together that he makes me feel like I'm the only girl in the world.

The only one he's cognizant of.

But that can't possibly be true.

Especially when we're surrounded by beautiful women in sexy strapless dresses that barely skim their asses and leave a mile of toned legs on display.

Instead of glancing around, his gaze stays pinned to mine as if he's completely oblivious. It stirs up the exact kinds of feelings I'm trying to avoid.

The way he stares makes my pulse thrum beneath my skin. Especially when he pulls me against him and whispers in my ear, "What are you thinking about?"

The truth isn't something I'm ready to disclose.

"That this is fun," I say with a forced smile.

It's not a lie. The time I've spent with Ryder has been enjoyable. Even when I'm scared shitless while staring out at a crowd right before I belt out karaoke or when we're sneaking into the athletic center after hours to skinny dip. He pulls me out of my shell and forces me to do things I wouldn't normally contemplate.

"It is."

One song bleeds into the next and then another until I lose track of how long we're out on the dance floor. The thump of the bass vibrates through my bones and my eyelids feather shut as I tip my face upward, letting the notes and lyrics wash over me. My hands lift above my head. With Ryder's arms wrapped protectively around me, I feel safe and insulated.

Everything that normally rests on my shoulders gradually fades away. I don't think about my classes and whether or not I'll be able to pull off straight As this semester. I don't dwell on the MCAT or my med school applications. I don't worry about the possibility of Mom relapsing.

I can simply live in the moment and pretend the other stuff doesn't exist.

Even if it's just for an hour or so.

When was the last time I felt this free?

This alive?

It's even better than the party I attended a couple weeks ago because I'm perfectly sober and Ryder's with me. His hands stroke from the blades of my shoulders to my waist and then dip lower to the curve of my ass before slowly drifting upward again. They're so large and strong. The heat of his palms penetrates the fabric of my dress until it feels like I'm being scalded alive.

Branded.

That's the only word for it.

As we continue to dance, he twists me in his arms until my spine is pressed against his chiseled front. His grip tightens as he pulls me close enough to feel the hard length of his erection against my lower back. Images from the night at the pool flash through my brain like a slow-motion picture show. When my head grows heavy, I allow it to fall back until it can rest against the solid strength of his chest as his lips settle near my temple.

Heat explodes in my core before throbbing a harsh beat in perfect rhythm to the music. His hands glide along my ribcage before settling beneath the swells of my breasts. My teeth sink into my lower lip as my eyelids crack open and I glance around, concerned people might be watching. But no one is paying the slightest bit of attention to us.

The pads of his thumbs slowly slide over my rounded curves. I've never been one for PDA, but there's something deliciously sexy about him caressing me so openly with all these writhing bodies pressing in on us. I don't know if it's the club, the music, or the darkness that has lowered my inhibitions as all these thoughts pound rampantly through my brain, leaving me to feel turned on and achy for his slightest touch.

Or maybe it's just Ryder.

And the fact that I've secretly crushed on him since I was a kid.

"You're so damn sexy," he growls against my ear.

That's the thing...

I've never felt particularly sexy before. I've never been one to play up that part of my personality.

The hot rush of sensation thrumming through my veins makes me feel as if I've stepped out of my safe little world and into someone else's.

All I know is that I want more.

But only with Ryder.

That thought should scare the crap out of me, and on some distant level, bells are ringing shrilly inside my brain. Because I can't allow myself to fall for him. I need to enjoy this for what it is.

Fun.

An exercise in broadening my horizons.

As I move against him, his cock grows stiffer. His hands inch upward until he can cup my breasts, locking me against his muscular body as his fingers toy with my nipples through my dress.

The deep vibration of his groan echoes in his chest before reverberating throughout my body and settling in my clit. It's almost a shock to realize that it wouldn't take much to make me come.

Even in front of all these people.

He buries his face in my hair. "You have no idea how much I want you right now."

I twist my head until his mouth can crash onto mine. One stroke of his tongue along the seam of my lips is all it takes for me to open. And then he's delving inside, wreaking havoc, sending my senses into a tailspin.

Just when I'm on the verge of self-combusting, he pulls away enough to search my eyes. He spins me around until my front is once again pressed against his chest before wrapping his fingers around mine and dragging me through the gyrating crowd until we've turned a corner and find ourselves in a long, dark stretch of hallway. A group of women who look to be in their mid-twenties saunter past in sky-high heels and short glittery dresses, their interested gazes sliding over Ryder as he stalks past with me in tow.

"Lucky girl," one of them sighs.

Another agrees with the sentiment.

And then we're pushing through an emergency exit into a deserted alleyway. The chill of the breeze slaps at my overheated cheeks, instantly cooling them. I haven't had a drop of alcohol, but I feel strangely drunk.

Euphoric.

Ryder spins around and presses me to the building. The rough scrape of the brick against my back isn't enough to dull the heat that continues to rage within.

When his mouth crashes onto mine, our tongues tangle. There's absolutely nothing gentle about the kiss. He presses closer, his thick erection digging into my belly. My hand slides between us, wrapping around him through the khakis he's wearing and squeezing tight.

He pulls away just enough for a hiss of air to rush past his lips.

There's so much combustible heat filling his eyes.

Hunger.

For me.

For my touch.

It's a heady, powerful sensation.

One I've never experienced before.

Ryder might not realize it, but we're checking off so many other things that never made it onto the list. Things that only lived within my fantasies.

My palms settle on the sinewy planes of his chest before gently shoving him away. A frown morphs across his features as he retreats, and I slip around him. He turns, following me with a steady gaze. Then, I push into his personal space and press him against the brick wall, caging him in as much as I can given our size differences.

Our eyes stay locked as I reach up onto my tiptoes and press my lips to his. My kiss is gentler than the last one, but it turns me on just as much. His hands settle at my waist, lingering but never biting into my flesh.

When he opens, I draw his tongue into my mouth and suck the velvety softness until a growl rumbles up from deep within his chest. Once I release it, I nip at his lower lip and then the top before pressing a lingering kiss to each corner of his mouth. I slide lower to his chiseled jawline where there's a day or two worth of stubble.

My teeth scrape over the sharp jut of his chin before descending along the thick column of his throat. A groan escapes from him as he willingly bares it and I lick my way along his masculine flesh. As soon as I press my lips there, the scent of his aftershave teases my senses. My hands drift along his sculpted chest. The muscles that lie beneath the dress shirt are hard and chiseled. He feels more like granite than flesh and bone.

When my fingers settle on the button of his pants, he stills. My gaze flickers to his, wondering if he'll stop me. When he doesn't, I pop it open.

"What is it you think you're doing?" he asks in a raspy tone that strums something deep inside my belly.

I glance around the dark alleyway, needing to confirm we're still alone. From deep within the building, the faint sound of music vibrates through the brick as my fingers slip inside the front of his khakis and boxer briefs until they can wrap around his thick erection. He's impossibly hard. The heat that radiates from his smooth flesh nearly singes me.

I suck in a harsh breath to steady my nerves before sinking to my knees and staring up at him. Barely am I aware of the concrete beneath them. I'm too intent on the moment unfolding between us and the erratic thrum of my pulse.

This isn't something I've done before.

Well, that's not altogether true. I've gone down on a couple of the guys I've dated but never out in the open where someone could stumble upon us. That knowledge only heightens the excitement that rushes through my veins.

"What does it look like?"

"Fuck." He draws out the low sound as his eyes widen.

My lips tremble. "Sort of."

That has him groaning as I lower the zipper. The grind of metal is the only sound I'm cognizant of. When I realize he isn't going to stop me, my attention drops to the thick length fighting to break free.

His fingers slide gently through my hair as he tips my head upward so that I'm forced to meet his eyes. "You don't have to do this."

"I want to."

It's strange to realize that I'm telling the truth. I want to do this. I want to give Ryder this pleasure. How could I not when he's already given me so much? I have no idea when all of this will come to an end, and I'm unsure if any other guy will be able to inspire these kinds of feelings. It doesn't seem possible, and I want to embrace it all before everything goes back to normal between us.

As soon as that thought pops into my brain, I shove it away, not wanting to dwell on the lifespan of this relationship. I want nothing more than to live in the moment and squeeze every drop that I can from it.

My fingers grip the elastic band of his underwear before dragging down the cotton until his cock is able to spring free. The masculine scent of him invades my senses as I press my lips to the mushroom-shaped head. His hard flesh is hot to the touch. A groan rumbles up from deep within his chest as my tongue darts out to lick at the crown before drawing him between my lips. As I do, his fingers tighten around my scalp. The touch isn't punishing. He exerts just enough pressure for me to understand that he's holding me firmly in place and likes what I'm doing.

That's all the encouragement I need to draw him in deeper. My gaze lifts, locking on his as my hands slide around the backs of his muscular thighs to press him closer.

"You have no idea how fucking hot you look on your knees. The way you're staring at me like I'm your fucking everything..." His deep voice trails off as a guttural sound falls from his lips and fills the chilled night air.

At the moment, it's one hundred percent true.

Ryder *is* my everything.

There's just him.

And me.

Nothing else.

None of the usual constraints that keep us locked in the roles we've always played. Especially with each other.

Him the hot, talented hockey player wanted by everyone.

Me the studious bookworm who prefers to hole up in her apartment on the weekends.

There's a small part buried deep down inside that secretly wonders if Ryder has always been my everything.

His cock grows impossibly hard as I draw him deep inside my mouth until he can nudge the back of my throat. I've never blown anyone like this.

I've never wanted to.

In the past, it was more of a chore. Something I did to please the person I was with. It never turned me on or excited me. This experience couldn't be more different. My clit feels like it's thumping to the steady pulse of the music.

One hand slips from the back of his thigh to cup his balls through his boxers. A harsh hiss falls from his lips as I do.

"You keep that up much longer and I'm going to come."

That would be the end goal.

It's gently that he attempts to push me away. "Juliette…"

His voice is tortured.

My mouth turns voracious, pulling him deeper inside me until it feels like he's halfway down my throat. Tears prick my eyes as I keep them pinned to him, wanting to see every flicker of pleasure that crosses his face.

"Fuck baby…that feels so damn amazing."

With a groan, his muscles stiffen as he arches. His hips continue to piston as his fingers tighten around the sides of my head. Only then do I feel the warm spurt of his release. Utter bliss floods his expression as his eyelids feather closed and his head tips back, exposing the thickly corded muscles of his throat.

Have I ever seen anything sexier than Ryder losing control?

The fact that I'm the one who made him come undone only heightens my own arousal.

It's a heady sensation.

Being on my knees is what brought him to his.

Once he softens in my mouth, I release him and press a gentle kiss to the tip of his cock. His gaze fastens onto mine as he carefully tucks himself into his khakis. Then he reaches down and hauls me into his arms until his lips can crash onto mine. His tongue invades my mouth, mingling with my own as my arms tangle around his neck.

He pulls away just enough to growl, "I fucking love that you taste like me."

I like it too.

More than I thought possible.

"Let's get the hell out of here," he says.

Without waiting for a response, he swings me up into his arms and carries me to his truck. I rest my head against his chest, knowing that in this moment, there's nowhere else I'd rather be.

CHAPTER 24

RYDER

*H*er hand stays locked in mine as we drive back to her place. As much as I want her in my bed, that's not possible. Not with Maverick there.

I glance at Juliette. Her lips are still swollen from our kisses and when she went down on me in the alleyway.

Fuck.

I've had my fair share of BJs over the years, but none ever felt like that. In a matter of minutes, I was blowing my load. The image of Juliette kneeling before me as my length disappeared between her lips is enough to stir need inside me all over again.

I can't get enough of her.

Even though I wanted to wait to have sex, I can't hold off any longer.

I need to be inside her tight heat.

I want to feel her pulsing around me.

By the time we pull into the parking lot of her building and jump out of the truck, we're both on edge and vibrating with pent-up desire. I slip my arm around her waist and tug her close as we head to the entrance. Her hand trembles as she punches in the code and shoves open the door. Once inside the lobby, she hits the button for the elevator and within thirty seconds, the doors are sliding open and we're stepping inside the car.

Unable to hold back another second, I yank her into my arms and press her spine against the wall as the doors close, locking us inside before rising to the third floor. My mouth crashes onto hers. The fact that she still tastes like me only heightens the arousal pumping wildly through my veins. She blew me less than twenty minutes ago and already, I'm hard as steel. The thought of burying myself deep inside her pussy makes me want to explode.

I can't remember the last time I was this turned on. It shouldn't come as any surprise that Juliette is the one girl who's able to tie my insides up into a series of painful little knots. It's always been that way. Whether I was willing to acknowledge it or not.

She's been my Achilles heel for as long as I can remember.

When I force my thigh between her legs, a whimper escapes from her.

"That feel good, baby girl?"

"Yes."

I press against her core until she's practically riding my leg. A moan that sounds as if it's been dredged from deep within escapes from her softly parted lips.

By the time the elevator dings, announcing our arrival on the third floor, and the doors slide open, I have a fully-fledged boner. My fingers wrap around her wrist as I drag her from the car and down the hallway. She stumbles in her heels, trying to keep pace.

I hold out my hand as we reach her apartment. "Key."

After she drops it into my palm, I jamb the thin metal into the lock and twist the handle, shoving open the door. The inside is shrouded in darkness. Luckily for us, it looks like Carina is out for the night. I drag her to the bedroom and lock us inside. As soon as I do, she spins around to meet my eyes with dazed ones. Her cheeks are stained with color and her hair is disheveled from my fingers running through the thick mass.

Have I ever seen her look so stunning?

I've spent years wanting to muss her up. Satisfaction pounds through me that I've finally done it. Instead of rushing forward and taking her the way every instinct demands I do, I force myself to lean against the door and simply drink in the sight of her. I want to tuck this moment away in the back of my brain for eternity.

"You want this, right?" I ask, needing her to reconfirm that taking this further is a mutual decision.

The delicate column of her throat works as she swallows before nodding. "Yes, I do."

Relief floods through me. What would I have done if she'd said no? That she wasn't into it. That she didn't want me.

I probably would have fallen to my knees and begged her to change her mind.

Thank fuck that's not necessary.

My muscles tense as I push away from the door and swallow up the distance between us until I'm no more than a foot away. A fine tremble racks her body as I reach out to caress the side of her face. She's so fine boned.

Delicate.

How many times throughout the years have I longed to do exactly that but denied myself the urge because I didn't have any right to touch her?

Too many to count.

"You're so beautiful."

Her eyes soften as she presses the side of her face into my calloused palm.

"I'm not."

"Yeah, you are." My voice deepens, unable to believe that she doesn't realize how gorgeous she is. "Just looking at you steals my breath away."

I step closer until my lips can hover over hers. Unlike in the alleyway or elevator, this kiss is gentle. I want her to understand that it's not passion fueling the compliments but the truth.

As soon as my mouth slides over hers, she opens. Our tongues tangle, twining together as my hands gather up the fabric of her dress,

178

dragging it up her torso and chest. We splinter apart long enough for me to pull it over her head and drop it to the floor.

My gaze slides greedily down the length of her.

She's wearing another matching set.

This one is pink with little white polka dots.

I don't know how it's possible for my cock to grow any harder, but that's exactly what happens. This girl has no damn idea how sexy she is. All I want to do is worship her with my lips, tongue, and hands until she understands just how much she affects me.

How much she's always affected me.

"Gorgeous," I growl before my lips slant over hers again.

Instead of winding her arms around my neck and pressing closer, she pops the button of my khakis for a second time this evening before dragging down the zipper and untucking the dress shirt.

"I want your clothes off," she whispers against my mouth.

My fingers make quick work of the buttons before yanking off the pressed cotton and then the white T-shirt beneath. I shove the pants down my legs before stepping out of them until there's nothing more to cover me than my boxers. My hand snakes out, nabbing her fingers before towing her to me. I want to feel the warmth of her body pressed against mine.

Once she's in my arms, I force her back until the delicate flesh behind her knees hits the mattress and she falls onto it with a soft bounce. As she scoots up and settles in the middle of the bed, I can't help but stare at the pretty picture she makes.

I wasn't lying when I said she's gorgeous.

She absolutely is.

More than I imagined.

Even though this isn't the first time I'm seeing Juliette without her clothing, I'm just as bowled over by the sight. The suppleness of her thighs, the gentle flare of her hips, the softness of her belly, the roundness of her breasts cupped by the silky material, and the slope of her shoulders.

Not to mention, all that dark hair cascading around her.

She's a fucking wet dream sprung to life.

Unable to resist a moment longer, I crawl onto the bed and cage her in with my bigger body before settling on top of her so my cock is nestled between the silkiness of her thighs. I want to yank off my boxers and stretch her panties to the side until I can bury myself deep inside her sweet heat. It's the only thought that pounds through my head.

I've never wanted another girl more than I want her.

It seems almost crazy. Juliette has been a part of my life forever, but I never imagined this happening between us.

Fantasized about?

Sure.

Of course.

But she always seemed out of reach.

Too damn smart and put together for a guy who just wanted to play hockey.

I take her mouth, licking and nipping at her lips before sliding along the curve of her jaw and then sinking further down her bared throat until I reach her collarbone.

I pull away long enough to growl, "As much as I love this bra, it needs to go."

Her lips quirk and her back bows as I slip my hands around her ribcage and unhook the clasp. When it springs apart, I pull the sexy garment away so my gaze can lick over her chest.

She's got the most perfect tits.

And her nipples...

They're rosy and hard.

My cock twitches in response.

I just want to mark this girl as my own.

That thought is jarring enough to give me pause.

This isn't a long-term arrangement. We both went into this knowing what the situation was. I'm helping her tick items off a list. And I get to lay my hands on her in the process, which is something I've wanted to do for years.

It's a win-win for both of us.

I refocus my attention on Juliette before those thoughts can ruin the moment by making me question everything. I've never wanted a serious relationship. I don't need someone weighing me down at this point in my life. Making demands on my time.

My tongue flicks over one turgid tip before drawing it inside my mouth and sucking it. Her spine arches off the mattress as her fingers tighten around the sides of my head to hold me in place.

As if that's necessary.

Wild horses couldn't pull me away from her.

It's only when she's writhing beneath me that I release her nipple with a soft pop and focus my attention on the other side before crawling further down her body. As I arrive at the elastic band of her panties, my fingers dip beneath the silky material, pulling the front down enough to press a kiss against the top of her slit.

I flick a glance up, only to find her watching me with lids at half-mast. "These need to go as well."

"Yes, they do."

I want to rip them off with my fucking teeth. Instead, my fingers wrap around the delicate fabric before yanking it down her legs and tossing it over my shoulder.

And then she's gloriously naked.

A groan of appreciation rumbles up from deep within my chest as I shoulder my way between her thighs, parting them so that I can see her glistening softness. Even in the shadowy darkness of the room, my gaze is able to lick over every pink inch of her. The scent of her arousal is intoxicating.

I can't imagine being more turned on than I am at this moment.

I run the tip of my nose over her core before burying it against her pussy and inhaling. She smells so damn good.

Good enough to eat. Which is exactly what I'm going to do this evening.

My plan is to make a meal out of her.

My tongue dips inside her slick heat before lapping at her slit with the flat of my tongue. I do this little maneuver half a dozen times until she's writhing beneath me before nibbling at her clit. Her moans fill the silence of the room as I continue gorging myself.

She's so damn responsive.

"I just want to eat you up all night long until you scream my name," I mutter against her softness.

"Please," she whimpers. "Please don't stop."

I'm not sure if I'll ever be able to stop. Imagining a day when I'm completely sated is impossible.

She's so close to splintering apart.

I love the feel of her fingers sliding through my hair, locking me in place as I nibble and lick at her. She's so damn perfect. The way she moves her hips, spreading her thighs wide, as she attempts to hold me close.

Her muscles grow impossibly tight right before she screams out my name.

It's the best fucking sound in the world.

Her hips gyrate as I pin her firmly to the bed.

It's only when she melts into the mattress that I press one final kiss upon her swollen pussy before straightening. I lift my hand and wipe my mouth with my thumb and forefinger. There's a dazed expression in her eyes as a contented smile curves her lips.

My cock is so damn hard as it throbs with painful awareness.

"Are you sure about this?" I ask again, not wanting to force her into anything she's not ready for.

"I'm sure, Ryder. I want you. And I want this."

I release a slow breath, relieved she feels the same as I do.

I grab my khakis from the floor and dig around in the pocket for my wallet before pulling out a condom and ripping open the package. I slide the latex over my dick with one swift movement. There might not be anything sexy about condoms, but chancing an STI or unwanted pregnancy is even less so.

I've never fucked a girl without wrapping it up tight.

Have there been times during the heat of the moment when I wanted to forego protection?

Fuck yeah.

But I've never actually done it.

Once I'm covered, I turn back to the bed and meet Juliette's dark eyes. Staring into them is like tumbling down a rabbit hole and never surfacing again.

I stop and stare at her for just a heartbeat. Just long enough to commit this moment to memory.

Her beauty is like a gut punch.

Every thought circling through my brain leaks out of my ears as she spreads her legs wide. Her hands drift to her breasts as she squeezes the soft flesh before tweaking the stiff little nipples.

Ummm…

I might have just blown my load.

Damn, that's hot.

I stalk to the bed and settle on top of her. Not wanting to crush her with my weight, I prop myself up on my elbows as the head of my cock nudges her slick entrance. At the same time, I press a kiss against her lips.

"I've never wanted anyone more than I want you," I admit before I can think better of it.

Her eyes carefully search mine as if sifting through them for the truth.

"I feel the same," she whispers, echoing the sentiment.

My gaze stays pinned to hers as I slowly press into her body. As much as I want to drive inside and bury myself to the hilt in one swift motion, I don't.

Can't.

I need to take my time. It's her pleasure that takes precedence over my own. I want to rock this girl's world and ruin her for all other men. That's not something I've ever cared about before. Every girl I've slept with has left my bed satisfied, but my pleasure was always uppermost in my mind.

Those girls were there for me.

To tend to my needs and relieve my stress.

This couldn't be more different.

A wave of ecstasy crashes over me as I continue to sink inside her tight body. My gaze stays pinned to hers the entire time. I couldn't look away even if I wanted to.

When her teeth sink into her lower lip, I ask, "Am I hurting you?"

Even after her earlier blowjob, I'm still wound tight. It wouldn't take much for me to go off like a shot, and that's the last thing I want. I need to draw this out and make it as good as I can for her.

"No. It feels amazing."

I blow out a steady breath, trying to keep my baser impulses under control when all I want to do is fuck her into oblivion.

"Good."

With one flex of my hips, I sink inside her pussy until I'm buried balls deep. For just a moment, I squeeze my eyes tightly shut and enjoy the sensation of her heat wrapped around my dick, squeezing the life out of it.

She's so damn tight and hot.

And soft.

So fucking soft.

If I focus too much on it, I'll come.

I grit my teeth and force my eyes open. It's only when I'm firmly under control that I pull out before sliding back inside. A spike of pleasure rushes through my veins as I drive inside her for a second time.

When I do it again, she raises her pelvis to meet my thrust. It doesn't take long for us to fall into a steady rhythm. More pleasure spirals through me as I steadily pick up the pace.

There's so much arousal darkening her eyes as she widens her legs before wrapping them around my waist and locking me against her. I didn't think it was possible to slide in any deeper.

I was wrong.

As soon as I bottom out, my balls draw up against my body and I realize that I'm moments away from losing it. One thrust and I splinter apart into a million pieces. My gaze stays locked on hers as I take her mouth. A groan rumbles up from my chest as her pussy spasms around my dick, milking it as I drive my tongue inside her mouth and mimic the movements of my cock.

My release seems to last forever. The sounds of her coming undone are sweet music to my ears. My hips continue to piston until I soften. With a huff, my body loosens, and I press one last kiss to her lips before resting my forehead against hers. Our labored breathing is the only audible sound that can be heard in the silence of the room.

I pull away just enough to search her eyes.

It would kill me to find shards of regret lurking within them.

Instead, a soft smile spreads across her face. "Guess I'll be checking off number six."

Relief spirals through me. I didn't realize how tense I'd become until now. "And number seven. Tonight was a two-for-one special."

Even though I'm reluctant to leave the warmth of her body, I pull out and roll off the side of the bed before grabbing a couple pieces of tissue and removing the condom. I tie the end into a tight knot and wrap it up before tossing the used rubber in the small garbage can near her desk. Then I'm back, sliding beneath the sheets and tugging her into my arms until her head can rest against my chest.

As hazy as my brain is, I can't get over how perfect this feels.

How good being buried deep inside her body was.

Or holding her close after sex.

Normally after blowing my load, all I want to do is devise an escape plan before the chick I'm with can mention getting together again. The last thing I want is to get sucked into a quasi-relationship, which is another reason I only sleep with a girl once or twice before moving onto the next.

But with Juliette?

That's not how I feel.

In fact, the urge to lock her down tight is the only one thrumming through me at the moment. It's on the tip of my tongue to broach the subject. To make this more of a permanent situation. I don't want her even looking at other guys. And if that isn't some scary shit, I don't know what is.

A burst of anxiety explodes inside me at the idea of heaping even more expectation and responsibility onto my plate.

Don't I have enough going on with school and hockey?

How can I handle adding something else to the mix?

Unease spirals through me and it all starts to feel like...*too much.*

The avalanche of confusion that buries me alive is what propels me to blurt, "It's late. I should probably get going."

For just a second, she stiffens before pulling away. As soon as her warmth vanishes, a sharp sense of loss fills me. It's so damn tempting to drag her back into my arms, but I don't. I force myself to rise from the bed and collect my scattered clothing before getting dressed. The entire time I do, regret churns inside me.

Once my shoes are on, I reluctantly turn back to the bed.

I have no idea what to say or how to leave this.

I plow a rough hand through my hair. "I'll see you around?"

"Sure." There's a pause. "Thanks for tonight."

"Yeah, it was fun."

That adjective doesn't even come close to describing what this evening meant.

We might be crossing off a lot of firsts for her, but this was one for me. The connection I felt while being buried inside her body isn't something I've experienced before. Nor have I ever placed someone else's pleasure above my own.

It's on the tip of my tongue to say something…

Something that will change the trajectory of this night.

"Take it easy."

When she gives me a tight smile in response, I slip quietly from the room.

CHAPTER 25

JULIETTE

I push my way inside the arena and find the place already swarming with fans. It's a sea of orange and black. The Western Wildcats have a massive following not only on campus but in the city itself. When there's a game, people show up in droves to support their hometown team. There's more than a few girls sporting McAdams jerseys. An ache flares to life beneath my breast and I unconsciously raise my hand to rub the area as if that alone has the power to make the pain disappear.

It doesn't.

It's been five days since we slept together.

Hands down, it was the best sex of my life.

No surprise there.

Was I expecting anything less from Ryder?

Nope.

What I didn't expect was to be ghosted afterward.

Have I reached out to see what's going on?

Hell no. In fact, it was tempting to skip the game altogether. The last thing I want to do is sit in the bleachers along with his other groupies and stare at him on the ice for the next three hours.

Can you imagine anything more tortuous?

Me neither.

Except…

How could I not show up and support my brother?

Carina links her arm through mine as we navigate our way through the concourse to the section where both sets of parents will be sitting.

"Sure you don't want to sit in the student section?"

I shake my head. "Are you kidding? It gets way too crazy over there. All the yelling and screaming."

"I know," she says, flashing a grin. "That's what makes it so fun."

A reluctant smile curls around the edges of my lips as I squeeze her close. "I'm glad you came with me tonight. I'm sure Ford will be thrilled to see you."

She rolls her eyes. That comment is enough to have the smile vanishing from her face.

"That guy is such a pain in my ass."

"Oh, stop. He'll appreciate the support."

"Please, he gets enough of that from the puck bunnies that stalk his every movement. Did you see the groupie at the other game that wore his jersey and then flashed her tits?" She wrinkles her pert little nose. "Show a little self-respect, for fuck's sake."

I arch a brow. "And you really want to sit in the student section along with them?"

The Western Wildcats fangirls are a rabid bunch, and they'll do whatever it takes to get a player's attention. Like flash their boobs during the game.

"Hmmm." Her expression turns decidedly thoughtful as she mulls over the comment. "As much as I hate to admit it, you make a valid point."

"Thank you."

Once we're inside the rink, I search the stands for my parents. Mom and Dad always sit around the red center line so we can watch the action on both ends of the ice. As soon as she spots us, Mom rises to her feet and waves. Stella and my grandfather are seated next to them.

I'm sure Stella is here to support Maverick but also her bestie, Riggs.

I return Mom's greeting before grabbing Carina's hand and dragging her up the aisle. I say hello to a few of the other families I've gotten to know over the years. It's a tight-knit bunch.

As soon as I shimmy my way down the row, Mom wraps her arms around me. "Hey, sweetie. How are you?"

"I'm good."

Her gaze slices to my roomie. "Hello, Carina! I'm so glad you could join us."

"She's here to support her stepbrother," I add, knowing it'll irk her.

Mom flashes her an *Aww, aren't you the best stepsister in the world* look.

Carina gives me a bit of side eye before grumbling, "He's my ex-stepbrother."

"Is there really such a thing? You can't divorce siblings," Mom adds.

"Sure, you can. I did it. Successfully, too."

"You're so funny," Mom says with a chuckle and a pat on her arm.

When I shoot her a grin, Carina glares at me.

And the best thing?

I'm not even thinking about the players who are circling the ice for warmups. I'm focused on my family and Carina. Hopefully, that's exactly the way it'll stay for the next three hours.

Ryder who?

That's right.

That's exactly right.

I hug Stella and we chat a little bit since I haven't run into her on campus lately. Carina settles between the two of us.

"We should have gotten snacks," my roomie says, leaning closer to be heard over the blare of music and the noise of the crowd. "I'm starving."

I shake my head. I have no idea how Carina stays so slender. This is one chick who doesn't survive on leafy greens and diet soda. Sure, she spends hours a day in the dance studio, but the bitch can eat.

I'm envious of her metabolism. Sometimes it feels like all I have to do is look at a piece of chocolate cake and I gain five pounds.

"I'm going to run to the bathroom before the game starts. I'll stop at the concession stand on my way back."

"Want me to come with you?" she asks.

"Nah." I rise to my feet. "I'll be back in five. This will give you time to watch Ford."

"Shut up."

With a chuckle, I shimmy past the line of seats to the aisle. Unable to help myself, I glance at the ice. The entire team is out there warming up. That's more than fifty guys. And yet, my gaze slices to Ryder. His stick is resting across the blades of his shoulders and his arms are hanging over the length as he takes long strides, stretching the muscles in his legs.

The sight of him is almost enough to steal my breath, and my heart picks up tempo in response as an unwanted rush of longing floods through me. As soon as our gazes collide, a zip of electricity sizzles through my veins and I rip my attention away, swinging around and hurrying up the concrete stairs to the concourse. First, I hit the restrooms and take care of business before locating the concession stand and ordering three bottles of water and two large boxes of popcorn to share with Stella and my parents.

With my arms loaded down, I head back to the bleachers.

"Hey, stranger," a deep voice says.

I flick a glance to the side and find Sawyer grinning ear to ear.

For just a second or two, his presence throws me off. "Hi! What are you doing here?"

"I thought I'd check out one of Mav's games."

"Oh, that's so sweet. He'll appreciate you showing up to support him."

Sawyer shrugs before pointing toward the bottles and boxes. "Looks like you could use a hand."

"That would be great." I pass him the three water bottles as we enter the arena.

My roomie's brows rise when she gets a look at the handsome, dark-haired guy trailing behind me.

"Carina, have you met Sawyer? He's an old family friend."

Stella waves before Mom rises and pulls him in for a warm embrace. She's always liked him. When I first started at Western, she made a couple of comments about how fun it would be if the two of us got together since our families have always been close. We grabbed lunch at the Union a couple times, but nothing more transpired.

"It's so good to see you again," Mom says. "Are your parents planning to make it? I didn't get a chance to touch base with your mom during the week."

Regret flashes across his face as he shakes his head. "No, sorry. They're having dinner tonight with one of Dad's associates."

"That's too bad. Maybe next time."

Sawyer's green eyes flicker to mine. "Definitely."

I settle next to Carina before passing over two of the drinks and both boxes of popcorn.

"Thanks." She immediately pops open the lid and digs in. After munching a few pieces, she leans closer and whispers, "Damn, he's hot. I totally approve."

With a laugh, I shake my head. "It's not like that. We're just friends."

She glances past me to the handsome guy who has settled on the seat next to mine. "I wouldn't be too sure about that."

Carina doesn't know what she's talking about. He's more like a cousin than anything else. Wanting to shut down the conversation, I refocus my attention on Sawyer as the puck is dropped and the game gets underway.

My gaze stays fastened on Ryder every time he's out for a shift. Because I'm paying close attention, I notice when he gets passed over in the lineup and another player takes his place. Even from here, I can feel the pent-up agitation rolling off him in heavy, suffocating waves.

Sawyer leans close in order to be heard over the rock music blasting through the speakers. "I spoke to Ryder for a little bit at your mom's party. It's been a couple of years since I've seen him."

I rip my attention away from the ice long enough to meet his eyes and force a smile. "Oh, yeah?"

He nods, his gaze flicking to the action in the arena before slicing back to me. "Is there anything going on between you two?"

"Of course not," I lie. "He's always been more Mav's friend than mine."

With an easy smile, he drapes a muscular arm around the back of my chair. "Yeah, that's what I thought but wanted to make sure."

We continue to chat, talking about stuff from our childhood and then his job, until the first period ends. It's almost a surprise to realize how quickly time is flying by. In all honesty, I was dreading tonight's game. Dreading having to sit here and watch Ryder on the ice. Sawyer has been the perfect distraction.

I glance at the scoreboard and realize that the Wildcats are in the lead by a solitary goal. It'll be a nailbiter. Already the crowd is going crazy, jeering at the refs for bad calls.

"Your mom mentioned that you're in the process of applying to med school."

I drag my attention away from the Zamboni as it resurfaces the ice to meet Sawyer's inquisitive stare. "So far, I've applied to three colleges. Hopefully, I'll get accepted to at least one." Even thinking about it makes the muscles in my belly spasm with nerves. It's what I've spent all these years working toward. Until I know the outcome, I'm in limbo, and that's a difficult place to be.

"Oh, yeah? Which ones?"

"John Hopkins, Duke, and the University of Chicago."

He whistles. "That's a pretty impressive list."

I force out a laugh. If there's one thing I hate talking about, it's my accomplishments. "I haven't been accepted yet. So, it might not be that impressive at all. We'll see."

He nudges my shoulder with his larger one. "Please, your mom was telling me that you have a near four point oh and that you'll graduate Magna Cum Laude. That's a real achievement. You should be proud. I only made Summa Cum Laude." He flashes a lopsided smile.

"So, you beat me out. My parents always said you'd do amazing things, and here you are."

With a groan, I bury my face in my hands. "Oh my god, how embarrassing."

My mortification makes him chuckle. "What's wrong with that? She's proud of you." He glances at the ice. "Of both you and Maverick."

My heart softens. Neither of my parents have ever held back their praise. They'd shout it from the rooftops if they could. And I love them for it. They've always been our biggest cheerleaders and champions.

"I know."

When the crowd erupts into whistles and applause, I glance around and realize with a start that people have swiveled in their seats and are openly staring at us.

Sawyer points to the jumbotron perched high above the ice.

"We're on the Kiss Cam," he says with a laugh.

What?

My eyes widen as I see our faces on the giant screen. Sawyer's arm is wrapped around my shoulders as he grins at the camera. More whistling and cheers erupt.

"Come on, you two," Carina says. "Don't disappoint the crowd!"

"Yeah," Stella shouts. "Lay a wet one on her, Sawyer."

Embarrassment claws at my cheeks. It feels like everyone in the arena is staring, encouraging us to kiss. Even my own family and friends. When I glance at him, he arches a brow in silent askance and I give him a helpless look in response, unsure what to do.

Maybe I'm making a bigger deal out of this than is necessary.

It's just a peck on the lips.

"Well, what's it going to be?" he asks softly as if he understands that I'm uncomfortable with all the attention.

I suck in a harsh breath before jerking my head into a tight nod and closing the distance between us. It's gently that his lips brush over mine. Unlike Aaron, they don't feel dry and papery. But it's nothing like when Ryder kissed me either.

There's absolutely no spark.

It's…*pleasant.*

Could it be more than that if another guy's kisses weren't so fresh in my mind?

Maybe.

The crowd explodes into cheers and whistles as Sawyer pulls away and searches my eyes before staring at the camera and waving.

Air rushes from my lungs. I have no idea if I'm relieved or disappointed that I didn't feel more of a connection with him.

I blink away those thoughts and refocus my attention on the ice, only to find Ryder glaring at me. If I didn't know better, I'd say he looked pissed.

But that can't be.

Can it?

CHAPTER 26

RYDER

*W*hat the actual fuck was that?

Did she seriously just kiss that guy?

Even though my head should be in the game, it's not. My attention is locked on Juliette and the *Wolf of Wall Street* wannabe sitting next to her.

Goddamn it. I *knew* he was interested in her. I should have set him straight at the party, but I kept my trap shut because...

Well, what was I going to say?

That we're together?

An item?

A legit couple?

We aren't.

I have no idea what the hell we are...if anything.

After we slept together, I decided it would be best to take a giant step back from the situation. It had been the best damn sex of my life, and everything had started to feel a little too intense.

It's more than I'm used to.

And that had scared the shit out of me.

Ford knocks into me with his shoulder, drawing my attention back to the present and the game.

"You good, man?" His brows pinch as he searches my eyes.

"Yeah, I'm fine."

And if I'm not, then I need to get good real quick. I can't afford any distractions. Not when any fuck-ups on the ice will make my situation even more precarious than it already is. At this particular moment, Juliette shouldn't be a thought in my head. The girl shouldn't even be on my radar.

That, unfortunately, is not the case.

"Let's shut these motherfuckers down once and for all." He pats my shoulder with a gloved hand before skating to the red line.

He's right. That's *exactly* what we need to do. We need to shut them down and make them our bitch. They're in our house. In front of our fans. This has gone on long enough.

When Hayes glances at me from his faceoff position, I jerk my head into a nod. For just a fraction of a second, I squeeze my eyes tightly shut and refocus my attention on the moment playing out in the arena.

Nothing else matters.

My eyes fly open in time to see the puck get dropped and Hayes swipe it away before passing it off to Ford, who digs his blades into the ice as he takes off toward our opponent's net. Defensemen swarm from both sides. He passes it back to Hayes and then Colby as they battle their way to the goal. There's a lot of back and forth until one of them takes a shot. The goalie blocks it, and the other team's defenseman picks it up before passing it to their right wing who races down the ice. I keep my gaze pinned to the guy rushing toward me. We've squared off plenty of times before. I've also watched enough game film to anticipate the moves he'll make. I sweep my stick in front of me as I continue to skate backward.

From the corner of my eye, I see the asshole talking with Juliette and for some reason, I turn my head to get a better look.

That's my first mistake.

When the right wing fakes to the left, I fall for it.

Hook, line, and sinker.

That's my second mistake.

If I were solely focused on him the way I should have been, that never would have happened. I would have realized his intentions a couple seconds before he made the move. I would have read it on his face or intuition would have kicked in. I've always been able to trust my instincts.

As soon as he whizzes past, I know I won't be able to catch him. He's too fast and has too much momentum. But that doesn't stop me from giving chase. My blades dig into the ice as I attempt to close the distance between us.

I can already hear Coach's irate voice filling my head. It's just another thing I'll get my ass chewed out for in the locker room after the game. I can feel the disappointment of his stare boring into my back as I attempt to rectify my mistake.

It only messes with my mojo.

Although, this time it doesn't have anything to do with me second guessing myself and everything to do with not being focused on the game.

Just as Bridger races across the ice to catch him, the guy rips off a shot. Wolf slides before dropping to his knees, attempting to block it. The puck hits the tip of his glove and ends up going in.

Fuck.

As the guy circles the ice, a smile pasted across his sweat-soaked face, I lower my shoulder and knock him into the boards. There's a grunt as he slams against the Plexiglass. My shoulder crashes into it and for just a second, I meet Juliette's wide gaze. Her mouth tumbles open in shock. The guy I hit whips around and plows his hands into my chest.

"You want to fucking go?" he roars. "Then let's do it, McAdams!"

It's so damn tempting to throw my gloves to the ice and beat the piss out of him. I'm being a dick and we both know it.

He outplayed me.

Outmaneuvered me.

It doesn't happen often, and I fucking hate that it did now.

The sharp blast of a whistle rents the frigid air of the arena.

"Get your ass in the box, McAdams," Coach bellows.

I don't bother glancing at him. My gaze remains locked on Juliette as I take my sweet damn time skating to the penalty box before throwing myself onto the bench and tearing off my helmet. I toss the gloves to the rubber mat and plow my fingers through my damp strands.

My gaze remains pinned to Juliette as the penalty clock is set.

Even when the asshole next to her attempts to regain her attention, her eyes stay fastened to me.

It's exactly where I want them.

Where I've always wanted them.

Only now can I admit that to myself.

It takes a moment to realize that the emotion burning a painful hole at the bottom of my gut is jealousy.

I don't like it. All it's doing is messing with my head. And that, I don't need. Not now. Not when I have everything to lose.

With me cooling my ass in the box for two minutes, our opponents are now on a power play. We're a man down and the other team will attempt to capitalize on that by scoring another goal. My attention should be focused on what's happening on the ice.

If we end up losing this game because I allowed two goals to be scored, it'll be on me.

Instead, I stare at Juliette.

CHAPTER 27

JULIETTE

"*T*hat was weird. What do you think got into Ryder?" Carina whispers as I chew my nails.

It's a bad habit I've tried to kick over the years. In times of great stress, I gnaw my fingernails.

And right now, standing in the lobby, waiting for Ryder to exit the locker room, I'm an anxious mess. Nerves swirl at the bottom of my belly like an impending storm, causing all sorts of havoc.

When I fail to respond, she wraps her fingers around my hand and gently lowers it from my mouth. I don't bother looking at my nails. I'm sure they're a pulpy mess.

Ever since Ryder was sent to the box, I've been chewing on them.

The look on his face as he'd glared at me...

A shiver trips down my spine.

It's not an expression he's ever aimed in my direction, and I'm unsure what to make of it.

"I don't know," I mumble, not wanting to field any more questions. Both her and Stella kept shooting me speculative looks during the rest of the game.

All right...

Maybe that's not altogether true.

Maybe I do have a clue as to what's going on, but that doesn't mean it makes sense. Ryder is the one who scrambled out of my bed like he couldn't get away fast enough.

And the capper?

It's been stereo silence from him.

I'd actually gotten used to his daily texts and started to look forward to them.

By the way Carina's blonde head is tilted as she studies me says that she suspects I haven't given her full disclosure.

Which is, unfortunately, the truth.

What exactly am I supposed to tell her?

That Ryder and I have been messing around while we check items off the silly list I made after high school graduation?

For the first time in my life, I don't know what I'm doing and feel completely out of my depth. Worse than that, I'm not sure how we move forward.

There's a flurry of activity as a few of the guys trickle out of the locker room. Their hair is damp and shiny from the showers. The game ended in a tie, so no one appears particularly happy.

Another wave of anxiety crashes over me as I nibble my lower lip, scanning each face but not finding the one I'm searching for. My belly trembles in anticipation, or maybe it's dread. I feel almost sick inside.

Am I supposed to act normal?

Ignore him?

I have no idea, and it's stressing me out.

As soon as Ford saunters out with Wolf, his gaze locks on Carina. The goalie's remark from a couple weeks ago in the apartment hallway pops into my brain as sexual energy crackles in the air. It's a surprise when neither of them bursts into flames. Now that he's pointed it out, it's shocking that I never picked up on the underlying tension that vibrates between them like a live wire.

Madden and Riggs are the next to walk out. Stella quickly gravitates to her bestie before throwing her arms around his neck.

"I was wondering if you wanted to grab something to eat after this and we can spend a little more time catching up."

Jerked from my thoughts, my gaze settles on Sawyer.

How terrible is it that I forgot he was still here?

My mind spins as I turn the invitation over in my head. "I'm, ah, not sure. Let me check with my parents to see if we're doing anything after this."

I'd much rather hightail it from the arena. I would have taken off after the final buzzer rang if not for Carina. We always wait around for the players afterward. To deviate from that would have raised suspicions, and once that girl picks up a scent, she won't let it go until she ferrets out the truth. She can be persistent and single-minded. Kind of like one of those yappy little dogs.

And I'm a terrible liar.

She'd see right through me, and then I'd be blurting out the truth along with everything else that's transpired over the past few weeks.

"Sure. Of course." His gaze never falters as he shoves his hands into the pockets of his expensive looking camel-colored overcoat.

I can't say he doesn't look handsome in his suit. My guess is that he came straight to the game from work.

If none of this had happened with Ryder, Sawyer would be exactly my type. He's handsome with bright green eyes and hair that's cut a little longer on top and buzzed shorter on the sides. It's stylish yet professional. Both times we've run into each other, he's been friendly, witty, and funny.

The perfect gentleman.

Plus, he's older. More mature. And smart. Like me, he prioritized academics over partying and having a good time.

I should be jumping at the chance to get to know Sawyer on a different level. Instead, I can't stop thinking about Ryder. I keep comparing Sawyer to the hockey player with the shaggy blond hair. There's no denying how everything in my brain goes eerily silent when his lips settle over mine.

Or when he lays his hands on me.

Ugh.

Ryder McAdams is the last person I should be falling for.

And I know it.

But how do I stop the fall when it already feels like I've tumbled over the edge and am in mid-descent?

Is it even possible?

My greatest fear is that it's not.

Maverick is the next to stroll out with Bridger and Hayes. My brother beelines for our parents and everyone slaps him on the back, congratulating him on having a good game. Even though Maverick doesn't talk about it, I know there's a ton of pressure on him to perform at a higher level. Mav wants coaches and the other players to recognize him for his own talent, not because he's the son of Brody McKinnon.

If there's anyone on the team who understands what that's like, it's Colby. His father, Gray McNichols, played professional hockey and is now a broadcaster for ESPN.

Dad pats Mav on the back before pulling him in for an embrace and whispering something in his ear. As he does, I watch my brother's muscles loosen as a smile curves his lips.

By now, it seems like most of the players have trickled out of the locker room. It's on the tip of my tongue to ask about the blond defenseman.

Thankfully, Dad beats me to the punch and voices the question so I don't have to.

"Where's Ryder? Is he still in the locker room?"

Maverick's gaze flickers to me for a second before settling on Sadie and Cal. "Yeah, Coach wanted to have a few words with him."

I wince, knowing exactly what that means. Maybe it would be best for everyone involved if I took off with Sawyer. Ryder has already helped tick off a good portion of the list. It's way more than I thought I'd accomplish on my own. I can finish the rest by myself. If that thought has a burst of sadness sparking within me, I shove it away before it can take root.

Decision made, I clear my throat. "Sawyer?"

He steps closer, angling his face toward mine. "Yeah?"

"I was thinking—" My voice trails off as my phone dings with an incoming message. Thrown off, I slip the small silver device from my jacket pocket before peeking at the screen.

Meet me in the locker room ASAP

With a blink, I reread the message more carefully before throwing a quick glance over my shoulder at the empty hallway that leads to the locker room designated for the men's hockey team.

"Juliette?" Sawyer's voice breaks into the whirl of my thoughts.

My attention snaps back to him. "Yeah?"

"What were you about to say?" A hopeful expression lights up his face.

"Oh." I glance at the screen again. "I, ah, need to use the restroom."

Disappointment fills his eyes as he gives me a quick nod. "Then we can talk about taking off?"

"Sure." I force a smile. "Be right back."

"I'll be waiting."

Guilt swamps me as I swing away and hustle down the corridor. Instead of heading to the bathroom, I fly by the door, speedwalking past it to the locker room. Even though the hallway is empty, my heart jackhammers a steady tattoo against my ribcage.

I pause outside the door and throw a cautious look over my shoulder to make sure no one's around to see me sneak into the men's locker room. The heavy metal door closes behind me with a soft rush of air as I slip inside the space.

It's a surprise to find the place shrouded in darkness and shadows. Humidity from the showers and the pungent scent of sweat hang heavy in the air. Another shiver scampers across my flesh as I take a tentative step inside. It's tempting to call out his name, but I have no idea if anyone else is around.

As I inch my way farther inside the area, I peek cautiously around the corner until the benches that run parallel to the lockers come into sight. The cinderblock walls are painted golden orange and the long rows of lockers are a shiny black. There's a mural of the university mascot—a wildcat with its teeth bared and claws out.

The place is empty. No other players linger.

My heart continues to ratchet up as I step further inside the room, passing by more lockers. That's when the sound of water catches my attention. There's a thick stack of white towels off to the side as I peek around another corner and spot Ryder standing beneath the spray of water. His face is tipped upward toward the shower head and his arms are lifted to his hair. His shoulders are broad, and his chest is all finely honed muscle. His traps are equally defined as they taper in a V to his waist.

A punch of lust hits me square in the gut.

All right...maybe it hits a little lower.

Have I ever seen anything as sexy as Ryder, in all his naked glory?

My mouth turns cottony in response.

In the days that have passed by with no communication from him, I've repeatedly tried to convince myself that Ryder McAdams wasn't anything special and I haven't developed feelings for the guy.

Only now, as I eat him up greedily, do I realize I've been lying to myself.

Even though I've remained silent, he must feel the intensity of my perusal. His eyelids flutter as his gaze locks on mine, skewering me in place. Air gets wedged in my lungs as every muscle turns rigid. This must be what it feels like to be a prey animal sighted by a predator.

His arms slowly lower to his sides, the play of muscles bunching and flexing with the motion. "Come here, Juliette."

It's not a conscious decision on my part to slink closer. My feet automatically move with the need to follow his gruff command.

"Take your clothes off."

My pulse quickens as I hesitantly glance over my shoulder. "What if someone walks in?"

My voice is so low and husky that it doesn't sound like it belongs to me at all.

"That's not going to happen." Before I can throw up another road-block, he says, "Get undressed."

His demand arrows straight to my core before exploding like a firework as I shrug out of my jacket and toss it near the stack of towels before pulling off the sweater. My jeans are next as I toe off my shoes and then socks until I'm left in my panties and bra. Even though the shower room has turned steamy, gooseflesh erupts across my arms and I lift my hands to rub it away.

His gaze slides over me, heating every inch where it lingers. "Take off all of it."

A thick lump wells in my throat, making it impossible to swallow. My fingers tremble as I reach around my ribcage and unfasten the snap at my spine. The stretchy material springs apart before the straps slink down my shoulders and arms, revealing the tips of my breasts before falling away. His gaze tracks each movement as the garment is tossed onto the growing stack of clothing. His cock turns hard before lengthening until it's standing perfectly at attention.

I can't stop staring. I'm mesmerized by the sight. All I can think about is what it felt like to sink to my knees in the alleyway and take him in my mouth for the first time.

"Panties," he rasps.

I shove them down my hips and thighs until they puddle around my feet before kicking them away.

And then, I'm just as naked as he is.

It's tempting to cover my breasts as the tips harden, but I force my arms to remain at my sides. I can tell by the way his gaze licks over me that he likes what he sees.

The massive boner is a dead giveaway.

I reach up and pull the elastic band holding my hair in a ponytail. The dark strands fall around my shoulders and down my back. I quickly gather the thick length into a bun at the top of my head so it doesn't get soaked.

"Come here," he growls, losing patience.

My belly hollows out at the rough demand.

For days, I've been reliving the time we've spent together. Fantasizing about all the ways he touched me.

Just thinking about it was enough to turn me on.

Full disclosure—I've had more than one self-love session.

But none compared to what it felt like when he laid his hands on me.

I force myself to close the distance between us. As soon as I'm within striking distance, his hand snakes out, locking around my fingers before dragging me to him until I'm pressed against all that steely strength. Before I can suck in a full breath, his mouth crashes onto mine. When his tongue slides across the seam of my lips, I open so he can plunge inside. There's a mixture of pent-up hunger tinged with anger in that caress. It's as if I'm being eaten alive.

Devoured.

I could feel it pouring off him in hot, suffocating waves while he sat in the penalty box, his gaze pinned to mine.

He spins me around before forcing me back until my spine is pressed against the smooth tile. His hands rise, the palms settling against the sides of my head as if to hold me in place.

His gaze searches mine. "Are you on the pill?"

"Yes."

He releases a steady breath as an internal debate is waged within him.

"I've never fucked a girl without a condom, but I don't want anything coming between us when I take you. Are you good with that?"

Air leaks from my lungs as his words somersault in my head. If I'm smart, I'll shoot down that idea. Like him, it's not something I've ever done either. My mantra has always been *no glove, no love.*

Maybe I'm foolish for trusting him, but I don't think he'd do anything to put either one of us at risk.

"Yes."

The rigid set of his shoulders loosens. "Good. I want you bare. I want to feel your soft pussy wrapped around me."

That's the only warning I'm given before he slides deep inside my body with one swift movement. A gasp escapes from me before ending on a drawn-out moan that echoes off the walls.

"Fuck," he growls.

With every piston of his hips, pleasure reverberates throughout my entire being. It sparks to life deep in my core before resonating outward to the very tips of my fingers and toes as he holds my head firmly in place.

When my eyelids feather closed, he growls, "Open them. I want you to watch as I fuck you so you know exactly who's getting you off."

As if I could ever doubt it.

His gaze stays pinned to mine as he fucks me against the wall. Water pours from the shower head, misting us as the thick humidity wraps around us, cocooning us in warmth. It doesn't take long before I'm falling apart, splintering into a million jagged pieces that will never be put back together again.

He quickly follows me over the edge. His cock jerks as warmth floods my womb. The feel of his hard flesh throbbing inside me with nothing to stand between us is unbearably intimate.

His breathing is harsh as he rests his forehead against mine and stares into my eyes. "I didn't like seeing you with that guy."

Honestly, I'd forgotten all about Sawyer and the Kiss Cam.

"It didn't mean anything."

"I don't care. I didn't like it. I didn't like him parked next to you during my game and I sure as shit didn't like watching him take your mouth."

When I remain silent, his palms tighten around the sides of my head before tipping my face upward so that there's no other choice but to meet his eyes. "I don't want anyone else touching you, Juliette. Period."

Warmth ignites in my chest before spreading outward. "Are we setting conditions? Is that what we're doing now? Because I don't want anyone else touching you either."

"Done." Tension ebbs from his voice and body as he presses his lips to mine. "Let's get out of here. One time wasn't nearly enough."

The man hasn't even pulled out of my body and he's already talking about sliding back inside.

"McAdams, you still here?" a deep voice calls out, echoing off the tile.

I freeze as my eyes widen at the gruff male voice that comes from somewhere within the locker room.

Ryder's lips lift into a smirk as his gaze stays fastened to mine. "Yup. Still in the shower."

"All right. Hit the lights on your way out."

"Will do, Coach."

Footsteps fade before a door in the outer area closes.

"Guess you can cross sex in a public place off your list."

"I suppose so," I say with a smile before pressing my lips against his.

CHAPTER 28

RYDER

*E*veryone grabs their empty trays from the table. Just as Bridger swings around, his gaze gets snagged by something. The easygoing expression he'd been wearing throughout lunch vanishes as a fierce look flares to life in his eyes. I glance over my shoulder at the chick who's glaring just as intensely at him.

Huh.

Well, that's interesting.

Normally, Bridger has the opposite effect on the ladies. That thought is only reconfirmed when she lifts her hand and flips him off before stalking away.

I glance back at him with a raised brow. "Let me guess, that's your number one fan?"

He snorts. "Sure looks that way."

"What happened? You take her to bone town, and she was less than impressed with the ride?"

His upper lip curls. "Something like that."

"Don't most of the girls you screw feel that way? I'm sure there's enough of them to start a club or, at the very least, a support group." I jerk my head toward the chick who has disappeared through the crowded Union. "That one can be the president."

"Hey, I have an idea—why don't you fuck off."

A smile stretches across my lips. "You first."

Now it's my turn to be treated to a one-fingered salute before he saunters away. Although, he takes off in the opposite direction of the girl with his tray in hand.

"What's his problem?" Ford asks, staring after our teammate. "It's like there's a giant stick wedged up his ass."

Colby slips his phone from the pocket of his jeans before pulling up a message from Western.

Except...

It's not the official kind we get regarding the university.

My brows pinch together as I scan the photo of Bridger making out at a party with a chick and the caption beneath it.

Look what the son of Chancellor Sanderson is getting up to this weekend. A different night, a different puck bunny. Sometimes more than one. Eww. My advice to the groupie in this photo as well as all the others—get tested ASAP. God only knows how many STIs this manwhore is spreading around campus.

My eyes widen. "What the fuck is that?"

Colby shrugs. "Dunno. There was a different one that hit my phone last week as well. His father lost his shit and summoned him into his office to rip him a new one. He's been in a crap mood ever since."

My hand rises to scratch the scruff on my jaw. "Whoever hacked into the university system and posted that BS must be tech savvy."

"I'm sure Coach caught wind of it as well."

I wince. "That's almost worse than his dick of a father."

"Yeah. I know my way around a computer pretty well, but even I couldn't pull off anything like this," Colby adds.

Just as I grab my tray, a flash of long dark hair catches my attention and my gaze slices to Juliette as she walks through the Union. The sight of her is like a punch to the gut, and the force of it nearly steals my breath away. My reaction to her has always been visceral, but now it's even more so.

Now I know exactly what she feels like beneath my hands. And the floral scent of her skin when I bury my face against the delicate hollow of her throat. I know exactly how it feels to have my cock surrounded by her tight heat and the way her inner muscles clench, milking every last drop from my dick when she orgasms.

Even thinking about it is enough to have a semi stirring in my jeans.

"Hey, you coming or what?" Colby asks, shifting his weight and raising a brow.

I force my gaze back to him. "Nah. Go without me. There's something I gotta take care of."

"All right. See you at practice."

"Yeah, later."

As soon as he takes off, I dump the tray and beeline for Juliette. She hasn't caught sight of me yet. Anytime she's around, everything else falls away until she's all I'm cognizant of. I've been with my fair share of girls, and none of them have ever made me feel this way.

When it comes down to it, none of them have ever made me *feel*.

Period.

Just her.

But isn't that one of the reasons I've always steered clear? Because I knew deep down that everything would be different with Juliette?

She glances up from her phone as I pull up alongside her.

"Hey." It's so damn tempting to haul her into my arms and press her close. To bury my face in her hair and inhale a giant breath. It never fails to calm the inner turmoil roiling beneath the surface.

Fuck.

"Hi."

Instead of giving in to temptation, I ask, "What are you up to this afternoon?"

"I have class in twenty minutes. I was just about to grab a coffee at the Roasted Bean."

"Blow it off and let's do something." The words are out of my mouth before I can fully think them through.

"You want me to skip class?" There's a pause as surprise morphs across her features. "Now?"

When she continues to stare like I've grown a horn on my head, I shrug. "Why not? It's on the list, isn't it?"

It takes a second or two before she admits, "Yeah. But..."

"You do realize the world won't end just because you don't show up to one class, right?

She shifts before sucking the fullness of her bottom lip into her mouth and chewing it. "Are you sure about that?"

My gaze drops to the movement and my cock twitches. Where she's concerned, it doesn't take much. I want her all the damn time.

"Yup, positive. Come on, spend the afternoon with me," I cajole, wrapping my fingers around hers so I can play with them. I don't give a damn who sees us. I just care about...

Her.

I just care about Juliette.

Fuck.

Her eyes soften as she gives in. "Okay. What do you have in mind?"

Before I can respond, she says with a spark of humor dancing in her eyes, "Let me guess, I'll have to wait and see."

With a quick grin, I tow her from the building.

CHAPTER 29

JULIETTE

*E*ven after we make a quick pitstop at my apartment and then his house to grab gloves and a hat, Ryder refuses to tell me what he has up his sleeve. In all honesty, I don't care. I just enjoy spending time with him. It doesn't matter what we do or where we go.

The way he looks at me sends shivers careening down my spine and makes my belly do a little flip flop. It's impossible to imagine another man rousing these kinds of feelings within me.

I'm trying to temper my expectations. Even though he demanded exclusivity, I'm not sure what that means, and I'm hesitant to ask for clarification. I want to ride this wave for as long as possible before it comes to its inevitable end. Then, I'll pick up the fragmented pieces of my heart and glue them back together again the best I can.

Until then, I try not to focus on it.

There are only two more items on the list.

Skip class (number nine), which is what we're doing right now. So, that one will definitely get checked off when I return home.

And number five, a romantic date.

I blow out a steady breath, unable to imagine Ryder planning something like that. We're not actually going out. When sadness tries to push in at the edges, I ignore it. The last thing I want to do is dampen my mood. It takes effort to force myself back to the present as Ryder pulls the truck into the gravel parking lot of a local outdoor skating rink that's open during the winter months.

After killing the engine, he swivels toward me. "You've been awfully quiet. Already having regrets about not attending bio stats?"

I force a bright smile, refusing to admit the truth. I'm sure Ryder's more than used to girls falling head over heels for him.

The last thing I want to be is one of them.

"No. I just need to text Aaron tonight and ask for notes."

"Aaron?" I can almost see the wheels in his brain spinning. "Isn't that the guy you kissed in the hallway?"

"If you mean the kiss you interrupted outside my door, then yes."

"You still haven't thanked me for saving you from that unfortunate situation," he says with a snort.

I arch a brow. "Who said I wanted to be saved?"

A low growl erupts from him as he slides his hand around the back of my head and drags me forward. A second later, his lips crash onto mine before his tongue thrusts inside my mouth.

Like the other night in the locker room, it's forceful and possessive. As if he's trying to prove exactly who I belong to. Just as I grow lightheaded from lack of oxygen, he pulls away enough to search my eyes and nip my lower lip with sharp teeth. He sucks the fullness into his mouth before releasing it with a soft pop.

"You were saying?"

"Thank you," I whisper.

One side of his mouth hitches. "That's what I thought."

Even though it's early afternoon, there's a dozen or so people on the ice. A few older couples, some parents with preschool aged children, and then a few high school kids.

"You ready?" he asks.

"As I'll ever be."

We exit the vehicle before meeting up around the hood. When he reaches out and snags my fingers with his own, I can't resist dropping my gaze to our clasped hands. A month ago, I couldn't have dreamed of this happening and now...

Here we are.

My heart clenches.

I don't want this to ever end.

"Do you remember how to skate?"

I shake that disturbing thought away before running my tongue across the front of my teeth. "It's been a while. I'm sure I'll be rusty, which actually means I'll probably fall on my ass a lot."

"Guess it's a good thing you have a professional with you."

I quirk a brow. "A professional, huh?"

"Yup." He tugs me to him before dropping a kiss against my lips.

I never realized just how affectionate Ryder is. When I've caught sight of him around campus with other girls, they've always been the ones hanging on him.

Not the other way around.

We stop at the little wooden shack and grab a pair of rental skates before settling on a bench. Then, we slip off our shoes and slip on the skates, making sure to lace them up tight.

"It's funny," I muse. "Skating has never been a huge part of my life. Dad had me take lessons when I was a kid and asked if I wanted to play hockey, but I never had any interest."

Once he's finished, he rises to his feet and extends a hand for me to take hold of. "I remember you spending a lot of time at the arena when you were a kid."

"Yup. Anytime Mav had practice, we were there. I always made sure to bring lots of books to read. Once I was older, I'd bring home-work and study on the bleachers, or I'd grab a snack at the concession stand and work at a table in the lobby. It wasn't so bad."

"Most of my childhood memories involve you, one way or anoth-er," he admits softly.

I glance at him. "Same."

Our gazes stay locked as his hand tightens around mine and I rise to my skates.

Just when I think he might continue the conversation, he says, "You ready to do this?"

"I hope so."

As soon as we hit the ice, my muscles tense, and I wobble. He pulls me closer before wrapping an arm around my waist and whispering against my hair, "I won't let you fall. Promise."

I release a steady breath and force myself to relax. Hopefully what they say is true and this is just like riding a bike. With each pass, my strides lengthen and the breeze rushes past my cheeks as I slowly pick up speed. It's not long before my movements begin to feel more natural.

"You doing all right?" he asks.

A wide smile spreads across my face. "Yeah. It's actually kind of fun."

He squeezes my hand. "Good."

We fall into a comfortable rhythm as we circle the oval sheet of ice in the center of town. There's something strangely freeing about being on skates. It's kind of like flying.

A couple of people point and stare when they recognize Ryder.

It's not difficult.

He has a presence about him. Especially with the long blond hair and natural ability on the ice. During the season, his picture is plastered in the papers or on the Western University athletic home page.

"Has the situation with your coach gotten any better? You haven't mentioned it lately." Not even when we almost got caught in the locker room shower.

The way his smile fades makes me wish I hadn't broached the subject.

"It's fine, I guess."

This time, I'm the one squeezing his fingers, wanting to offer comfort and support. "I'm sorry."

"It's fine. I'm trying not to get in my head about it." His voice turns wistful. "I wish it were possible to go back to last season when hockey felt more like a reflex rather than me second guessing every move I make on the ice."

"It will. You just need to keep playing your game. That's all."

One side of his mouth hitches as his gaze fastens onto mine. "You think so?"

"Yeah, I do. You're such a talented player. I have no doubt that Chicago will sign you after graduation."

"I really hope that's the case. I don't know what I'll do if it doesn't pan out."

Before I can say anything more, he tugs my fingers, drawing me closer until he can wrap his arms around my body. I gasp when he lifts me off my feet so that our faces are scant inches apart.

"I don't want to talk about hockey," he mutters, his warm breath drifting over my lips.

"Then maybe you shouldn't have brought me to a skating rink."

He grins. "Probably right about that. I just thought it would be fun."

"It has been." Actually, it's been a blast.

He holds me close as we circle the rink. "Ready to take a break? Maybe get a cup of hot chocolate?"

"That sounds amazing."

With me still wrapped up in his arms, he skates to the edge of the ice before jumping onto the rubber mats and then carrying me to the bench to change back into our shoes. Ten minutes later, we both have cups of cocoa in hand and are sitting near a gas fire pit as orange flames dance and twist in the air. The heat wafting off of it feels so good and the fire is mesmerizing. One of Ryder's arms is wrapped around my shoulders and my head is tucked against his chest as we sip our drinks.

I don't think I've ever felt happier.

That's when I realize I'll be crossing off number five after all.

In fact, I couldn't have envisioned a more perfect date.

CHAPTER 30

RYDER

*M*y eyelids crack open, and it takes a couple of seconds to remember where I am.

Juliette's room.

I glance down only to find her curled up beside me. Her dark hair is spread out around her. Unable to resist, I pick up a lock and caress the silky strands before twining them around my finger. They're as dark and shiny as a raven's wing.

There were so many years when I yearned to do exactly this. When I wanted to reach out and stroke my hands over her any damn time I craved it.

When I wanted to be the one who could claim her.

Not once did I ever believe those fantasies would come to fruition.

Hell, I never thought she'd look sideways at me.

I mean, come on. The girl is gorgeous and so fucking smart she makes my brain hurt. She could be or do anything she wanted in this world. All the choices are hers to make. Not once did I think I'd be one of them. That I was anywhere near good enough for her. Even though this relationship has barely begun, I don't want to let her go.

I want to keep her with me.

I want this to grow into something more.

Air leaks from my lungs as those thoughts churn through my brain.

This is the first time I've ever wanted something permanent.

And Juliette?

She doesn't think this is a relationship. If you asked her, she'd say that I'm helping her check items off a list. Somehow, I'll have to convince her that this is so much more than either of us anticipated.

But I'll have to be cagey about it.

Maybe trick her into thinking we're just casually chilling and then, when the time is right, I'll spring it on her that this is a relationship and lock her ass down tight.

I glance at the clock on the nightstand. It's not even six in the morning and already my brain is spinning.

This is exactly what that girl does to me.

Before I can concoct a solid plan, I decide to use the bathroom. It's carefully that I ease from the bed so as not to wake her before rising to my feet. I can't help but glance at the pretty picture Juliette makes. The sheet has slipped down her chest and her delectable nipples are clearly on display. My mouth waters as a tortured groan rumbles up from my chest with the need to suck the rosy little tips into my mouth.

The second I return, that's exactly what I'm going to do. Then I'll slip deep inside the heat of her body. Even the thought is enough to stiffen me right up.

I scour the floor for my boxers before spotting them crumpled in the corner. We came home last night and immediately tore each other's clothing off before falling into bed and making love twice.

That thought is enough to give me pause.

When have I ever considered sex love?

Never. Not one damn time.

My gaze slides back to Juliette as she continues to snore softly, oblivious to the thoughts circling through my brain. Her cupid's bow of a mouth is parted as her chest rises and falls rhythmically. That's all it takes for my heart to clench, squeezing so hard it becomes painful, because that's exactly what it was.

For the first time in my life, I didn't have sex.

I made love.

I was more concerned with her orgasm and giving her every bit of pleasure that I could than getting off myself. Those thoughts are like a revelation as I drag a hand over my face and swing away, heading toward the door.

Looks like we'll be having that convo sooner rather than later. I need her to realize this is serious.

We're serious.

Decision made, I crack open the door and peek into the hallway. Until we sit down and hash out the state of our relationship, I need to keep this on the down low. Although, moving forward, that'll need to change. I don't want to continue sneaking around like we have something to hide. In the beginning, it was all fine and good.

Kind of fun.

But now?

I want everyone to know that Juliette belongs to me.

I'm her man.

Me.

Not that family friend who was eyeing her up like she's a sweet treat.

He needs to lose her number and never talk to her again.

I give my head a slight shake to clear it of these thoughts. Never in my life have I experienced even a whiff of jealousy where a female was concerned. It just goes to show you how different my feelings for Juliette are.

With those thoughts circling through my head, I slip inside the bathroom and take care of business before washing my hands and then putting a small dollop of toothpaste on my finger and scrubbing it over my teeth. When they're passably clean, I rinse my mouth out. The quickest way to turn someone off is with dragon breath.

I open the bathroom door, ready to head back to Juliette's room and wake her up with my dick, only to stumble to a halt as Carina leans all casual-like against the doorjamb with her arms crossed against her breasts. Her blonde hair is mussed and tumbling wildly around her shoulders.

"Well, well, well," she says almost conversationally even though the expression on her face is anything but. "Isn't this a surprise."

I raise my brows. "A pleasant one, I hope."

My attempt to lighten the mood with a bit of humor falls flat.

Her eyes narrow. "That has yet to be determined."

Before I can say anything else, she straightens to her full height. Carina is tall. Probably somewhere in the vicinity of five foot ten. She takes a step forward and invades my personal space before stabbing a pointed finger at my bare chest.

"You hurt that girl, and I'll come for you. Understand?" She cocks her head. "You don't even want to know what I'll do. But rest assured, you'll never be the same again."

I gulp. Carina can be scary when she wants. Like now. "Isn't it a little early in the morning to be threatening my manhood?"

"It's never too early for that. And make no mistake, it's not a threat. More like a promise of retribution."

I hold up my hands in a gesture of surrender. The last thing I want is for her to get ramped up. "I'll do everything in my power not to hurt her, all right?"

She pokes me a second time, but it lacks the previous aggression. "Better not. Now get out of my way, I need to use the bathroom."

I quickly step aside and extend my arm. It's tempting to tell her that I'm not the one who initiated this convo, but I'm afraid she'll drill her finger into me for a third time. I have a feeling that what she already did will leave a mark.

With one last glower, she closes the door behind her. I shake my head and slip back inside the bedroom. My gaze immediately falls to Juliette.

And her naked breasts.

So fucking delectable.

Already my mouth is watering for a taste of her.

All of her.

She's seriously sweet all over.

As I beeline toward the queen-sized bed, my gaze flickers to the nightstand. When a folded-up piece of paper catches my eye, I pivot at the last moment. I know exactly what it is. There's a screenshot on my phone.

And to think…

That list is what sparked everything between us.

Seems crazy.

Even though I have the damn thing memorized, I reach out and pick up the paper before carefully unfolding the sheet and staring at the list. My gaze slides over each number.

Bucket List for College

1. ~~Make out at the library~~
2. ~~Skinny dip~~
3. ~~Karaoke~~
4. ~~Get drunk at a party~~
5. ~~Romantic date~~

My heart swells when I see that she crossed off the romantic date. Honestly, I hadn't been thinking about it when I took her to the outdoor rink. I'd just wanted to spend a little time alone with her.

6. ~~Orgasm~~
7. ~~Dance at a club~~
8. ~~sex in a public place~~
9. ~~Skip class~~

And then it stutters painfully when I see the very last item has been ticked off, even though we agreed to remove it from the list.

10. ~~Fall in love~~

My wide gaze flies to her. She's still snoring softly and sleeping soundly.

Does that mean she actually…

Loves me?

I didn't think that was possible.

I mean, sure…I have those feelings for her. Even though they were buried deep down inside where I couldn't dwell on them, I've loved this girl for as long as I can remember.

"Juliette?" Her name comes out sounding hoarse, as if it's being choked from my body.

With a lazy stretch, her eyelids flutter open. A soft smile tugs at the corners of her lips when her sleepy gaze locks on mine.

"Morning," she says, voice all low and husky. It only twists my insides up more.

My gaze stays fastened to her as I hold up the list. "Everything's been ticked off?"

She blinks. I can almost see her trying to play mental catchup and the exact moment it hits her. When she props herself up on her elbows, the sheet slides even further down her torso until it crumples around her waist.

All that creamy flesh on display isn't nearly enough to distract me from discovering the truth.

Her expression turns cautious. "Yes."

It feels as if my throat is closing up as I push out the question. My heart thuds a painful staccato against my ribcage until it echoes in my ears. Any moment, it's going to bust free and flop around on the carpet at my feet. "You love me?"

A deafening silence falls over us before she straightens her shoulders and lifts her chin an inch or so as a steeliness enters her voice. "Yes, I do."

Every muscle weakens until it feels like my knees will turn to jelly. "I love you too."

Her eyes widen and her mouth pops open. *"You do?"*

Shock colors her expression as I carefully fold up the list and set it on the nightstand before slipping beneath the covers and gathering her up into my arms.

"Honestly? I don't remember a time when I didn't love you."

"I...don't know what to say."

I press a kiss against the tip of her nose before pulling her closer. "You don't need to say anything."

And then I do what I've been aching to since I woke up twenty minutes ago and make love to her.

CHAPTER 31

RYDER

I rap my knuckles against the frosted glass door before poking my head inside the cramped space. The muscles in my gut constrict. It's almost comical that there was ever a time when sauntering into this office and plunking down on a chair felt normal.

Enjoyable, even.

Now?

It's anything but.

I fucking hate getting called in here. If it were possible to avoid Reed Philips for the remainder of the season, I'd do it in a heartbeat.

I clear my throat. "You wanted to see me, Coach?"

He glances up from the computer before waving me in. "Yeah." Then he points to the chair parked in front of his desk. "Have a seat."

It takes effort to force my feet into movement. It feels like those last couple steps are a slow march to my impending doom.

My gaze slides over the interior, mentally taking note of the changes since Coach K packed up all his shit and left me high and dry. There are photos of this new guy with the NHL teams he played with. Framed articles, memorabilia, awards, along with a smattering of family photos.

One in particular catches my eye. It's a glossy eight by ten of him with a dark-haired woman who looks to be around the same age and a petite younger girl wearing a glittery skating outfit. All three have their arms wrapped around each other as they beam at the camera. The girl holds up a gold medal that hangs from a thick ribbon around her neck.

He has a daughter who's an ice skater?

Interesting.

My gaze slides back to him as I drop onto the vinyl chair.

Unlike with Coach K, there's zero camaraderie. He's just a guy who's come in and blown my world to shit. I can't help but wonder if he even realizes the catastrophic damage he's inflicted with his mere presence.

Better yet, would he care?

Doubtful.

It only makes me dislike him more.

I just want this season over with and then…

I guess we'll see where the chips fall.

With a frown, he drums his fingers against the metal desktop as he continues to stare. The uncomfortable silence that stretches between us is brutal.

Just when I begin to squirm, he clears his throat. "You know, when I took this job, I spent hours talking with Coach Kasminski. He gave me a rundown of all the guys. Even the new players he'd recruited the previous year. He knew exactly where everyone in this program fit in. And I respected that."

Yup, that sounds exactly like Coach K, and it only makes me miss him more.

His serious gaze bores into mine. "You were a big part of those plans."

Unsure what to say, I fold my arms across my chest and remain silent. Kind of sounds like he's going to launch into one of those *I couldn't be more disappointed* speeches. Quite frankly, after the rough season I've had, I don't need it. All this guy has done since day one is fuck with my head.

"And I watched enough of your game film to know that he wasn't wrong. You're a talented defenseman. I can understand why Chicago wants you."

I'm sorry...what?

The unexpected compliment has my brows snapping together in confusion.

"But I'm not seeing that translate onto the ice."

Ah. There it is.

That's more of what I was expecting.

"So tell me, what happened? Why aren't you playing at the level we both know you're capable of?"

That softly spoken question feels like someone pulling a plug until I'm deflating before his very eyes. I can only slump in my chair as that question circles viciously around in my brain before dragging a hand down my face. "I don't know what's going on."

As difficult as it is to admit, even privately to myself, he's not wrong. I'm not playing at the same level as last season. My game is off.

When I remain silent, lost in the chaotic whirl of my thoughts, he continues. "That's something you need to figure out. Your performance needs to improve. You're better than what you're showing me out there and we both know it. The problem is that Chicago knows it too. I don't need to tell you how important this season is in regard to your future. The last thing I want is to apply more pressure."

Yeah, well...it's a little too late for that.

Sometimes it feels like the entire fucking world is resting on my shoulders.

And him acknowledging it doesn't make it better.

Only heavier.

More soul crushing.

"You've been distracted. And I get it. You're young and this is college. It's the last year before you play in the pros or find a job."

A pit the size of Rhode Island takes up residence at the bottom of my belly. The thought of Chicago not signing me after graduation makes me gut sick.

"There's school and hockey," he continues. "That's it. Eliminate the other distractions."

When I open my mouth to argue, he holds up a hand and cuts me off.

"I don't want to hear it. Bullshit will always creep in at the edges. You're to the point where you need to decide what's important and that's what you focus on. If you're out partying every weekend, knock it off. At least until you get your shit figured out."

"Yes, sir," I mumble. There's no point in arguing.

"And if you ever pull that BS on the ice again, I'll bench you." His steady gaze stays pinned to mine. "Do I make myself clear?"

"Crystal." I glance down at my hands as they twist together in my lap. "I'm sorry about that. It won't happen again."

"I'm going to hold you to that promise."

When there's another knock on his door, I pop to my feet, ready to get the hell out of here.

One of the assistants sticks his head into the office. "Hey, Coach. You got a minute?"

"Yup. McAdams was just on his way out."

No need to tell me twice.

"Thanks, Coach," I say as I cross over the threshold.

"No problem." There's a pause. "And Ryder?"

I grind to a halt and meet his eyes. "Yeah."

"If we got off on the wrong foot at the beginning of the year, I apologize for that. This position has been a transition for everyone. I want you to know that my door is always open if there's anything you want to talk about. All right?"

For the first time since he summoned me into his office, the tension in my shoulders drains and the corners of my lips hitch.

"Thanks. I'll keep it in mind."

He nods. "You do that. Now get out of here."

As I walk into the locker room, everything Coach said circles through my head. Ever since I was a kid and fell in love with hockey, it's been my number one priority. What I've recently realized is that there's more to life than school and the sport I love.

There's Juliette.

Now that we're finally together, the last thing I'm going to do is fuck it up.

But Coach is right.

All the other bullshit needs to go.

CHAPTER 32

JULIETTE

I yank open the door to the Union and rush through the entryway. Even with a winter jacket, scarf, and hat, I'm still chilled to the bone. The temperatures have dropped, and the wind is whipping through campus. The heat from the building isn't nearly enough to warm me.

It's a little before noon and the place is already packed with students looking to grab lunch before afternoon classes start up again. As I scan the tables, looking for Mom and Dad, I catch sight of Brooke and her boyfriend, Crosby. A smile lights up his face as he swallows up the distance between them and playfully nips at her neck. She squeals in response before shoving him away. Laughter simmers from both of them.

As soon as my gaze locks on Brooke's, she lifts her arm in a wave. I return the greeting. Seeing them together makes my heart sigh. They're so perfect for each other.

And to think…

It wasn't all that long ago that she was dating his roommate, Andrew. Or, as I like to call him, Andrew the douche. At that point, she and Crosby couldn't stand each other. Could barely tolerate being in the same room together. It just goes to show you how quickly everything can change.

I suppose Ryder and I are a perfect example of that. We've never really been friends and now...

Now I can't imagine my life without him in it.

I refocus my attention on Brooke and her friends. The table is packed with football players and their girlfriends. Demi and Rowan, Sydney and Brayden, Sasha and Easton, Elle and Carson. And then there's Asher Stevens.

There's more than one girl vying for his attention.

I've known most of these guys since freshman year, and a good number of them have always been players. Now that they've found girlfriends, that's all changed.

Well, except for Asher. Looks like he's the last holdout.

I don't realize I'm staring until our gazes catch. He gives me a chin lift along with a smirk. We had a few gen ed classes together sophomore year and have always been friendly.

Would I ever consider dating the guy?

No way in hell.

Plus, I don't think he actually dates. He more or less likes to spread the love around, if you know what I mean.

I shoot him a smile and continue on my way before spotting Mom and Dad at a table off to the side near a large picture window. Even though Mav isn't here yet, a handful of his teammates are crowded around Dad. Everyone knows who he is, and a few are even repped by his management agency.

Mom quickly rises to her feet and pulls me in for a warm embrace. She's always been affectionate but is even more so after battling cancer. It's like she wants everyone in her life to know just how much they mean to her and how loved they are.

For just a second, I squeeze my eyes tightly closed and sink into her warm embrace before unwrapping myself and giving my father a hug.

"Hey, pretty girl. How's everything going?" Dad asks.

"Good. How about you?"

"Can't complain. Work's keeping me busy as usual."

I drop my bag to the tile floor near the table and unzip my black puffy jacket. Ford, Madden, and Riggs give me chin lifts in greeting. They've always been nice, treating me more like a sister than anything else.

Wolf shoots me a smirk.

He's always been friendly, but there's something about him that seems almost dangerous. Because of that, I've always been cautious where he's concerned. He's kind of like a lion lounging on a sunny rock, biding his time. It lulls you into a false sense of security before he leaps and rips your jugular out.

Or maybe I'm letting my imagination run wild. What I do know is that the guy is a force to be reckoned with on the ice. He's one of the best goalies playing Division I hockey. Like Ryder, he entered the draft during his sophomore year in college and was picked up by Milwaukee. Once he graduates, he'll sign his contract and play professionally.

"Hey, little McKinnon," Colby says with a smile. One flick of his baby blues and girls drop their panties, no questions asked.

I can't help but flash him a smile. It's tempting to pinch his dimpled cheeks. "You realize that I'm the older sibling, right?"

"I meant in stature," he shoots back easily.

Well, he's got me there. Next to these guys, I'm a pipsqueak.

All of them say goodbye to my parents before taking off. Heads swivel as they saunter through the Union.

I pull out a chair and take a seat. "Where's Mav? Isn't he meeting up with us for lunch?"

Mom searches the crowded space before pointing toward the entrance. "Speak of the devil, he just walked in."

The guys all knock fists with Maverick on the way past before he hugs Mom and settles next to me. Since our parents arrived earlier, they grabbed a few sandwiches, two soups, and a couple salads along with drinks.

Mom glances around the Union before meeting Dad's gaze. "It doesn't seem like all that long ago when we were at college, does it?"

"Tell that to my joints," Dad grumbles. "Some days I wake up and it feels like I'm eighty."

Mom's lips quirk. "I know, but still...sometimes it feels like yesterday."

His eyes soften before he reaches out and squeezes her slender hand. "You look the same as you did then."

She snorts before smiling. "Nice try."

"I'm serious. You're just as beautiful as the day we met."

When they lean in for a kiss, Mav makes a few gagging noises. "If you two start going at it, I'm leaving."

A smile simmers around Dad's lips. "How do you think you and your sister got here?"

"Jesus..." Mav mutters. "Are you trying to make me lose my appetite?"

Mom chuckles before passing out the sandwiches and giving us all a choice of soup or salad. Our parents opt for the salads and Mav and I grab the containers of soup. The bowl is still steaming when I lift the spoon to my lips.

They try to stop by campus once a month to have lunch or take us out to dinner. During hockey season, it's easier to grab something in the afternoon between classes rather than work around Mav's practice and game schedule.

"How's it going with the new coach?" Dad asks.

Mav jerks his shoulders. "The guy was a real hardass when he first came in, but now that we're a month into the season, he's beginning to mellow."

Dad nods before musing, "I played against Reed Philips in college and when he was in Chicago. He was one hell of a player back in the day."

"Did they have helmets way back then, old man?" Mav asks, lips twitching.

"Hardy har har. You're hilarious."

He smirks. "I try."

"I spoke to him last week about a couple of players I'm representing, and then we talked at length about Ryder."

I pause before taking a bite of my sandwich as Dad continues. "I'd assumed that playing another year in college would help solidify his confidence, but it's had the opposite effect. I think Kasminski leaving and Philips coming in has messed with his mojo. He needs to get his head on straight if he wants Chicago to sign him.

Surprised by the comment, I blurt, "Do you really think there's a chance they'd drop Ryder?"

Dad's serious gaze settles on mine. "I don't know. The season has just gotten underway and there's still a lot of time, but knocking that guy against the boards after the play was over wasn't a smart move. No one wants to pick up a loose cannon. I know Cal and Sadie are concerned. He's talented. I'd really hate to see Ryder not play professionally."

I've never heard my father express concern for Ryder's future. A thick lump settles in the middle of my throat as my appetite pulls a disappearing act.

When I remain silent, Dad refocuses his attention on my brother. "You haven't noticed anything going on with him, have you?"

Mav's gaze flickers to mine for a heartbeat before locking on our father. "Nope. Nothing at all."

"I'll reach out tonight and talk to him. Maybe see what's going on."

I stare at my half-eaten sandwich as talk turns to Maverick's classes and how they're going. Like Dad, Mav was diagnosed with dyslexia in elementary school. As soon as he showed signs of struggling when learning to read, they had him tested and hired private tutors. It was never something that was looked upon as a disability. He just learns differently. Sometimes that means accommodations or modifications. For as long as I can remember, getting my brother to sit down and study or complete homework has been a challenge.

It still is to this day.

He'd much rather be on the ice than stuck in a classroom.

Ever since Maverick was old enough to skate, Dad would flood part of the backyard during the winter months to make a small rink where he could go and practice after finishing up his homework. It was the perfect incentive.

Sometimes our parents would lace up their own skates and we'd all fool around before heading indoors to sit by the fireplace and sip mugs of hot cocoa. Those memories of our childhood are some of the most cherished ones I have.

Mav would have pickup hockey games with kids from the neighborhood. Maybe Ryder and I weren't friends back then, but he was always there, part of my life.

Mom reaches out and lays a hand over mine. "You've been awfully quiet. Is there something on your mind?"

I force a smile, unwilling to admit the truth about my relationship with Ryder. "I was just thinking about how we would have pickup games in the backyard."

Her expression turns wistful as she squeezes my fingers. "Oh, I miss that."

"Me, too."

Dad and Mav continue talking about the season and the Wildcats' upcoming schedule as my mind once again turns to the blond hockey player.

And what I need to do.

CHAPTER 33

RYDER

I spot her dark head from twenty yards away as she moves through the flow of student traffic and pick up my pace. I'd know Juliette anywhere. For as long as I can remember, I've been attuned to her presence. Almost like she was already a piece of me. Fighting my desire for her has always been a losing battle.

I have no idea how I lasted this long without laying hands on her.

Thank fuck I don't have to keep my distance anymore.

Her dark hair has been pulled up into a messy bun at the top of her head, leaving the nape of her neck bare. My fingers itch to pull the elastic from her hair so that it falls around her shoulders and down her back in a thick curtain. I love wrapping the silky length around my fist until it becomes necessary to arch her spine when I'm fucking her from behind. The thought of being inside her tight heat is enough to have me popping wood.

Even when I'm buried deep inside her body, all I can think about is the next time I'll be able to do it. When we're joined together, the world around me falls away and it's just the two of us. I don't have to think about school or hockey. I can just focus on Juliette. She eclipses everything else in my life.

I almost stumble as that thought circles in my head, because it's one hundred percent true. Nothing matters more than she does.

Not even hockey.

And that's a frightening prospect. Nothing and no one has ever mattered more than my chosen sport.

It's my reason for living.

For breathing.

Who am I without it?

I have no idea.

What I do know is that Juliette sees more than just hockey when she looks at me. She sees all the possibilities that I'm unable to. Because of that, the future doesn't seem quite so scary with her by my side.

It only takes a handful of seconds before I eat up the distance between us. People call out my name as I jog past, but I don't pay them any attention. How can I when she's in the vicinity?

As I pull alongside her, my fingers fasten around her smaller ones as I tug her close. I just want to bury my face in the delicate hollow of her neck and breathe her in. I want to take her mouth and not come up for air for hours. The need I feel for her is unlike anything I've ever experienced before.

A gasp escapes from Juliette as I haul her into my arms, and she quickly glances around. One palm settles on my chest as she gives me a slight shove. "Ryder, we're in the middle of campus. Anyone could see us."

I shrug. "Why do we have to hide our relationship? Maybe we should bite the bullet and tell our families. Do you really think they'd have a problem with it?"

Then I could touch her any damn time I wanted, and people would realize that she belonged to me. The first order of business is to get her a jersey with my name on it so she can start wearing it.

That would get the word out quickly.

I make a mental note to pick one up at the campus bookstore before the next game.

Her eyes widen as surprise morphs across her features.

"In fact," I say, warming to the idea, "we could all go out after Thursday's game. We'll spring it on everyone then. What do you think? Does that sound like a plan?"

She sucks her lower lip into her mouth and chews it as we continue moving along the wide path that cuts through campus.

One heartbeat passes and then another.

When she remains silent, a prickle of unease blooms in the pit of my belly as I steer her onto the grassy knoll so we're no longer caught up in the flow of student traffic.

"What's wrong?" My brows pinch together as I search her face. I really thought she'd be on board with this. She's never been someone who likes to hide things or be less than truthful. Especially with her family. The four of them have always been tight knit.

Kind of like my own.

She draws in a steady breath before slowly forcing it out again. "Nothing's wrong."

There is. I can tell by the way her eyes flicker away as if she's unable to hold my gaze.

"It feels like there's a but coming," I say carefully.

There's a flash of emotion on her face before she forces her eyes to meet mine. I'm unsure what the look in them means.

Or maybe I do, and I'm hoping like hell that I'm wrong.

"I think we might be moving too fast." Her voice trails off on a whisper.

It takes a heartbeat or two for her soft words to fully sink in so that my brain can make sense of them.

"Too fast?" I echo as if from far away. It's like I'm staring at her through a long tunnel. Where we used to feel so close, she's nothing more than a distant speck on the horizon.

"Yeah. I think this relationship is moving a bit too quickly and we should take a step back. A little space will do us both some good."

"Space?" I wince as I echo another word.

Sorrow fills her eyes as she jerks her head into a tight nod. "With finals coming up, I need to focus. I received a low B on one of my tests and that's never happened before. This is such an important year. I don't want to see anything get in the way of either of us reaching our goals, you know?"

What I hear is that Juliette doesn't feel the same way as I do. If she did, there's no way in hell she'd be willing to take a step back from our relationship or spend any time apart.

"I guess," I mutter, feeling like a humongous asshat.

She reaches out and wraps her fingers around mine. "It's not what I want, but I think it's what we both need. I don't want either of us to have regrets."

I hear what she's saying loud and clear. She needs to focus on what's important.

FYI—that's not me.

Even though it feels impossible to clear the thick emotion clogging my throat, I force myself to say, "I know how much med school means to you, and I don't want to get in the way of that."

"And I don't want to derail hockey or your dreams of playing in the NHL," she says softly, blinking away the tears that sting her eyes, making them look shiny in the sunlight.

I drag a hand through my hair and glance away, staring at the red brick building that looms in the distance. When I caught sight of Juliette ten minutes ago, I never imagined this was how our conversation would play out. It's so damn tempting to argue. To tell her that we can find a way to balance everything in our lives.

We don't have to let this go.

Or walk away.

But…

I refuse to do anything that will jeopardize her future. She's worked too hard to get where she is. Whatever her dreams are, I want her to achieve them.

Whether they include me or not.

That's the bitch of it, right?

Only now do I understand that loving someone means putting their wants and needs ahead of your own.

"Okay."

I force my gaze back to hers. There's so much heartbreak swirling through her dark depths.

I don't understand it.

She's the one breaking up with me.

Not the other way around.

With our gazes locked, I force myself to take a step away. Just as I'm about to take another, my hand snakes out and my fingers wrap around her wrist before hauling her into my arms. As soon as my lips crash onto hers, she opens enough for my tongue to slip inside and tangle with her own. The sweet taste of her floods my senses and pounds through my veins.

How am I going to go without this for the rest of my life?

Part of me expects her to fight the intimate embrace, but that doesn't happen. Instead, she clings to me as if she's in just as much pain as I am.

Again, it makes absolutely no sense.

I have no idea how long we kiss.

Minutes?

Hours?

All I know is that it's not enough.

It'll never be enough.

It takes every ounce of self-control to sever the physical connection. Instead of pulling away completely, I rest my forehead against hers and stare into her eyes. Before she can tell me to back off or how sorry she is about the breakup, I swing around and stalk away without a second look.

And that, more than anything, just about kills me.

CHAPTER 34

JULIETTE

"*T*hanks again for the ride," I tell Carina, standing near the driver's side window with my overnight bag in hand. "Sure you don't want to come in and stay for dinner?"

She shakes her head. "No, I've got some studying to do and a piece of choreography that needs work. I'll see you tomorrow morning."

"Sounds good."

For just a moment, I watch her sleek BMW pull out of the circular driveway before I swing away and head to the house. I push open the heavy front door and glance around the double story foyer before calling out, "Mom? Are you home?" My voice echoes off the cavernous walls.

Her silver Range Rover is parked in the drive, so I'd just assumed she was here. Maybe I'm wrong.

"Jules?" Her surprised voice floats down the hallway. "Is that you?"

"Yup." I peel off my jacket before draping it over the banister and then toeing off my Converse.

She peeks her head out from the spacious kitchen at the back of the house. "I wasn't expecting you to show up this afternoon. What's going on?"

I shrug and force a smile. "What? I can't pop home to see my parents without something being wrong?"

She wipes her hands on a dishtowel as she closes the distance between us. "Of course you can, honey. Any time you want."

When she reaches out and tugs me into her arms, I go willingly, resting my head against her strong shoulder. I'm just a smidge taller than she is.

"Come on, Jules. Tell me what's going on," she whispers against my ear. She's always had a sixth sense about these things.

I shrug, unsure if I want to open up that particular can of worms. There's so much she doesn't know. So much I've been keeping from her. Now that Ryder and I agreed to back away from our fledgling relationship, there doesn't seem much point in rehashing the situation.

When I remain silent, she pulls away enough to search my face before threading a slender arm around my waist. "Come talk to me while I finish preparing dinner."

That's when the tantalizing aroma of beef and mushrooms hits me. It's enough to make my mouth water. "Stroganoff?"

"Yup."

"That's one of my favorites."

She gives me a wink. "Your dad's, too. I remember the first time Grandma Karen made it for him. I thought he was going to lick the plate clean."

That image does the impossible and has the corners of my lips lifting into a smile.

Once inside the spacious kitchen, I settle at the marble island while Mom adds a shake or two of salt and pepper to the stroganoff.

"What can I get you to drink?" she asks.

"Just water, please."

She grabs a glass from the cupboard before filling it from the dispenser on the fridge and setting it down in front of me. Then she preps a colander of green beans, chopping off the ends and rinsing them in the sink before filling a stainless-steel pot with water and setting it on the stove.

"All right, spill." She glances up and catches my gaze. "Tell me what's going on. Did something happen with Carina?"

I scrunch my face and shake my head. "Of course not. I can't even remember the last time we had a disagreement." Unless of course, it's about how I spend too much time studying and not enough going out and living my best college life.

"Is it school?"

"No." I draw in a lungful of air before reluctantly admitting, "Although, I did get a B minus on an exam the other day."

"Did you talk to the professor and go over the exam, so you understand where you went wrong?"

"Yeah. I made a few careless mistakes."

She glances at me. "Doesn't exactly sound like a problem then."

"No, I guess not," I murmur in agreement, muscles incrementally loosening.

"You don't have to be a straight A student for your father and I to be proud of you." There's a pause. "You understand that, right?"

"Yup." I've always known it. They're not the ones who put all the pressure on me.

I am. It's one hundred percent internal. It's something I realized in high school. I'm the one who sets high standards for myself.

Not them.

And I'm the one who beats myself up when I'm anything less than perfect.

As I lift the glass to my lips, she says, "Then it must have something to do with Ryder."

My hand pauses midair as my eyes flare wide. "What?" My voice comes out sounding choked.

Her expression never falters as her steady gaze stays pinned to mine. "I assume if it's not school or your roommate, then whatever's going on has something to do with Ryder."

"Why would you say that?" I whisper.

With a smirk, she shakes her head. "Because I have eyes and I've seen the way you two have been looking at each other." There's a pause before she tacks on, "Especially lately."

My mouth tumbles open. *"You have?"*

"I've always seen the way he looked at you, Jules. The way he'd stare when he thought no one was watching. It was sweet."

Those comments have my throat closing up, making it impossible to breathe.

"So, I'm right? This has something to do with Ryder?"

"Yeah."

"Were you two seeing each other?" she ventures with a guess.

"For a little bit, but I broke it off."

Her brows draw together as she pauses her prep. "How come?"

I jerk my shoulders and shift restlessly on the stool. "I don't want to be a distraction. You heard Dad at lunch. Ryder needs to be one hundred percent focused on hockey." Even though it hurts my heart, I force out the rest. "Not me."

She sets the knife down on the plastic cutting board before rounding the massive island and slipping onto the stool next to me. "You're absolutely right. Ryder needs to focus on his priorities. But I think you're one of them, sweetie. And that's not a decision you should make for him. He's a grown man." There's a lengthy pause as she searches my eyes. "I made a similar mistake when your father and I got serious. I broke up with him because I'd thought I was making the right decision, and you know what? It turned out to be the wrong one. For both of us."

"You did? Really?" This is one part of their story I've never heard before. I'd assumed that once they got together it was all roses and rainbows.

Her expression grows solemn. "Yup. It's one of the worst mistakes I ever made."

I lean closer. "How did you resolve it?"

"Once I finally realized what I'd done, I booked a ticket to Milwaukee. Then I tracked him down at the hotel where he was staying with your grandfather and begged him to forgive me."

My lips lift as I imagine the scenario playing out. Mom rushing through an airport and then hauling ass to the hotel. "Since you've been married for almost twenty-five years, I assume he forgave you?"

A chuckle escapes from her before she sobers. "He did. But I could have easily ruined the best relationship of my life because I allowed outside influences to get in my head. What I should have done was sit down and discuss the situation with him like a grown adult."

Everything she just admitted churns inside my brain. Even though I'd been so sure I was making the best decision for both of us, now I'm not so sure.

"Do you think I made a mistake?" I ask softly, almost afraid of the answer.

Her hand flutters over mine. "I don't know. That's something you'll have to decide for yourself."

I release a steady breath until my lungs are completely empty. For the first time since I broke off my relationship with Ryder, I feel like I have clarity. "Thanks, Mom."

As she pulls me in for another hug, the door in the mudroom bursts open before slamming shut as Dad's loud voice booms throughout the kitchen.

"I smell stroganoff! My guess is that someone's looking to get lucky tonight!"

Mom presses her lips together as her shoulders shake with silent mirth.

Just as Dad rounds the corner, he grinds to an abrupt halt when he catches sight of me in Mom's arms.

"Oh." He glances from me to Mom and then back again as a dull flush crawls up his cheeks. "Well…this is certainly awkward."

Unable to contain ourselves any longer, we burst out laughing.

CHAPTER 35

RYDER

I toss my stick into the holder before unsnapping the strap on my helmet and yanking it off my head. My practice jersey is the next to go before I rip off the pads and toss them inside my locker. Even though the past couple of days have sucked major ass, practice has gone better than expected. The talks I had with both Coach and Brody have helped me to find my footing once again. Instead of second guessing every move I make, I try to follow my instincts and play with the confidence I've always had on the ice. Once I started doing that, everything else seemed to fall back into place.

Am I still making mistakes?

Yeah.

But not like before. I'm not freezing up and dumping the puck. I'm able to slow the game down in my head, evaluate my choices and make the best decision I can.

It's a relief.

More surprising than that, Coach actually complimented me. The first time it happened, I nearly stumbled and ate the ice.

And school's fine. I'm passing all of my classes. I've never been an A student. But I have a solid B GPA and I'm good with it.

So, yeah…

I should be flying high.

The problem is that I'm not.

In fact, I've never felt lower.

I drop onto the bench to unlace my skates. As I do, someone grinds to a halt in front of me. I don't have to glance up to know who it is. I'd recognize Maverick's scuffed-up Bauers anywhere. The guy could afford the best ones money could buy every six months if he wanted.

He doesn't.

Mav is superstitious. It's not all that uncommon for a hockey player. He's been using the same practice jersey since last year, even though we have new ones. If he wears a pair of socks and wins a game, then he'll keep wearing them until we lose.

And no, they don't get washed.

It's gotten to the point where they can sometimes stand up on their own.

Fucking disgusting.

He's had these particular Bauers since freshman year of college. Thankfully for him, his feet stopped growing senior year of high school or he'd have a real problem on his hands. Brody's tried telling him that he's a talented player and it has nothing to do with luck.

Mav refuses to listen.

In fact, his lucky penny is glued to the bottom of his left skate.

Heads up.

When he shifts his weight and clears his throat, I finally glance up and meet his gaze. "Yeah?"

He crosses his arms over his broad chest and glares. We've been friends for a long time. Because of that, it only takes one look for me to know what's on his mind.

"What the hell did you do to my sister?" he growls just loud enough for me to hear as laughter and chatter explodes around us now that practice has ended.

I almost bark out a laugh.

Me?

What the hell did *I* do?

Is this guy serious?

"Not a damn thing."

He narrows his eyes. "She's been upset. And I think it has everything to do with you."

I glance around at our teammates who are stripping off their gear to hit the showers before dropping my voice. "Just so you know, she's the one who broke up with my ass. Not the other way around."

Surprise flickers across his face. Guess he wasn't expecting that bomb.

"You do something to piss her off?" Even though he cocks his head, he sounds a little more unsure of himself.

I huff out a tired breath. "No, I didn't. In fact, I told her I wanted to come clean with our families. That I was tired of hiding our relationship." The words shoot out of my mouth before I can stop them. It only makes me sound more pathetic, and that's the last thing I need.

The remaining anger drains from his expression and he hesitates before dropping down beside me on the bench. "How long was something going on between you two?"

"About a month." Although, it felt much longer.

In my heart, it's always been Juliette. Mav can't possibly understand that.

"Do you care about her?"

I drag a hand over my face before waving it around the locker room. "Are we really doing this here?"

A smile quirks the corners of his lips as humor sparks in his eyes. "Yup."

"Fine," I grumble. "I care about the girl. I've always cared, but I didn't think she'd ever give me the time of day." I give him a bit of side eye before admitting, "She's too damn smart for me."

He nods in agreement. "That's just straight-up facts."

A grunt escapes from him when I ram my elbow into his side.

"What the hell was that for? All I did was agree with you," he says with a chuckle.

"It wasn't necessary. I'm more than aware of the situation."

"All right, so what are you gonna do? Just let her walk away?"

Yeah…that was the plan.

I mean, she's the one who broke up with me.

I arch a brow. "You think I shouldn't?"

He presses his lips together before jerking his shoulders. "I don't know, man. It kind of seems like you're just as mopey as she is. So, if neither of you want to be apart, then maybe you should be together."

Even though he makes a fair point, I need time to think it through. As much as I want Juliette in my life, I need to do what's best for her.

Am I what's best?

That would be the million-dollar question.

CHAPTER 36

JULIETTE

*N*erves dance at the bottom of my belly as Carina and I walk up the concrete stairs to where both my parents and Ryder's are camped out in the bleachers. We stopped at the concession stand on the way in. So, my roomie is set for the game with a box of popcorn and a drink.

I hug my parents and then greet Sadie and Cal. I've known them for as long as I can remember and they're like second parents to me. I love how close our families have grown throughout the years. When Mom was sick, Sadie cooked meals for us and brought over a diffuser to use with essential oils that were supposed to help with nausea and pain.

As soon as Carina and I settle on our seats, she immediately digs into the popcorn before holding out the box. I shake my head as my knee bounces a steady tempo. The game hasn't even gotten underway, and I already feel sick to my stomach. The buttery saltiness will probably make me throw up all over the place.

After a couple of minutes tick by, she leans closer. "Are you certain about going through with this?"

Hell, no.

At the moment, I'm not sure about anything. I could end up

making a huge ass out of myself in front of an arena full of fans. And you know damn well that people will whip out their cell phones to video the entire thing.

With my luck, it'll go viral.

That thought makes me nauseous.

For all I know, Ryder has moved on.

Or worse, I really hurt him, and what I say won't mean a damn thing.

I'll have single-handedly thrown away the best relationship I've ever found.

Or will find.

The fear that grips me is almost paralyzing. Thick emotion clogs my throat as the Western Wildcats take to the ice, circling their half for warmups. As soon as Ryder skates past our seats, my gaze latches onto him. He's the only thing I'm cognizant of.

I've missed him so much that my heart aches.

My gaze licks over him greedily as he skates by. It feels more like weeks or months rather than days since I last laid eyes on him. It doesn't make sense that I've known him my entire life and we barely had anything to do with each other, and in the span of a few short weeks, he's become my everything.

"Are you all right?" Carina asks softly.

I rip my gaze away from Ryder long enough to meet her concerned eyes before they bounce back to him. Not once has he glanced in this direction, and I know that has everything to do with the fact that I'm sitting here. He understands that no matter what happened between us, there's no way I'd miss Maverick's game.

"I think so."

"When were you planning on doing it?"

I jerk my shoulders and gnaw my lower lip. "I'm not sure. When the time feels right, I guess." That thought has a horde of angry butterflies winging their way to life inside the confines of my belly. Any moment, they'll escape.

"Do your parents have any idea what you're up to?"

I shake my head.

"Well, this should definitely be interesting," she says, tossing another piece of popcorn into her mouth.

That's the least of what it will be.

After fifteen minutes, both teams return to their benches and the lights dim. A spotlight falls in the center of the arena as music blasts throughout the building. The visiting team roster is announced first. The atmosphere becomes even more amplified as the Wildcats take to the ice one player at a time. The hometown crowd goes wild, cheering and clapping.

Bright light once again floods the large space as the first lines for both teams take their positions. Ryder skates to the blue line. All the insecurities he's admitted over the past few weeks circle through my head. More than anything, I want him to have a good game and find the same kind of joy he used to have while playing hockey.

The puck is dropped and both centers fight for possession. At first, our team has it, but then the small black disk is knocked loose and stolen by the other team's right wing as he races down the ice. Ryder skates backward, keeping his attention focused on the guy. Air gets trapped in my lungs as the other player attempts to deke him out, faking one way and then the other.

Ryder leaps forward, his blades digging into the ice as he knocks into him. The puck goes flying as they scrabble over it. Everyone in the stands jumps to their feet and cheers as Ryder scoops up the small black disk and takes off, flying across the ice. He winds up, looking like he'll try to place it in the upper left corner of the net. When the goalie starts to slide, Ryder pivots to the right. But it's too late for the goalie to catch it, and the puck whizzes past him before hitting the back of the net.

The fans filling the arena go crazy.

A horn blasts as Ryder slows, circling around the back of the net. Even from the stands, I can see the grin lighting up his face. It's not uncommon for a defensive player to score, but it's been a long time for him, and I couldn't be more thrilled. What I notice throughout the rest of the game is that he plays with more confidence. I don't know what finally clicked in his head, but I'm happy for him.

Just as the buzzer rings, signaling the end of the third period, the players clear the bench and swarm the ice. The Wildcats pulled off another win. Ryder gets a bunch of slaps on the back from his teammates.

I draw in a lungful of air to steady my nerves before quickly unzipping my jacket and tossing it to my seat so that my McAdams jersey with Ryder's number is clearly visible. Then I hold the poster-board I'd rolled up and carried into the arena.

The sound of my heartbeat fills my ears like the dull roar of the ocean as a few of his friends catch sight of me before nudging him and pointing. His eyes widen behind the cage as he slowly skates toward the bleachers and comes to an abrupt halt in front of me. My heart kicks up its tempo, slamming painfully against my ribcage. Heat floods my cheeks as people swivel and stare. A cartoon figure of a wildcat dancing on the jumbotron is replaced by livestream feed of me.

Holding my sign with shaky hands.

Bile gurgles up in my throat.

There's no question about it—I'm definitely going to be sick.

This was a mistake.

Had I been thinking clearly, I would have texted instead to see if we could meet up for coffee and talk. I wouldn't have publicly humiliated myself by trying to make a grand gesture to win him over.

I'm not sure how I'll ever show my face around campus again.

Ryder's gaze stays pinned to mine as his smile blooms into more of a grin. He taps his chest twice before pointing a gloved hand at me. When cheers go up, my knees weaken until it feels like I'll slide to the sticky concrete beneath my feet.

"Breathe," Carina says, pitching her voice just low enough to be heard over the roar of the fans. "He's totally into it."

For the first time in days, I flash her a grateful smile as relief pumps through my veins.

It doesn't take long for the crowd to disperse. Most head for the exit and into the crisp night air. People will definitely be out en masse celebrating at the bars tonight. Dozens of friends and family wait for the players to shower and change. Small groups of girls wearing jerseys are there as well.

I chew my nails, impatient for Ryder to make an appearance. The moment he walks out of the locker room, my heart kicks into overdrive. His expression remains inscrutable as his gaze locks on mine.

What if he changed his mind?

What if he wants to let me down easy so that I'm not publicly humiliated in front of ten thousand spectators?

The more distance he eats up with his long-legged strides, the more nauseous I become.

When we're only a handful of steps away, my tongue darts out to moisten my lips. I need to get in front of this.

Now.

"Ryder—"

Before I can force out the rest, he captures my fingers with his larger ones and tugs me close until I'm pressed against the steely wall of his chest. Then he lifts me off my feet and spins me around in a tight circle until I'm dizzy.

As soon as he grinds to a halt, his mouth crashes onto mine. When his tongue steals across the seam of my lips, I open so that they can dance and mingle. Everyone around us fades away until the only person I'm aware of is Ryder and how good it feels to be back in the warm circle of his arms.

I've missed this so much.

I've missed *him* so much.

Just when it feels like my lungs will burst, he pulls away enough to search my eyes.

"So, you're sorry and you love me, huh?"

"I am, Ryder. I'm so sorry for hurting you. I thought I was doing what's best for both of us. The last thing I want to be is a distraction, but nothing feels right without you."

His eyes soften. "Say it again."

"I love you."

"I love you too."

He rests his forehead against mine and stares deep into my eyes. It would be all too easy to drown within their blue depths.

It's only when someone clears their throat from beside us that we splinter apart. Although, Ryder hauls me against him as if he'll never let go.

Dad arches a brow as he folds his arms across his chest.

Ryder straightens to his full height. "I probably should have been upfront with you about what was going on with your daughter. If you no longer want to represent me, I understand." He glances at me, and his arm tightens, pressing me closer. "But I'm not breaking up with Juliette."

When he falls silent, my dad narrows his eyes. "Is that so?"

The younger man lifts his chin and holds his ground. "Yes, sir. It is."

"All right, I guess there's only one thing to say—"

I wince and steel myself for what's about to come. Mom knows about my relationship with Ryder, but I failed to mention anything to my father.

"It's about time you got your head out of your ass where my daughter's concerned."

My eyes widen as my mouth falls open.

Ryder blinks before a slow grin slides across his face. Then he stretches out a hand and shakes my dad's. "Does that mean we have your blessing to see each other?"

My parents share a look before he says, "I wouldn't think of trying to keep you apart."

"Seems like this night is one for celebrations. Let's grab dinner and make it official," Cal says with a slap to Dad's shoulder.

"How about Taco Loco?" Sadie throws out and everyone agrees.

"All right. We'll all meet up at the restaurant," Dad says. "Last one there foots the bill."

As everyone heads for the exit, Ryder and I hang back, needing to steal a moment alone.

He presses his lips to mine again before whispering, "I would much rather take you home and make love to you."

"Me too, but there's no way we can bail on our parents."

He glances at them. "Nope. It'll have to wait until after."

I reach onto the tips of my toes and whisper, "Did I happen to mention that I started another one of Carina's books and there was a pretty interesting position I wouldn't mind trying out?"

He groans before smacking another kiss against my lips. "Are you sure we can't just ditch them? We could always say that you have a headache or something."

My lips tremble around the edges as I shake my head. "Yeah, it's doubtful anyone would buy that."

"I think you might be trying to torture me," he grumbles.

With a shrug, I nip his lower lip between my teeth and give it a gentle tug. "Maybe."

"Maybe my ass. You're definitely trying to torture me. But you know what?"

I raise my brows in askance.

His voice softens and his expression grows serious. "It doesn't matter, because I love you."

"I love you more. And I have a sign that proves it."

Before I can say anything else, he sweeps me up into his arms and carries me out of the arena.

And yeah...we end up at Taco Loco for an hour or so before heading home, where Ryder makes sweet love to me.

CHAPTER 37

RYDER

The house is jampacked as we move through the first floor. My arm is draped around Juliette's shoulders. What I've found is that I can't keep her close enough. Even when we're having sex, it's never enough.

I want closer.

I want everything with this girl.

I always have.

And now she's mine.

It might have taken a while, but Juliette McKinnon belongs to me. And if I have anything to say about it, that's the way it'll stay. I kept my distance for years until it was no longer possible. And then I did the only thing I could and claimed her as my own.

Thank fuck she claimed me right back.

"Love you, babe," I whisper against the outer shell of her ear.

She turns her face until our gazes can lock and hold. A smile simmers around the corners of her lips.

"I love you, too."

Her softly spoken words have the power to settle something deep inside me.

It's like that every time.

Breaking eye contact, Juliette glances over her shoulder at Carina and the new guy she's been seeing. He's a douchey baseball player. Justin something or other. As far as I can tell, the guy seems kind of full of himself. All he does is talk about baseball. His stats and how great he is...blah, blah, blah.

For fuck's sake, he's not even in season.

Chill out, man.

"Let's get something to drink," Justin shouts before plowing his way toward the kitchen and dragging Carina behind him like a ragdoll. She glances at Juliette before shrugging and going with the flow.

Once she disappears through the sea of people, I ask, "How long do you think this one will last?"

Juliette narrows her eyes and scrunches her nose. "Hopefully, not long. I don't particularly care for him. Brooke is friends with a girl on the soccer team who he cheated on."

Not a surprise.

"Did you tell Carina about it?" I ask with a popped brow.

"Not yet, but I will." She presses her lips together before admitting, "The guy is kind of an ass."

"Really?" I say with a snort. "I hadn't noticed."

A chuckle erupts from me when she whacks me on the chest.

It takes about ten minutes before we finally make it to the kitchen. Everyone is there and having a good time. Luckily, the party isn't too rowdy or out of control. This hasn't turned into a clothing-optional evening and no one's putting on a sex show in the living room.

Some of these people just don't care about having an audience.

Or maybe that's the kind of thing they're into.

It's the sound of raised voices over the music that pulses throughout the first floor that catches my attention. Fights erupt here just as often as they do on the ice. These are a bunch of guys who are used to throwing punches.

Hell, I've thrown a few myself.

My gaze sweeps over the packed space until it lands on the guy Carina brought with her.

And Ford.

I should have known this would happen. Even though all these two do is bicker, their wicked barbs seem more like foreplay than genuine dislike.

Ford glares at the ballplayer. "What the fuck are you doing here, Fischer?"

The other guy's jaw stiffens as he takes a drink of his beer. "I was invited."

"Who the hell did that?"

He wraps an arm around Carina before smiling at Ford. "Carina did."

I lean closer to Juliette before muttering, "You realize that if these two get into it, I'm gonna have to jump in, right?"

The corners of her lips wilt.

Ford straightens to his full height before flicking a glance at Carina. "She shouldn't have done that. This isn't her party. Maybe you should do us all a favor and take off."

Justin drags her even closer before pressing his lips against the side of her face. "Nah. Don't think I will."

Just when it seems like all hell will erupt, Ford's gaze swings back to Carina and he grits out between clenched teeth, "Can I talk to you outside?"

Her cheeks have pinkened from the near altercation. "Is that really necessary?"

"Yeah, it is." He jerks his head toward the back door. "Let's go."

She presses her lips together before glancing at the douche at her side. "Give me a minute and I'll be right back." Then she flicks a steely look at her ex-stepbrother. "Apparently, Ford has decided to be an inhospitable dick tonight."

"He's a dick every night," Justin says with a smirk.

Before she can say anything else, Ford locks his fingers around her wrist and drags her away from the other guy. The look he shoots over his shoulder at the baseball player is feral.

I shake my head as they disappear through the back door before glancing at Juliette. "Well, it looks like one crisis has been averted."

Even though Carina and Ford have vanished from sight, her gaze remains locked on the back hallway. "I wouldn't be too sure about that."

I snort.

She's probably right. It seems like tension has been ratcheting up between those two for months. Ever since we returned for senior year. Guess it'll be interesting to see if anything actually happens between them.

Dismissing the ex-siblings, I pull Juliette closer before pressing my lips against the crown of her head. Normally when the house throws a bash, I'm all about it. I've done my fair share of partying and screwing around with groupies, but as I scan the crowded space, I realize that I no longer have the same need. The person who truly matters to me is already in my arms, and as long as we're together, life is good.

I got the girl.

I got hockey.

And good friends who have my back.

What more could a guy ask for?

EPILOGUE

JULIETTE

*ix months later...*

I SMILE at Dr. Ashford as I hand over my final exam for medical microbiology and hightail it from the lecture hall before pushing through the glass doors into the early May sunshine. For just a second, I pause at the top of the wide stone stairs and tilt my face toward the sun, allowing it to stroke over my flesh.

That was my last exam of the spring semester.

And college.

It's finally over, which feels surprisingly bittersweet. Carina and I have slowly been packing up our apartment, getting ready to move. I'm going to miss her like crazy. We've lived together for three years, and she's turned out to be my best friend. One I'll have for the rest of my life. Sometimes I have to remind myself that no matter where we are, we're only a phone call away.

I draw a deep breath into my lungs before jogging down the stairs. I'm supposed to meet up with—

"Hey Juliette!"

I swing around and find Aaron walking toward me.

A smile lifts my lips. "Hi."

It might have taken a month or so for our relationship to get back to normal, but it eventually happened.

"How'd the exam go?"

"It was hard, but all the hours we put in studying really helped. Thanks for the notes and prep material you created. You're the best."

He shrugs. "It wasn't a problem. Glad it was useful."

My gaze flickers away to search the grassy knoll and trees that dot the landscape for Ryder. We've been so busy with finals and packing that we haven't been able to spend much time together.

I'm impatient to see him.

Although, that's nothing new.

Just as that thought rolls through my head, I spot the muscular defenseman stretched out on a blanket with a paperback in his hand. Bright sunshine pours down on him. He's wearing a gray Wildcats hockey T-shirt that looks to be a smedium and black athletic shorts. All those delicious muscles on display are enough to have my feet stuttering to a halt as a punch of arousal hits me square in the gut.

All right, so maybe it hits a little lower.

It doesn't matter if my brain is fried from studying around the clock and a two-hour exam.

I want Ryder.

Just like always, the world around me melts away until he's all I'm cognizant of. My breath stalls as he turns his head and meets my eyes. As soon as our gazes lock, a slow smile spreads across his face and a horde of butterflies explodes in the pit of my belly.

"Juliette?"

It takes effort to blink out of the stupor that's fallen over me before forcing my attention away from my boyfriend to meet Aaron's muddy brown eyes. There's a lopsided smile on his face.

"Sorry. What did you say?"

"Just that I stand corrected about chemical attraction. You were right. It exists."

A blush hits my cheeks as a grin lifts my lips. "Yeah, it does."

And I'm proof of that.

His gaze flickers to Ryder as he takes him in for a second or two. "If he makes you happy, then everything worked out for the best."

"He does." More than anyone else ever could. More than I ever thought possible. I spent years looking for love and here it was, right beneath my nose.

Aaron leans a bit closer before dropping his voice. "So...does he have any buff friends who might be interested in going out with a nerdy med student?"

My eyes widen and I'm just barely able to keep my lower jaw from coming unhinged. After swallowing down my surprise, I say, "I'm not sure, but I'll check and get back to you."

"Excellent. Keep me posted."

With a nod, I throw my arms around his wiry form and hug him tightly. "I'm really going to miss you next year."

"Same."

We say our goodbyes before I beeline for Ryder. His gaze stays locked on me as I eat up the distance between us.

"Hey, babe," he says when I'm close enough. "How'd your final go?"

"I don't know. Hopefully, I passed."

His blue eyes spark with humor as he shakes his head. "Please. We both know you'll ruin the curve for everyone else."

Maybe. We'll see.

He sets the paperback down and I catch a glimpse of the cover. It's one of those pretty special edition ones that are so popular right now.

"I'm glad you're here. I was just getting to the good part." He waggles his brows. "Chapter twelve."

"Oh yeah?"

"Yup." His voice dips. "It's definitely giving me some ideas."

I drop down beside him before pressing my lips against his. "What kind of ideas?"

"The sexy kind," he growls.

His tone is enough to have my core dampening with need. "Those are the very best ones."

"They are, aren't they?"

"Maybe we should take this back to my place so we can explore them in more depth."

"Jeez, can't I go anywhere without seeing you two all over each other?" my brother yells from the cement path that cuts through campus.

We both turn and stare as he shakes his head in disgust. A couple of his teammates grin as they pass by. While Mav doesn't mind us being together, he has zero desire to see any PDA.

And I can't blame him for that.

Ryder's lips bow. "I think getting out of here sounds like an excellent idea."

It takes fifteen minutes to get back to my apartment. Thankfully, Carina is out, and we have the place all to ourselves.

And then Ryder makes love to me.

Several times.

And yeah…chapter twelve.

It's some good stuff.

SECOND EPILOGUE

RYDER

Two years later...

I drop my athletic bag in the entryway of our apartment and kick off my shoes. After being on the road for a ten-day stretch, it's good to be home again. I missed my girl.

Fuck, did I miss my girl.

The only thing I can think about right now is getting my hands on her.

Even though we FaceTimed as much as we could, it wasn't nearly enough. And it sure as hell isn't the same. There's nothing better than the feel of Juliette wrapped up tight in my arms.

Unless it's sliding deep inside her sweet heat.

Then, yeah, that's better.

Being inside her body is like coming home. And after a stint on the road, it's the first thing I want to do.

My guess is that it's the same for her.

"Jules," I call out, raising my voice to be heard throughout the three thousand square foot apartment that has amazing views of Lake Michigan. After graduation, Chicago signed me to a three-year contract.

It's one of the teams that Coach Philips played for. Our relationship might have started off rocky, but over the course of the season it improved drastically.

Was I as close to him as Coach K?

Nah.

But he's still someone I call for solid advice when I need it. Maybe he broke me down after my last coach left, but he also helped build me back up. If there's one thing I've learned through all of this, it's that adversity makes you stronger. Senior year ended up being one for the record books.

Hello, Frozen Four Championship.

Best damn way to end my college career.

My brows draw together when the apartment remains silent.

Is it possible she's out?

Maybe studying at the library?

Med school takes up a lot of Juliette's time, but she's thriving on the challenge. So far, my girl has straight As.

Disappointment floods through me at the realization that she's not home to greet me.

That's a first.

I pull out my cell and hit her number. It takes a couple of seconds for the call to connect. It rings in my ear before the distant sound comes from somewhere in the apartment.

I click it off and call out again, "Juliette, baby? Where are you?"

My steps quicken as I glance in the white marble kitchen with its gleaming stainless-steel appliances. It's a chef's wet dream. In Juliette's off time, she enjoys dabbling with recipes. She likes to tell me that cooking is kind of like science. It's all about following a formula. She's turned out to be pretty damn good—which is no surprise, since science is totally her thing.

But the kitchen is empty.

My gaze sweeps over the living room with its floor-to-ceiling wall of windows that look out over the blue depths of Lake Michigan. Million-dollar views, the realtor claimed when we toured the building. As soon as we walked inside, I knew it was the perfect place to start our lives together.

And I wasn't wrong.

The spectacular view is usually enough to calm me.

But not this time. Not when I don't know where my woman is.

I peek inside the study to see if she's camped out there but, just like the kitchen and living room, it's deserted. I loosen the tie from around my neck and walk into our massive bedroom. A noise from the bathroom draws my attention and I beeline in that direction. As I step over the threshold, my feet grind to a halt at the sight that greets me.

Juliette is stretched out in the massive porcelain tub. It's roomy enough for at least six people, which means that there's plenty of space to maneuver.

A groan rumbles up from deep within my chest as my gaze rakes over her naked body. Water laps at her rosy-tipped nipples. That's all it takes for my mouth to water and my cock to stir.

Damn, but I've missed her something fierce.

"Hey, baby," she says before bringing a glass of champagne to her lips and taking a sip. "I've been waiting for you."

When she extends the delicate stemmed flute, I take it and down the bubbly contents in one thirsty gulp.

"There's more," she says with a smile.

That's when I notice a dark glass bottle with an orange label sitting off to the side and a bowl of bright red strawberries.

My brows rise. "Planned a little romantic evening for us, did you?"

"Yup. I missed you while you were away." Her gaze slides down the length of my body. It feels more like a physical caress. "Are you going to take off your clothes and join me?" There's a pause before she rises from the water. "Never mind, I'll take them off myself."

My hungry graze roves over her nakedness. Juliette is so fucking beautiful. Especially wet with her long, dark hair piled high on top of her head. Her skin is all flushed from the warm water.

I set the flute down as she steps out of the tub. Rivulets of clear liquid roll down her delectable body before puddling on the thick bathmat. Unable to help myself, I reach out and pinch one stiffened peak. Arousal flares in her eyes as she steps closer before reaching out to slip the loosened tie from around my neck. It gets tossed onto the gray veined marble tile. The silk tie was an expensive gift from her last Christmas, and I usually take great care with it.

In this moment, I don't give a crap.

She unbuttons my pressed white shirt before parting the material and slipping it from my shoulders. Once the white T-shirt is discarded, she flattens her palms against my pectorals and strokes them across my chest.

There's nothing like the feel of her hands worshiping my body.

This right here is exactly what I've been craving.

Her palms make one last pass before settling on my belt. She loosens the silver buckle before starting on the button and then zipper. The material gets shoved down my hips and thighs before she sinks to the marble tile. I'm quickly divested of my wingtips, socks, and slacks until I'm in nothing more than my boxer briefs. From her position, she meets my eyes before rising to her knees. Her fingers settle around my rigid length through the cottony material before giving me a gentle squeeze. A few strokes later, she delves inside my underwear and tugs the fabric down until my cock can spring free.

Another groan rumbles up from my chest when she closes the distance between us and wraps her lips around the head of my dick before drawing it into the warmth of her mouth. Even though I want to keep my eyes open so I can stare at the pretty picture she makes, I can't.

The way she licks and sucks me feels too damn good.

I thrust out my hips, only wanting to feel the sweet suction. Just as she finds a steady rhythm, I gently push her away, knowing that if she keeps this up for much longer, I'll come in her mouth. And as much as I enjoy that, I want inside her pussy. I've been dreaming about it for days.

Ten to be exact.

Surprise morphs over her features as I reach down and lift her up until my mouth can settle over hers. Our tongues tangle. There's absolutely nothing sexier than the taste of myself on her lips.

"You cheated me out of giving you a proper greeting," she whispers, arousal bursting in her tone. "I've missed your cock." She nips at my lower lip, tugging it with sharp little teeth. "The vibrator isn't the same."

I groan, remembering the sight of her through the video as she spread her pretty thighs and let me watch while she pleasured herself.

Did I have to whack off a couple times after that?

Damn straight I did.

But it was totally worth it.

And do you know who we have to thank for that little suggestion?

Yup, a romance novel. It's not something I would have thought up on my own, and I have a pretty creative imagination. We have several shelves of sexy romance paperbacks in our study. Our collection might just rival Carina's.

It only takes a couple of long-legged strides to reach the counter where I carefully set her down before spreading her thighs wide.

"Fuck," I growl at the sight of her bare pussy.

She's so damn beautiful.

And mine.

This woman is mine.

She'll always be mine.

Deep down, I think she always belonged to me. Even when I was too young and stupid to realize it.

Thank fuck that's no longer the case.

My mind tumbles back to the bucket list she created before college. The one I found on her nightstand when I carried her home from that party.

That's all the prodding I needed to make her mine.

Unable to resist the lure of her for another moment, I press her legs even wider and hunker down until I'm eye level with her pussy. My dick throbs with the need to be buried deep inside her warmth.

We've been together for two years, and I understand exactly what she likes and what gets her off. I run the flat of my tongue from the bottom of her slit to the top before licking at her clit. The breathy sounds that escape from her tell me everything I need to know.

I spear my tongue inside her softness before repeating the maneuver. After about a minute, Juliette arches her spine with the need to get closer. As I nibble at her pretty little clit, her muscles tighten before she explodes. The way she chants my name over and over again is sweet music to my ears.

As soon as her orgasm fades, I press one last kiss against her swollen pussy before straightening to my full height. In one swift motion, I bury myself deep inside her welcoming body.

Only then does it feel like I can breathe again.

Less than a dozen strokes later, and I find my own release. My heart pounds a steady rhythm as stars burst behind my eyelids.

It's always like this when we're together, and I can't imagine it any other way.

When my breathing evens out, I open my eyes and stare into hers. Contentment fills her expression as I press our foreheads together.

"I love you, baby."

Her lips curve. "I love you, too."

"But I said it first, so I mean it more."

Her shoulders shake with silent laughter. "Is that so?"

"Yup."

"Promise that you'll always love me as much as you do now?"

"Damn right I will."

"Good. I can't imagine my life without you in it."

"You know I feel the same."

The need to hold her close thrums through me as I gather her up into my arms and carry her to the steaming tub of water before stepping inside and settling in the warmth. I reposition her until the back of her head can rest against my chest.

"Just in case you didn't realize it, you're my everything," I whisper. "The very reason I draw air into my lungs. *You.* And nothing will ever change that."

She turns her head just enough to meet my gaze. This time, when I slip inside her body, there is absolutely nothing frenzied or rushed about it.

I make love to her.

Slow and sweet.

Just the way she likes it.

* * *

Thank you so much for reading Hate You Always! I hope you enjoyed Ryder & Juliette's story as much as I loved writing it. Want a little more of Juliette & Ryder? Subscribe to my newsletter for a free bonus epilogue!

The Western Wildcats Hockey series continue with Carina & Ford!

One-click Love You Never now!

Want to read Natalie & Brody's story while you wait?
One-click Hate to Love You now!

"I LOVE Brody & Natalie! They're so adorable. Their sexual chemistry is off the charts.

Their witty banter is so hilarious and entertaining" -Chelsea, GoodReads

"I rarely give a book 5 stars, but this book was near perfect" -Oksana, GoodReads

Turn the page for an excerpt from Hate to Love You...

HATE TO LOVE YOU

BRODY

"*D*ude, I thought you'd be back earlier." Cooper, one of my roommates, grins as I walk through the front door. There's a half-naked chick straddling his lap. "We had to get this party started without you." He shrugs as if he's just taken one for the team. "It couldn't be helped."

I snort as my gaze travels around the living room of the house we rent a few blocks off campus. Even though there are only four of us on the lease, our place seems to be a crash pad for half the team. By the looks of the beer bottles strewn around, they've been at it for a while. I'm seriously thinking about charging some of these assholes rent.

Although, I guess if I were stuck in a shoebox of a dorm, I'd be desperate for a way out, too. I played juniors straight out of high school for two years before coming in as a freshman at twenty. I skipped dorm living and went straight to renting a place nearby. There was no way I was bunking down with a bunch of random eighteen-year-olds who'd never lived away from home. Not to mention, having an RA up my ass telling me what I could and couldn't do.

That sounds about as much fun as ripping duct tape off my balls.

Which is, I might add, the complete opposite of fun. Hazing sucks.

And for future reference, you don't rip duct tape off your balls, you carefully cut it away with a steady hand while mother-fucking the entire team.

My other two roommates, Luke Anderson and Sawyer Stevens, are hunched at the edge of the couch, battling it out in an intense game of NHL. Their thumbs are jerking the controllers in lightning-quick movements, and their eyeballs are fastened to the seventy-inch HD screen hanging across the room.

I can only shake my head. Every time they play, it's like a freaking National Championship is at stake.

I arch a brow as the girl on Cooper's lap reaches around and unhooks her bra, dropping it to the floor. Apparently, she doesn't mind if there's an audience. Cooper's lazy grin stretches as his fingers zero in on her nips.

I'd love to say this scene isn't typical for a Sunday night, but I'd be lying through my teeth. Usually, it's much worse.

Deking out Luke with some impressive video game puck handling skills, Sawyer says, "Grab a beer, bro. You can take over for Luke after I make him cry again like a little bitch."

"Fuck you," Luke grumbles.

I glance at the score. Luke is getting his ass handed to him on a silver platter, and he knows it.

"Sure." Sawyer smirks. "Maybe later. But I should warn you, you're not really my type. I like a dude who's packing a little more meat than you."

My lips twitch as I drop my duffle to the floor.

"Hey, you see that bullshit text from Coach?" Cooper asks from between the girl's tits.

I groan, hoping I didn't miss anything important while I was out of town for the weekend. I'm already under contract with the Milwaukee Mavericks. My dad and I flew there to meet with the coaching staff. I also got to hang with a few of the defensive players. Saturday night was freaking crazy. Next season is going to rock.

"Nah, didn't see it," I say. "What's going on?"

"Practice times have changed," Cooper continues, all the while playing with the girl's body. "We're now at six o'clock in the morning and seven in the evening."

Fuck me. He's starting two-a-days already?

"You think he's just screwing around with us?" I wouldn't put it past Coach Lang. I don't think he has anything better to do than lie awake at night, dreaming up new ways to torture us. The guy is a real hard-ass.

Then again, that's why we're here.

But six in the morning...that sucks. Between school and hockey practice, I already feel like I don't get enough sleep. And it's only September. That means I'll need to be up and out the door by five to make it to the rink, get dressed, and be on the ice by six. By the time eleven o'clock at night rolls around, I'll fall into bed an exhausted heap.

Sawyer shrugs, not looking particularly put out by the time change.

Cooper pops the nipple out of his mouth and fixes his glassy-eyed gaze on me. "Can't you have your dad talk some freaking sense into the guy?"

Luke grumbles under his breath, "I can barely make it to the seven o'clock practice on time."

"Nope." I shake my head. I'd do just about anything for these guys, except run to my father with anything related to hockey. Coach and my dad go way back. They both played for the Detroit Redwings. I've known the man my entire life. He helped me lace up my first pair of Bauers. So, you'd think he'd have a soft spot for me. Maybe take it easy on me.

Yeah...fat chance of that happening.

If anything, he comes down on me like a ton of bricks *because* of our personal relationship. I think Lang doesn't want any of the guys to feel like he's playing favorites.

Mission accomplished, dude.

No one would ever accuse him of that.

"Then prepare to haul ass at the butt crack of dawn, my friend."

With that, Cooper turns his attention elsewhere, attacking the girl's mouth.

Luke eyes them for a moment before yelling, "Hey, you gonna take that shit to the bedroom or are we all being treated to a free show?"

Not bothering to come up for air, Cooper ignores the question.

Luke shakes his head and focuses his attention on making a comeback. Or at least knocking Sawyer's avatar on its ass. "Guess that means we should make some popcorn."

I pick up my duffel and hoist it over my shoulder, deciding to head upstairs for a while. I love hanging with these guys, but I'm not feeling it at the moment.

"Hi, Brody." A lush blonde slips her arms around me and presses her ample cleavage against my chest. "I was hoping you'd show up."

Given the fact that this is my house, the chances of that happening were extremely high.

I stare down into her big green eyes.

"Hey." She looks familiar. I do a quick mental search, trying to produce a name, but only come up with blanks.

Which probably means I haven't slept with her recently.

When it comes to the ladies, I've come up with an algorithm that I've perfected over the last three years. It's simple, yet foolproof. I never screw the same girl more than three times in a six-month period. If you do, you run the risk of entering into the murky territory of a quasi-relationship or a friends-with-benefits situation. I'm not looking for any attachments at this point.

Even casual ones.

I'm at Whitmore to earn a degree and prepare for the pros. I'm focused on getting bigger, faster, and stronger. The NHL is no place for pussies. If you can't hack it, the league will chew you up and spit you out before you can blink your eyes. I have no intention of allowing that to happen. I've worked too hard to crash and burn at this point.

Or get distracted.

In a surprisingly bold move, Blondie slides her hand from my chest to my package and gives it a firm squeeze to let me know she means business.

I have no doubts that if I asked her to drop to her knees and suck me off in front of all these people, she would do it in a heartbeat. Other than a thong, the girl grinding away on Cooper's lap is naked.

My first year playing juniors, when a girl offered to have no-strings-attached-sex, I'd thought I'd hit the flipping jackpot. Less than five minutes later, I'd blown my load and was ready for round two. Fast forward five years, and I don't even blink at a chick who's willing to drop her panties within minutes of me walking through the door. It happens far too often for it to be considered a novelty.

Which is just plain sad.

When I was in high school, I jumped at the chance to dip my wick.

Now?

Not so much.

It's like being fed a steady diet of steak and lobster. Sure, it's delicious the first couple of days. Maybe even a full week. You can't help but greedily devour every single bite and then lick your fingertips afterward. But, believe it or not, even steak and lobster become mundane.

Most guys, no matter what their age, would give their left nut to be in my skates.

To have their pick of any girl. Or, more often than not, *girls*.

And here I am...limp dick in hand.

Actually, limp dick in *her* hand.

Sex has become something I do to take the edge off when I'm feeling stressed. It's my version of a relaxation technique. For fuck's sake, I'm twenty-three years old. I'm in the sexual prime of my life. I should be ecstatic when any girl wants to spread her legs for me. What I shouldn't be is bored. And I sure as hell shouldn't be mentally running through the drills we'll be doing when I lead a captain's practice.

I pry her fingers from my junk and shake my head. "Sorry, I've got some shit to take care of."

And that shit would be school. I have forty pages of reading that needs to be finished up by tomorrow morning.

Blondie pouts and bats her mascara-laden lashes.

"Maybe later?" she coos in a baby voice.

Fuck. That is such a turnoff.

Why do chicks do that?

No, seriously. It's a legitimate question. Why do they do that? It's like nails on a chalkboard. I'm tempted to answer back in a ridiculous, lispy-sounding voice.

But I don't.

I'm not that big of an asshole.

Plus, she might be into it.

Then I'd be screwed. I envision us cooing at each other in baby voices for the rest of the night and almost shudder.

"Maybe," I say noncommittally. Although I'm not going to lie, that toddler voice has killed any chance for a later hookup. But I'm smart enough not to tell her that. Chances are high that she'll end up finding another hockey player to latch on to and forget all about me. Because let's face it, that's what she's here for.

A little dick from a guy who skates with a stick.

Just to be sure, I run my eyes over the length of her again.

Toddler voice aside, she's got it going on.

And yet, that banging body is doing absolutely nothing for me.

Which is troublesome. I almost want to take her upstairs just to prove to myself that everything is in proper working order. But I won't.

As I hit the first step, Cooper breaks away from his girl. "WTF, McKinnon? Where you going?" He waves a hand around the room. "Can't you see we're in the middle of entertaining?"

"I'll leave you to take care of our guests," I say, trudging up the staircase.

"Well, if you insist," he slurs happily.

My bedroom is at the end of the hall, away from the noise of the first floor. As a general rule, no one is allowed on the second floor except for the guys who live here. I pull out my key and unlock the door before stepping inside.

My duffel gets tossed in the corner before I open my Managerial Finance book. I thought I'd have a chance to plow through some of the reading over the weekend, but my dad and I were on the go the entire time. Meeting people from the Milwaukee organization, hitting a team party, checking out a few condos near the lakefront. Just getting the general lay of the land. On the plane ride home, I had every intention of being productive, but ended up sacking out once we hit cruising altitude.

Three hours later, there's a knock on the door. Normally an interruption would piss me off, but after slogging through thirty pages, my eyes have glazed over, and I'm fighting to stay awake. This material is mind-numbingly boring, and that's not helping matters.

"It's open," I call out, expecting Cooper to try cajoling me back downstairs.

When that guy's shitfaced, he wants everyone else to be just as hammered as he is. I've never seen anyone put away alcohol the way he does. It's almost as impressive as it is scary. And yet, he's somehow able to wake up for morning practice bright-eyed and bushy-tailed like he wasn't just wasted six hours ago. Someone from the biology department really needs to do a case study on him, 'cause that shit just ain't normal.

When I suck down alcohol like that, the next morning I'm like a newborn colt on the ice who can't keep his legs under him.

It's not a pretty sight. Which is why I don't do it. Been there, done that. Moving on.

The door swings open to reveal Blondie-With-The-Toddler-Voice. And she's not alone. She's brought a friend.

I raise my brows in interest as they step inside the room.

In the three hours since I've seen her, Blondie has managed to lose most of her clothing. The brunette she's with appears to be in the same predicament. They stand in lacy bras and barely-there thongs with their hands entwined.

My gaze roves over them appreciatively.

How could it not?

Their tummies are flat and toned. Hips are nicely rounded. Tits jiggle enticingly as they saunter toward the bed where I'm currently sprawled.

I should be a man of steel over here. I haven't gotten laid in three weeks. Which is almost unheard of. I haven't gone that long without sex since I first started having it.

But there's nothing.

Not even a twitch.

Which begs the question—What the hell is wrong with me?

It must be the stress of school and the skating regimen I'm on. Even though I'm already under contract with Milwaukee and don't have to worry about the NHL draft later this year, I'm still under a lot of pressure to perform this season.

National Championships don't bring themselves home.

I'd be concerned that I have some serious erectile dysfunction issues happening except there's one chick who gets me hard every time I lay eyes on her. Rather ironically, she wants nothing to do with me. I think she'd claw my eyes out if I laid one solitary finger on her.

Actually, all I have to do is stare in her direction, and she bares her teeth at me.

Maybe these girls are exactly what I need to relieve some of my pent-up stress. It certainly can't hurt.

Decision made, I slam my finance book closed and toss it to the floor where it lands with a loud thud. I fold my arms behind my head and smile at the girls in silent invitation.

And the rest, shall we say, is history.

One-click Hate to Love You now!

CAMPUS GOD

BROOKE

"**G**irl, I'm in desperate need of a break," my bestie says as we hustle our way through the crowd of students traveling across campus like a herd of slow-moving cattle.

"Easton wearing you out already with all that sex?"

Sasha's eyes widen as she knocks her shoulder into mine. "What? Of course not!"

I grin as her face turns beet red.

Uh-huh, sure…

I know *exactly* what's going on in the room across from mine. Those two are so loud it would be impossible *not* to know. Although, I can't begrudge Sasha for finding her happily ever after and enjoying every moment of it.

That girl deserves it.

She's been crushing on her best guy friend since they were kids and didn't think there'd come a time when Easton saw her as anything more than his soccer-playing gal pal. But dreams really do come true, because here we are. They've been going strong for about a month now.

And it's all thanks to yours truly. I'm the one who pushed her into going out with my hockey-playing cousin, Ryder. That was all the prompting Easton needed to see her for the gorgeous woman Sasha has grown into. And the rest is relationship history.

They fit so perfectly that it's almost like they've been together for years. Two pieces of the same puzzle.

Am I a wee bit jealous of what they have?

Of course not.

All right, maybe a little. Who wouldn't want to be with a guy who looks at you like you hung the moon in the sky especially for him? That's exactly the way it is with Easton.

My last relationship ended in spectacular disaster. We're talking flames, plumes of black smoke, and no survivors.

Andrew Hickenlooper.

Football player.

More like all-around player.

We were together for almost a year when I'd learned that he'd been cheating.

A nasty chlamydia diagnosis was the ultimate tip-off. Imagine sitting on a table in a doctor's office, only to be told you had an STI. And since I wasn't screwing around on the side, I knew exactly where it had come from.

The only thing worse than that was when he tried to deny it. When that didn't work, he'd attempted to tell me that I caught it from a toilet seat.

Ummm…no.

It's not called a sexually transmitted infection for nothing.

The situation jackhammered to an all-new low when I found out that almost everyone at Western knew he was screwing around behind my back, and that it had been going on throughout most of our relationship. I won't lie, for a few minutes, I'd considered transferring colleges.

But here's the thing—I didn't do anything wrong.

Even though it wasn't easy, I held my head up high and ignored all the ugly gossip until it eventually died down. Now, if Andrew would take a hint and leave me alone, I could finally put the whole nasty mess behind me, where it belongs.

"You might not have noticed, but the walls in our apartment are paper thin."

"Oh, god," she groans, cheeks growing more flushed with every step we take.

I can't resist the chuckle that slips free.

"If we could go to his place, I would. But you know what it's like over at the football house. Constant parties and cleat sniffers looking to get laid. I'd prefer to keep them away from my man."

"Like you have anything to worry about. That guy only has eyes for one girl and that's you, my friend."

It's sweet.

The smile that blooms across her face tells me that she knows it as well. Just as she opens her mouth to respond, strong arms wrap around her from behind and sweep her off her feet.

Literally.

Speak of the devil...

Sasha beams as Easton presses her against his muscular body. By the besotted look in my bestie's eyes, the world around her has completely fallen away. People jostle past, shooting irritated looks in their direction, but neither cares. It wouldn't surprise me to see little red and pink hearts dancing above their heads.

Ugh.

They're seriously too cute for words. It's enough to induce vomiting.

Just as I'm about to sigh, movement catches the corner of my eye. A shiver of awareness slices through me and the delicate hair at the nape of my neck prickles as my gaze lands on the figure loitering a few feet away.

Crosby Rhodes.

Left tackle for the Western Wildcats.

My initial reaction is to step away and put more distance between us, but I refuse to give him the satisfaction. Instead, I steel myself for a confrontation. I've spent too much time around him not to know exactly how this interaction will play out.

And that's badly.

The funny part—if there's anything amusing about this situation—is that he has a reputation on campus as a real player. The guy doesn't *do* girlfriends. To my knowledge, he's never entertained the idea of one. Even with his surly disposition, he can still charm the panties off any female within a ten-mile radius.

Except me.

To me, he's a total dickhead.

As soon as I make eye contact, his gaze drops, slowly crawling down the length of my body. Even though he's not physically touching me, that's exactly what his perusal feels like. It takes every ounce of self-control to remain motionless, so he doesn't see how much his scrutiny bothers me. Instead, I straighten my shoulders and grit my teeth before jutting out my chin in defiance. If he thinks he can burrow under my skin that easily, he's seriously mistaken.

By the time his onyx-colored depths return to mine, there's a slight curl to his upper lip and a dark look filling his eyes.

"Nice tits, McAdams. New push-up bra? They look bigger than usual. I like it."

"Fuck off, Rhodes." It takes effort to resist the urge to hunch over so that my breasts aren't as noticeable. Although, let's face it, when you wear a D cup, that's difficult to do. I've always been sensitive about the size of my boobs, and somehow, Crosby has figured it out.

He smirks as if pleased by my reaction. I have no idea what I did to provoke his ire, but it's been directed at me since Andrew first introduced us. If it had been possible to avoid the surly boy with the messy dark hair and lip ring, I would have done so after just one meeting. Unfortunately, that was impossible given that Andrew and Crosby are teammates, friends, and roommates. They share an apartment together off campus.

In the beginning, I went out of my way to be nice, figuring that with enough time and kindness, his attitude would thaw and he'd soften his stance. That never happened. If anything, his temperament grew nastier. Once it dawned on me that we were never going to sit around a campfire and sing Kumbaya, I avoided and ignored him.

Even though Andrew and I broke up six months ago, I still run into Crosby on campus and at parties. Sure, I could avoid the football players all together, but I refuse to give either of them that much power over my life. That being said, am I going to miss any of them, with the exception of Easton, when I graduate from Western in the spring?

Nope. Not even a little.

That's not to say they're all bad dudes. A couple of Sasha's soccer teammates are dating football players and they seem like nice guys. But after Andrew's total mindfuck, I have zero interest in getting wrapped up with another self-absorbed jock. There are too many girls at Western throwing themselves at their feet. Most of the ones who hooked up with Andrew knew he had a girlfriend and didn't give a crap.

So much for girl code.

After I dumped his ass, a good number of them came out of the woodwork to share all the gory details. Then they were all about pussy power and solidarity. Not so much when they were hoing around with my man behind my back.

"What?" He grins. "It was a compliment. You should take it that way."

"Please," I snort, "nothing that comes out of your mouth could be misconstrued as complimentary."

His smile widens, and the tiny silver hoop pierced through the corner of his lip glints in the sun. Without realizing it, my gaze drops to the metal. His tongue darts out to play with it, and a punch of arousal explodes in my core.

His voice dips as he looms closer. "Is that what you want, McAdams? My sweet words?" He practically purrs the question.

My heart kicks into overdrive as my attention snaps to his eyes. An unwanted sizzle of electricity snakes down my spine. One would think from our contentious past, the only thing he would do is piss me off.

Turns out that's not the case.

For whatever reason, Crosby is the only guy on this campus capable of making my hormones sit up and take notice. If there were away to stomp out the unwelcome attraction rushing through me like liquid fire, I'd do it in a heartbeat.

But there's not. Trust me, I've tried. Which is precisely why I go to such great lengths to avoid him. I would say like a clap diagnosis, but…

That hits a little too close to home.

I clear my throat. "Hardly."

He eats up more distance between us until it becomes necessary to tip my chin upward to hold his flinty gaze. It takes every ounce of self-control to stand my ground instead of scrambling backward in retreat.

The buzz of attraction zipping through my veins is not only disconcerting but refuses to be extinguished. His bright white teeth flash in the sunlight, and my attention is reluctantly snagged by the small metal hoop. I've never been attracted to guys with piercings. Or who are dark and moody.

Crosby is—and has always been—the exception to the rule.

When he reaches out to trail a finger down the front of my sweater, I jerk out of the strange stupor that has fallen over me and knock his hand away.

"Don't touch me," I growl, baring my teeth like a rabid dog. He's lucky I don't take a chunk out of him. At the very least, he'd think twice about messing with me in the future. Then again, nothing seems to deter him. He enjoys taunting me.

A slow grin spreads across his face as dark humor dances in his inky-colored irises.

Unwilling to get drawn into any more of a verbal skirmish, I spin on my heels and stalk through the crowd. Now that Easton has captured Sasha's attention, it's doubtful she'll notice my abrupt departure.

There's only so much of Crosby Rhodes I can take.

One-Click Campus God now!

MORE BOOKS BY JENNIFER SUCEVIC

Princess of Hawthorne Prep

The Next Door Duet (football)

The Girl Next Door

The Boy Next Door

What's Mine Duet (Suspense)

Claiming What's Mine

Protecting What's Mine

Stay Duet (hockey)

Stay

Don't Leave

Standalones

Confessions of a Heartbreaker (football)

Hate to Love You (Hockey)

Just Friends (hockey)

Love to Hate You (football)

The Breakup Plan (hockey)

Collections

The Barnett Bulldogs

The Football Hotties Collection

The Hockey Hotties Collection

The Next Door Duet

ABOUT THE AUTHOR

Jennifer Sucevic is a USA Today bestselling author who has published twenty-four new adult novels. Her work has been translated into German, Dutch, Italian, and French. She has a bachelor's degree in History and a master's in Educational Psychology from the University of Wisconsin-Milwaukee. Jen started out her career as a high school counselor before relocating with her family and focusing on her passion for writing. When she's not tapping away on the keyboard and dreaming up swoonworthy heroes to fall in love with, you can find her bike riding or at the beach. She lives in the Michigan with her family.

If you would like to receive regular updates regarding new releases, please subscribe to her newsletter here-
Jennifer Sucevic Newsletter (subscribepage.com)

Or contact Jen through email, at her website, or on Facebook.
sucevicjennifer@gmail.com

Want to join her reader group? Do it here -)
J Sucevic's Book Boyfriends | Facebook

Social media links-
https://www.tiktok.com/@jennifersucevicauthor
www.jennifersucevic.com
https://www.instagram.com/jennifersucevicauthor
https://www.facebook.com/jennifer.sucevic

Amazon.com: Jennifer Sucevic: Books, Biography, Blog, Audiobooks, Kindle

Jennifer Sucevic Books - BookBub

Printed in Great Britain
by Amazon

45488859R00169